D0382935

Finding You

LYDIA ALBANO

Swoon READS
Swoon Reads | NEW YORK

V
TEEN
FIC
ALBANO

A Swoon Reads Book
An imprint of Feiwel and Friends and Macmillan Publishing Group, LLC.
175 Fifth Avenue, New York, NY 10010.

Finding You. Copyright © 2017 by Lydia Albano.
All rights reserved. Printed in the United States of America.

Our books may be purchased in bulk for promotional, educational,
or business use. Please contact your local bookseller or the Macmillan Corporate
and Premium Sales Department at (800) 221-7945 ext. 5442
or by e-mail at MacmillanSpecialMarkets@macmillan.com.

Library of Congress Cataloging-in-Publication Data is available.
ISBN 978-1-250-09858-0 (hardcover) / ISBN 978-1-250-09859-7 (ebook)

Book design by Brad Mead

First edition, 2017

1 3 5 7 9 10 8 6 4 2

swoonreads.com

ADA COMMUNITY LIBRARY
10664 W. VICTORY
BOISE, ID 83709

*For all the girls whose names and
stories will never be told*

prologue

There was no doubt that we were the two most opposite people in the world. But for all my failings, and the ways he balanced them, I loved him with my whole heart.

"Let's run away," he'd say when we were younger. "Think of all the amazing places there are, still secret and undiscovered, just waiting for us." And he'd spread his arms at the stars and breathe in deeply, eyes aglow with the lure of adventure. And if anyone could have ever made me try something reckless, it would have been him.

But I was the girl who took out a book instead: one about gemstones and minerals, industry in the past century, or the life spans of different butterflies. "Research," I'd tell him. "You know we can't go anywhere until we have all the facts."

And he'd shake his head at me and sigh. He'd groan, "You don't understand, Isla. The world isn't *in* books." He would climb off the roof outside my window, down the iron bars and gutters, and make his way across the street to his own home.

But the next day he'd be back.

I'd see his golden head appear at the railing, and my heart would start to pound, but I'd ignore it. *There's time,* I'd tell myself. *Time for him to realize I've been here all along. Time for him to see me the way I see him. Time for him to love me.*

And I was right, for so long. My life—*our life*—went on. Around us, things changed: Sickness swept through our corner of the city, and my mum died, and his, too. Miles away, someone named Nicholas Carr seized the principal city, Verity, and made himself our dictator. Copper became less valuable and my pa was paid less to mine it. Everyone wanted steel for the steam engines, and every day the noise and smoke of the city seemed to eat up more of the greenery that used to surround it.

Still, we had each other, and we had time.

Some things had changed, and would always be changing, I knew. But not us. Not the lazy afternoons on school holidays, talking about futures that still loomed far off. Not the way he'd move closer to me when we heard footsteps behind us on the street, or the grins he'd flash my way when he saw a funny advert in a shop window.

I would always have him. I was so sure.

Until the hottest day of the year I was sixteen, when the boy—who had somehow become a man, suddenly—climbed the rusty ladders to the roof outside my window, dressed all in brown.

one

"What are you dressed as?" I ask with a grin, lowering myself onto the hot shingles beside him.

Tam doesn't smile. "I have something for you," he says quietly, squinting up at the sun instead of meeting my eyes. I nudge him, and he takes something from the satchel slumped beside him and thrusts it into my hands. I watch him for a minute, my confusion growing.

He's early; there's no way he's done making deliveries for the grocer yet. "Tam, what—"

"Look at it," he prompts, strangely shy. I begin to unwrap the tiny paper package, which is heavy for its size. "It's nothing too great, really," he starts as I uncover a chain, delicate and a little tangled, with a small brass heart at the end.

My eyes widen. "Where did you get it?"

Tam's smile is proud. "I bought it." *It must have cost a fortune,* I think. *He must have gone to one of the antiques shops downtown.*

"Was it terribly expensive?"

He just shrugs, and I force myself to breathe, waiting for the explanation. The silence seems to last forever. "Oh! I've got the other piece, see?" he says eventually, holding up a similar chain that hangs about his neck. This one has a tiny key at the end.

"What's all of this for?" I ask finally. "My birthday isn't till winter and I've—"

"I might not be here." He's quiet, avoiding my eyes suddenly. A whole minute passes, my heart thudding in my temples.

"Tam . . ."

"That's why I came," he explains, talking very fast. "I—a man came to our house. A recruiter. He said that if I joined the army, then my family wouldn't be hungry through the winter, and with my pa not able to work what with his lungs getting so weak, and the kids . . . anyway, I registered." He takes a breath, and the silence is heavy on my chest, suffocating me.

All I can say is, "The . . . the army?" The sounds of the city fade in and out like a slow pulse. I feel like I've been struck. I can finally place the clothes—the crisp shirt and the boots with all their buttons—I've seen them in photographs, though I never knew what color they were. Pa always frowned and called the flyers propaganda, told me not to believe what they said about the borders starting trouble. "They can't make you—" I finally manage.

"They didn't, Isla. I decided. Good way to see the world,

right?" Tam can't lie to me—he's scared. He had a dozen plans of his own: joining the crew of a pirate steamer, building his own aeroplane, or stowing away on an expedition that would take him far beyond the stifling city walls to the wilds outside. . . . Joining Nicholas Carr's infamously brutal army was never on his list.

"Wait here," I command, choking back a sob. He's the strong one, the one who risks everything, endures everything.

I slip through the window behind us into my tiny room and rifle through the chest by my bed until I find the spyglass. "I meant to give this to you months ago," I tell him as I climb back onto the roof. "But I was afraid that if you could see far-off places, you wouldn't want to stay here, with me. Maybe . . . maybe now you can use it to look back home."

Hesitantly, I place it in his hands. I don't tell him about the day I got it, wandering about the flea markets with my pa. I felt guilty for letting Pa spend the money when I only wanted the spyglass for Tam, but he had insisted when he saw how I lingered at the table. He wouldn't tell me how much he paid, but I knew it was a lot. "I want you to keep it with you," I tell Tam.

Tam's arms envelop me. "You were supposed to come with me," he murmurs, but his voice is unfamiliar, strained, like he's going to cry. His arms tighten and I sink against him, my tears soaking his crisp, new shirt. Tam runs his fingers through my hair; they snag on the tangles, but he doesn't seem to notice, he just goes on about writing letters to me and coming home as soon as he's allowed, and I try to process every moment with him so I can keep them forever in my memory.

Finally he pulls away. I run my hands over my dress, smooth my hair, blink to clear my vision. "I have to go now," he says, his voice a little choked, his eyes a little swollen.

"Now? Right now?" I feel like I'll be sick. "Why didn't—"

"I came as soon as I could." *Time is running out right in front of me,* I think, starting to panic. *I've always had time.* Tam is looking at his feet again, and he trails his hand down the side of my arm, sending a shiver through me, even in the stifling heat. "We're leaving any minute; I can't stay or else they'll come looking. We've got to sign in at the train and all that." I try to breathe. *He'll be here again tomorrow,* a voice in my head insists. But suddenly the heat is unbearable, and I can feel everything unraveling.

"Good-bye, my dear," he whispers, his fingers brushing the side of my face and then lifting my chin a little. He leans in again, but this time he kisses me, his lips soft and cool in the heat of the day. My stomach flips and my eyes droop closed, and when he pulls back, I feel disoriented.

The rooftop seems dizzyingly high as I stare at him, not speaking. Tam smiles a little, like he's unsure again, and touches the little key around his neck. Then he disappears over the ledge, swinging down the rusty iron bars. A moment later, he's on the cobbled street, jogging backward, looking up at me. Then he's around the corner and gone.

My hand hovers at my mouth. He's gone. *Tam is gone.* Everything is in chaos. The locket and the kiss are at war with the longing and the pain, and suddenly all I can think is that I never told him I love him.

✦ ✦ ✦

I'm frantically buttoning my boots when Pa comes in, covered in the same gray dust as always.

"So hot today," he sighs, slumping into his usual chair in a cloud of what looks a little like smoke. Even his mustache is covered in it. "They told us that people up the line were passing out." He pauses and I realize he's studying me. "And what's your rush today, love?"

"Tam's leaving," I say hurriedly, starting on the second boot.

"Where to? Found a band of ruffians to see the world with at last?" Pa chuckles, shaking his head.

"Sort of," I mumble, and he looks at me sharply.

"Do you mean he's really going, darling?"

"He's joining the army, Pa." I tug viciously at the last hook on my boot, which won't button.

After a minute he says softly, "Did Ezra make him go?"

"I don't think so."

"And you're going now to see him off?"

I nod, sniffling loudly.

"All alone?"

"Please let me go, Pa. I'd ask you to come, but I know you're so tired."

"Don't be late, my love. If they're shipping out, the

crowds'll be fierce." I don't want to cry again, so I kiss his cheek quickly.

"Hurry! Don't let him leave without a pretty girl to wave to him from the platform!"

"I'll be right back," I say, slipping out the door.

It's three flights of stairs down, but today it feels like a hundred. I shove open the door at the bottom and a wall of sunlight hits me; heat wobbles up off the cobblestones and burns my skin.

Even before I can see, I'm running. The clacking of my boots echoes between the buildings of our complex until I reach open streets, where everything is strangely quiet except for a couple of buggies roaming here and there, looking for passengers. It never takes them long to realize that there's nothing in Industria except the struggling families of a couple of thousand miners. For a really good school or any capable medical treatment, it's an hour in any direction, and a full day's investment to visit a museum, posh shopping plaza, or playhouse in Verity.

There are rows upon rows of rectangular buildings housing the workers' families, but I know the short way through the maze. The sun bounces off bright buildings and glaring windows, and by the time I start to see the crowds, my dress is clinging to my skin with sweat. Pa was right about the madness; people swarm like ants to the station and the air is full of good-byes and demands for caution and letters.

I keep thinking about the family crowded into the flat next door to Pa's and mine whose eldest son joined the army. They tell me that he writes when he can, but even still, it's only once every month or two, and it's never good news: more skirmishes with what the government calls the restless, ungrateful people in the border villages.

I stretch on my toes to try to see above the crowd; I've always counted on Tam for his height, but the heat makes my head ache.

I don't see the soldiers themselves until I worm my way closer to the platform, and then they're everywhere: dressed in the same brick brown as Tam, shoulders straight, boots shining in the sun. I scan the rows: young men, mostly, with different faces and expressions. I don't see Tam. *I can't have already missed him,* I tell myself.

But then I catch sight of a head of familiar blond hair tossed about by the hot wind that's picking up. My heart jumps and I bob up and down on my toes, grinning. "Tam!" I shout. His head jerks up a little and he scans the crowd, still walking in line with the others. I wave, waiting for him to spot me, as they reach the steps of the train and the officers usher them inside. "Tam!" I try again, frantic.

He sees me.

His eyes catch mine and his face lights up in a grin that I know I'll be forever replaying until he comes back. I open my mouth to shout something—that I'll miss him, that I'll write to him, that I love him—and a hand slaps over my mouth. Someone grabs me around my waist, pinning my arms down, and I'm dragged backward, backward as I try to scream and kick and bite.

In a slow second I lose track of Tam's eyes; I see him stretch to find me again through the crowd, see the officer shove him toward the door of the train car. I thrash and fight, I try to writhe away, but I'm too small, too weak. I lose sight of Tam and the crowd pushes in around me, and still the arms are pulling me backward.

I throw my head back, wrenching it free, and try to scream, and something strikes my temple. My head explodes with pain, my ears ring, blackness clouds my vision.

two

I wake to a steady sense of motion beneath me and my head jostling against a wall, but when I open my eyes, it's still dark. Sharp pain bites at my hands; I try to move them and realize that my wrists are bound with something that cuts my skin when I struggle. *No, no.* I tell myself to breathe, to think, not to panic. But my heart is pounding. The air is stale and thick with something that tastes like mildew on my tongue.

I can't be calm. I can't, I can't, I can't. Questions crowd my head: *Where am I? Who was it that took me, and why? Where am I going?* I try the cords again, despite the sting, but in a moment I feel sticky blood between my hands, and I give up. Before I know it, I'm sobbing.

It's impossible to tell how much time has passed in the darkness, how long I sit curled against the corner of the wall, fear stripping me of my senses. Finally, I clamber painfully to my knees, then my feet. My boots squeak on the slippery floor, but I feel my way up the wall and run my fingers along it. Metal plates, it feels like, welded together in an overlapping pattern with thick rivets at the corners. We must be on a train. Probably in a cargo crate, like I see on the cars lined up at the station. Those hold coal and copper, grain and animals. Not people. Never people.

The only light comes from a rectangle on a far wall, an air vent, probably.

When I stumble toward it, I trip over something and go sprawling. My elbows burn and the cord cuts into my wrists again. I grope about to see what I tripped over and touch what feels like a shoe. It jerks away and someone exclaims.

I'm not alone. Of course I'm not.

I stand again, less steadily now, muttering an apology and straining my ears. Above the hum and screech of the train, I hear them: people all about me, girls, probably, crying and whimpering.

How many are there? My imagination snakes away with ideas about brothels and dark alleys. Everyone knows the stories of the girls who end up being found: the ones who had wandered off or gotten lost, or run away with a lover and then returned in shame. But there's not much to know about the girls who are taken, the ones who just disappear.

They don't tell stories.

They don't come back.

Is that my fate?

I blink again and again, as if that will help my eyes adjust to the darkness, and slowly pick my way toward the vent on the opposite side of the car. I count at least a dozen other figures, but there are probably more.

The vent, when I reach it, is pitiful: a hand's breadth tall and wide, made of warped and rusted metal that lets in only enough fresh air to tease me. I hold my wrists up to the light to see how they're tied, but my fingers can't reach the knots and my teeth are no good. I give up again, holding my hands together to relieve pressure and lessen the pain. For a while I stand there with my head against the grate, trying to will fresh air inside.

Then movement catches my attention; someone else appears, slowly entering the faint circle of light. A girl, a little taller than me, and a little stronger, too, I'd guess. She approaches me cautiously, her movements subtle, catlike.

She comes closer, keeping her balance perfectly in the moving car, and stops at the grate as I did. Now I can see her eyes: quick, light, maybe green. She watches me for a moment and then begins to work at the vent with her fingertips, her hands bound like mine.

"What are you doing?" I ask, and the words come out raspy and dry. She looks me up and down and doesn't answer. Then she goes back to what she's doing, pulling at the corners of the grate and the rivets. "I don't see what that will do," I mutter, slumping against the wall again.

"I don't care *what* you think," says the girl, not looking at me this time. "If there's a way out of here, I'll find it."

"Through a hole the size of your hand?" I ask. I regret the sarcasm instantly, even if she *is* wasting her energy.

Neither of us wants to be in here, or wants to know what comes next.

She narrows her eyes at me and continues to work at the metal. "You can give up," she says, just when I've stopped expecting her to speak again. "I never will. I'll do whatever it takes to get out of here." I sink to the ground, my back against the wall, which is warm from the sun.

Some time later, the cat-girl abandons her scheme and drops to the ground as well. She doesn't speak to me, or weep, or move at all, as far as I can tell. In moments of near silence, I hear her measured breathing.

But there are other voices around me, crying or muttering to themselves. Someone sings under her breath, a hoarse, raspy song in a language I don't know. Eventually the sound ceases. *What happens when the movement stops?* I don't want to think about it, and nothing changes for what feels like a lifetime.

I start to wish I were braver, like the strange girl beside me. I don't know what it is that allows her to keep cool, but it's foreign to me, and I wish I weren't weak and small. The realization that Tam has always been my courage is like a smack. Without him I have nothing to protect me, none of my own strength, no store of bravery to pull from. My help-lessness frustrates me.

A year must pass in the darkness. When we stop, it's sudden, and I'm thrown forward. Pain sears my wrists, and my elbows slam against the hard floor for the second time. I suck on the inside of my cheeks, trying to stop crying, trying not to think about what might be waiting. I press my eyes shut, wishing this were a dream that I could wake from.

Movement throws us again as the container rocks back and forth, is picked up, and then set down, adjusted and then adjusted some more. I take a slow breath in, and then out. With each breath, my chest shudders.

The moment that Tam kissed me replays behind my eyes when I close them. *His eyes, nervous when he leaned in, my lips more nervous still . . .* It was so *right. What if I never see him again? What if that was the last time?* At least I have the locket, tangible proof that he feels . . . something. That he cares. Gingerly, my hands bleeding and my wrists burning, I twist the chain about and unclasp it, holding on to it as if for my life.

✦ ✦ ✦

The stillness is worse than the movement was. We wait and wait. It might be hours or days. It might only be minutes. My stomach is hollow; the air becomes even closer, and toxic smells—sweat, urine—overwhelm me. I want to hold my breath, but the heat is oppressive; as the walls gradually get warmer, it feels as if we're being baked alive. My dress clings to me like a cobweb.

Time drags on, hot and damp and heavy.

I think back to the day Tam's father let us ride the elevator box in the tower he had been contracted to build. When the grating locked in place and the doors slid closed and we began to climb up, up, up, I was sure I would be trapped inside forever. But Tam wrapped one arm around me and he whispered in his excited way a hundred things we'd do when we got out, and he made the operator take us back to the bottom level. I knew how excited he had been to ride it all the way to the top.

That box was nothing compared with this one.

This is the end of me.

The thought comes out of nowhere, heavy enough to crush me. *Pa will have no way of knowing what's happened to me. I'm weak and helpless. I'm done for.*

But Tam . . . maybe he saw me, saw what happened. He might have broken away, come after me to help. For all I know, he's finding a way to save me right now. Hope, no more than a spark, is kindled inside me. Every novel I've ever read tells me it's possible, that the girl is always rescued from danger at the last minute.

I close my eyes and think of Tam. *His kiss, his voice tight with emotion, his fingers running through my hair. His eyes when he talks about the sea, the way he nervously drums his fingers when he's supposed to be staying still. There's no one I'm more certain of. He'll come for me. Of course he will.*

There is a creaking sound, old metal being wrenched open, and then a loud crack from the far side of the container. I shrink back against the hot wall, and the girls around me do the same.

There's an explosion of blinding white light. I cover my eyes, my head splitting. There are grunts and sounds of movement from outside, followed by banging against the walls. A fraction at a time, I open my eyes. Figures, like shadows against the bright light, pull girls from the crate, dragging them by their hair and their clothes and their limbs. Most of the girls scream and wail. I want to curl in on myself and pretend that none of this is real.

I can't press myself back any farther than I already am.

I can't disappear.

The figures climb into the crate and haul more girls out into the light. My heart races; I can feel it thudding in my throat, choking me. This is it. Tam's locket is still in my hand, my fingers clasped around it so tightly that it hurts. Somehow, I know they'll take it if they see it. One of the dark silhouettes crawls through the opening and toward me. I suck in a breath and shove the necklace into my mouth, inside my cheek, and clamp my mouth shut. The figure reaches forward and grabs my wrists in his hands, then drags me along the crate's rough floor.

The light is blinding. Coarse hands thrust me across a dirty floor, into a group of at least twenty other girls huddled on the ground. I can see the dried blood on my wrists and elbows, the dirt coating my skin and clothes.

I try to take in my surroundings. The room is giant and looks like a warehouse, square with a row of small windows lining a very high ceiling. There is little furniture: Stacks of boxes and crates sit here and there, a chimney and an enormous stove stand in one corner, and what looks like an automobile partially concealed by a tarp sits in another. The ground is covered in muddy tracks that might have come from a wagon; it reminds me of the storage yards where Tam's father purchases building materials.

Standing outside the shipping crate are at least a dozen people; I look from face to face, but instead of humanity, cruelty is splayed across each. The men are burly with scowling mouths and scarred hands, the women are hard and sharp, wearing breeches or tight skirts and fitted jackets. Their eyes are hollow.

Movement draws my eyes. Tall doors on one wall slide open and several boys carrying water troughs between them enter, stumbling from the weight. They put the troughs on the ground and leave, casting smirks over their shoulders and elbowing each other in the ribs. Slowly, the men and women form a circle around us. Their dark eyes make my skin crawl as some move between us, untying or cutting the cords that bind our hands. I have no time to be glad of the release.

Out of nowhere, another woman joins the group. She's different from the rest. She looks down at us the way bargain hunters at the market survey tables of cheap jewelry and half-rotten fruit. She is tall, with broad shoulders and a wide, red mouth, and her clothes are fine, elegant, and serious. A shudder runs through me.

She catches my eye, somehow.

Please, I mouth, as if it will do any good. *Please* seems like the only thing I have.

She just looks at me, her head cocked a little to the side, curiosity creeping into her expression. A long time passes, and I sit looking up at her, trembling. And then she blinks, and suddenly she smiles, a hateful and cruel smile.

"Start with that one," she says, pointing at me.

I try to squirm away as two of the younger men come forward and take me by my arms. They drag me, kicking and wriggling, toward the water troughs. I can't scream for fear of losing the locket in my cheek, and I'm sure screaming would do nothing anyway. A handful of women are gathered around the troughs and the men toss me onto the ground at their feet. My skin burns where I slide against the rough floor, and when I try to scramble back to get a look at the people around me, one of them grabs hold of me by the front of my dress and pulls me to my feet. With one jarring motion, she tears the fabric down the middle, sending buttons spraying in different directions. Then she yanks the dress off my shoulders, tugs it over my ribs, my hips, down my legs. Someone unhooks my boots and pulls them one by one from my feet, and then off come my petticoats.

I bite down, grinding my teeth, my face hot with tears. Someone starts on my corset and when I balk, a hand slaps my cheek, leaving my ears ringing. *Don't look around,* I tell myself. *They're probably watching. Don't find out for certain.* I tell myself that I can bear this, because Tam will come.

But standing there, naked and alone, wishing my hair could cover me better, I feel finished.

More hands pick me up and plunge me into a trough. The water is like ice, filling my ears and mouth and every crevice in my body. I struggle, but the hands hold me under, until finally, *finally*, I break the surface and air fills my throat and my lungs. I've hardly sucked in a breath before I'm under again, and again. Every time I come up, I clamp down on the locket in my cheek. The metal chain bites into my gums, and I taste blood.

One of the women begins to scrub me clean, the rough cloth tearing at my skin until it's raw and blotchy, like I've been burned. Her face is worn and uncaring, and I watch her and try to hate her and to be angry and strong, but nothing helps. I feel violated, stunned. They're pulling other girls over for the same treatment, I realize. Relief washes over me, that I'm not the only one any longer, but it's followed by guilt.

I'm yanked from the trough and another girl takes my place. Someone throws a blanket around my shoulders and I am hustled, along with half a dozen others, toward an empty corner of the building. I feel numb, standing still and staring at nothing, trembling even though it's warm. More girls file in around me, huddled in blankets like me, eyes wide. A few crumple to the ground, sobbing.

We're all close in age, as far as I can tell, and most of them look like city girls: skinny and strong, some pretty, all with serious faces. Most cry or, at the very least, shake. One girl, smaller than most, joins the group and clutches at me, weeping. I jerk away in surprise, but she holds on, her fingers white around my arm. *She can't be older than fourteen*, I think, my heart breaking for her, for all of us. Slowly, holding my blanket together with one hand, I wrap the other arm around her and pull her closer. I don't want to comfort her. I don't want to comfort anyone. I want to *be* comforted. I want Pa, and Tam.

The girl's sobs continue, and I recognize them from the journey here, in the train car. They grate on my nerves, loud and unharnessed, and I wish she would stop. My favorite memories of my mother are the way she smelled like bread even when we had none, and the times that she held me and traced spiderweb shapes on my back with her fingers when I needed comfort, telling me poems and stories to save up in my head for later. I close my eyes, wishing she were with me, and I trail my fingers along the girl's back the way I remember my mother doing. She heaves a shuddering sigh and leans closer, growing quiet.

When I look again, a beautiful girl with big, brown eyes and messy hair like wildfire smiles lopsidedly in my direction, as if thanking me. She doesn't cry, but her eyes are wide, and scared. *This is no worse for me than for anyone else,* I tell myself, and I try to believe it. And then I smell smoke.

A handful of men move toward us, and we shrink backward as one. The small girl who clings to my arm begins to weep more loudly than before, and her cries fill me with panic. *I'm helpless. Whatever they intend to do to me, I can't stop it.* I clamp my mouth even more tightly around the necklace in my cheek, and I notice the woman in command conferring with one of the men. She says something I can't hear and then nods toward me, her eyes glinting a little.

The man smiles crookedly and strides toward me; my

muscles tense and I nearly open my mouth to plead with him. *No. No, I can't lose the locket. I can't lose what I have left of Tam.*

I'm shaking when he reaches me, but I don't beg for mercy. My heart pounds as he takes hold of my wrists and pulls me forward, but I'm quiet. The younger girl grasps at me, sobbing, so I touch her cheek and try to smile, as if we'll be all right. It's not easy to believe.

Her grip loosens as the man yanks me away from the group, and I stumble to keep up so I won't be dragged. When he finally stops and draws me up beside him, we're on the opposite side of the building, by the stove.

Four men sit around a stone ring with a fire glowing hot and bright in the middle of it. There are metal rods resting around it, their ends among the embers. One of the men, wearing thick rawhide gloves, takes one of the rods from the fire and turns to me, his eyes full of something that looks like hunger. He wiggles the glowing end at me, grinning greasily. The iron makes the shape of the letter X, bright orange and twisted. *Wake up,* I tell myself. *Wake* up. *This isn't real.*

"Hold out your hand," the man says.

three

I can't. I seize up, pull back. The X is all I can see, glowing and bright and wicked like the smith's eyes. The hot metal leers toward me.

"No—" I cry, my voice slurred by the locket in my cheek. I try to run, but the men grab my arms, laughing at me and shoving me forward. I can't see through my tears, except to make out the glowing iron X. My chest hurts, my throat, my head. I crumple to my knees, the hot brand inches from my face.

I'm cattle to these people.

That's what this is.

They're marking me as their property.

One of the men wrenches my left fist from my side. He's stronger, bigger, more certain; his rough hands uncurl my fingers and splay them flat despite my struggling. He holds my hand with both of his, while the other man wrestles my body to stillness, his arms wrapped about me like a brace.

The smith comes a little closer, his eyes glowing. "Can't say it won't hurt, love." He grins, and I writhe with more feeble attempts to wrench myself free. I can't breathe through my sobs.

The brand touches my palm.

I scream and scream, until I can't hear myself any longer, until my throat hurts. I wish I were dead. I'm vaguely aware that they haul me out of the way, wailing and moaning, and leave me curled in a ball on the ground. I can't even think. All I know is the fierce, burning pain that screeches through my whole body. My hand and the screaming, screaming pain.

✦ ✦ ✦

My eyes flutter open, sticky with tears. *I must have passed out.* I lie still, looking at the world sideways with my head on the cool floor, wondering how much time has passed. My hand throbs and pulses, so I can't forget it; it twinges with pain at every movement.

I sit up, eventually. I pull my knees to my chest, rock back and forth as if that will help, clutch my blanket to me with my good hand. I can't move the other one.

Behind me, more girls are being branded. Their cries meld into one long wail, fraying my nerves. It's exhausting to pity them. My own pain fills my mind instead; I search my memory for something beautiful to focus on, but everything is tainted. I'm tainted.

And then I remember Tam.

He could still come. He *will* still come. Somehow, before

things get even worse. I close my eyes, pulling up his face in my thoughts. *The way his chin is cleft just a little at the center, and the way his copper-and-gold hair refuses to stay put, and the way his eyes never end.* I try to remember the feel of his mouth on mine, his hand on my back, his breath on my cheek. Already the memory feels a little faded, and I hate myself for letting it slip away.

For the first time since the train car, I take the locket from my mouth with the hand that can still move. I flatten the branded palm against the cool stone floor and press down on it, trying not to whimper. The locket is slick with my saliva, and the chain is tangled, but holding it, looking at it, is a kind of sanctuary.

I close my eyes again, holding the locket against my heart, forcing myself to breathe deeply, in and out. *Tam is here with me,* I tell myself. *He's with me the way he was in the elevator box. He's with me the way he was when I found out my mum wouldn't get better, and during the first thunderstorm after she died, when I thought the ceiling would come down and I didn't have her arms to hide in.* As long as I have the locket, he's with me. *And soon enough he'll come,* I add. And as long as I think it, I can bear anything.

✦ ✦ ✦

I fall asleep lying on top of my burning hand, and I only wake when one of the men jostles my shoulder sharply. A handful of them weave among the girls, waking the ones who are still sleeping, wrapped in blankets like me and coated in sticky tears. Their pretty faces are drawn and ugly with pain, and my good hand trails automatically over my cheek, my eye, my forehead, wondering if I look the same.

Tam used to tell me I was beautiful, in an offhanded way that I hated, because it made my heart race and yet he meant nothing by it. He told me a lot of things—that I was smarter than he was, that I should take bigger risks, that I shouldn't read at twilight because squinting at the pages would ruin my eyesight. He said I'd have to wear spectacles, and that other kids would turn my name into a joke and spell it "Eye-la" forever. Aching, I get to my feet, my whole body wailing at me.

As we're herded toward a heap of baskets full of clothing, the small girl who clung to me earlier appears at my side with a shudder, seizing my arm. I want to shrug her off, but I don't, trying to smile when she looks up at me. She's as thin as a skeleton, with haunted blue eyes that I can't look at for long.

There are women standing around the baskets, pulling the blankets off the girls and appraising their naked figures. They hand them various articles of clothing and tell them to dress, the words sharp and unattractive on their tongues.

When I reach them, one looks me over quickly. She rifles through the nearest basket and hands me different things. "Put them on," she says without feeling, pointing away from us, to an open area.

I take a breath and stay where I am, looking pointedly at the girl by my side and then back at the woman. She glares angrily at me. *She'll punish me for this,* I think, but I hold my chin higher. My heartbeat pulses in my head and through the scorched skin on my hand. But the woman narrows her eyes a little, watching the way the younger girl clings to me. She gathers a few more things and thrusts them at us, pointing again. "Now go," she says.

I drop my blanket, hiding my locket underneath, and stand shivering and exposed as I dress. The underclothes and corset are ordinary, and as I struggle to pull them on with only one hand, I'm surprised that they fit so perfectly. Then I understand the exactness of this business. They know their work by heart.

When I try to fumble with the hooks of the corset, the pain in my hand is blinding. I squeeze my eyes shut and try to push past it, but the swelling makes it impossible. My fingers fumble and shake and I can't make sense of what I'm trying to do without seeing it.

Suddenly I feel cool fingers close over mine, and a voice at my ear says, "Let me help you." A few quick movements later and my corset fits snugly about my ribs, hooked and tied. I turn to see who spoke, and it is the girl with the wild red hair who smiled at me. She is a little taller than I am, though her build is slight, and her eyes—deep, brown—are kind and sad and wise. "I'm Valentina," she whispers.

"Thank you," I say, feeling the weight of her kindness. "I'm Isla."

She nods and smiles a sweet, forced smile.

I turn so she won't see my tears and pull on the blouse I was given. It's made of lace only, hinting at the low-cut corset that does more to reveal my small breasts than bind them. The skirt is pale like the blouse, a creamy cotton with a high, wide waist and buttons up the side.

There are thin stockings that reach my thighs, made of lace more sheer than the shirt, and leather boots that cover my ankles and take me an age to button. When I stand and look down at myself, I feel like a different girl. I've been branded like an animal. Someone else has bathed me and chosen my clothes and decided who I'm to be. I don't have my family or the boy I love.

When no one is watching, I clasp my locket about my neck and tuck it beneath my shirt into my corset, a secret statement that a piece of Isla Powe still exists.

I try to count the number of girls but lose track as they're shuffled about. There are at least thirty, probably more. As the girls finish dressing, men approach with black cords in their hands. Some of the girls fight them, but I stand still, concentrating on the sliver of peace that comes from the weight of the locket about my neck.

The small girl moves closer to me when the men come toward us, and I stroke her hair gently and keep my head straight as a man kneels in front of me. He weaves the cord between my ankles, tying my feet together with only a foot or so of slack, enough to walk but not to run. I know without looking down that he steals a glance up my skirt as he works, but I don't flinch. *Tam will come,* I tell myself. I use the thought of him for everything it's worth, to strengthen my willpower. When the man binds the ankles of the other girl, she cries loudly, her fingers digging into my arm, but I say nothing.

They tie our wrists the same way and line us up against a wall, telling us we may sit. I sink to the ground and the little girl mirrors me. The cord around my ankles is tighter than it needs to be, biting into my skin through the stockings. The girl who helped me, Valentina, sits only a few feet away from me, and a little farther down the line, another face catches my eye: a taller girl, with a strong frame and bold features surrounded by fine blond hair. The cat-girl, I think. She doesn't sit. She stands erect against the wall and keeps her head level, her eyes direct. I wonder what she hopes to gain by her defiant attitude.

They've dressed us to look as young as possible, I realize in dismay. Frilly sleeves, lace bodices, ribbons, and bows. Flowers ornament some of the outfits. The skirts are all short like a child's and fail to cover our knees.

There are so many of us, but somehow I've never felt so alone.

After a time, a wide door on one side of the warehouse opens slowly, letting in a rectangle of brighter light, and revealing the silhouettes of half a dozen men. Most wear simple workers' clothes, but one man—striding ahead of the rest in a glinting silk suit—stands out. From his dark, neatly trimmed beard to the perfectly tied cravat around his neck, he's different. His eyes fall on me, twinkling when he smiles. I feel cold.

The way he walks is deliberate, his shoes making very little noise. He stops five or six feet from me, and another man appears at his side. This one is smaller—his head only reaches the first man's shoulder—and he coughs loudly as he runs nervous eyes over each of us girls. A valet, probably.

"Yours is first pick, of course," the commanding woman says, gliding over and arching her brows at the man in the suit. "If you're paying the usual price."

He ignores her last remark, meeting my eyes again. I try to look away, but his gaze is like a magnet. "Are they new?" he asks, his voice low and smooth.

"Brand-new. No one's touched them. Will you be wanting the usual number?"

"This lot is beautiful."

The woman scoffs. "A few of them maybe. We were hard-pressed, took some risks. How many? We do have other clients, you know."

"None who'll pay what I do," the man says smoothly. And still failing to answer her questions, he takes two gliding steps forward and looks down at me. Before I know what's happening, his manservant is hauling me to my feet. I press against the wall, breathing through my teeth; the man in the silk suit is too close, with his coal-black hair and glinting eyes that never blink. He strokes his beard for a moment, watching me, and then his gloved fingers graze the side of my face, trail along my cheek. I close my eyes. *I want Tam. I want Pa.* "This one," I hear him say in his silky voice, and his hand is gone.

He moves slowly down the line of girls, choosing whomever he likes best. Valentina is picked; the younger girl who clings to me is not.

The man's valet pays the woman, and she nods, smiling like a crocodile. And then the other men begin to advance, without orders, moving together in perfect unity. One of them approaches me, his smile full of jagged teeth. My heart thuds faster and faster, but the wall is at my back. I have nowhere to go.

His hand slides around my wrists and pulls me, stumbling, after him. As he does, the younger girl whimpers and surges forward, her small, hard fingers clawing at my arm. Immediately, one of the women appears and throws her backward, against the hard wall. *As if she would have gotten far with her ankles bound.*

I hope the girl can see how sorry I am, how I feel for her. I wish I could call out that it'll be all right, that she doesn't need to worry. But that would be a lie. I don't know what will happen to her, but I can imagine. The man hefts me onto his shoulder like a sack of produce, and I don't struggle; there's nowhere to go, even if I did get free. The little girl is held back, for the next round of buyers, no doubt. She gets smaller as I'm carried away, but her eyes, crazed and desperate, stay fixed on me for as long as I can see her, and her wails get louder and more miserable. And then I'm outside in the dying sunlight and I can't see her anymore, just the doors closing behind me. A second later, I'm hefted into the back of a cart, and there are arms and legs sticking into my back and just the sky above me.

The trapdoor in the cart is closed. I clamber into a sitting position, glancing around at my companions. There are about a dozen other girls in the cart. A few stare back at me and at each other with wide eyes. No one speaks. Some crumple against the sides of the cart, crying into their arms, and I cannot see their faces.

Movement is awkward with the cords around our arms and legs. I manage to scoot against one of the sides as three men climb into the driving seat. I don't see the fancy man or his attendant. *No doubt they have a much finer way to travel,* I think, anger pulsing through me.

With the crack of a whip, the cart starts to move. The road comes into view behind us, hard-packed dirt hemmed on either side by sickly looking trees. We must be outside the city, if not quite to the rich forests I've read about, then somewhere in between. If there's a place to make an escape, this might be it.

I pull my knees slowly up to my chest and begin to finger the knots that bind my ankles. I bite the inside of my cheek when my hand begins to throb, and I want to cry. Spy stories run through my head, filled with clever characters who get out of far worse situations than this all the time.

"Try anything"—my head jerks up as one of the men turns around to sit facing us, his feet resting on a row of crates—"and you'll be sorry." A pistol rests on his lap, the barrel pointing at us. I swallow and look at my hands, now still. *We'll be driving for a while,* I reason. *It looks like we're in the middle of nowhere. I can wait until he grows bored of watching us and then make my escape.*

For hours, the cart jostles on.

The man continues to watch us, though he sometimes converses with his companions. Every time I try to work at the knot, I feel his gaze drifting in my direction, and I stop.

The sides of the cart are too high to see over, and even the trap at the back only allows so much of a view. The heat is as bad as—was it only yesterday? Or the day before? As bad as it was when Tam left, when I last saw my pa, when I was taken, when everything went wrong.

The sky is the soft blue-turning-pink of a hazy summer evening; I would have gone to the city library, no doubt. Taken the long walk before the heat was so bad, buried myself among the encyclopedias that Tam could never see the need for, relished the long words and the artificial breeze from the slow-turning fans on the tables.

When I look around, Valentina's brown eyes catch mine. Her face droops with uncertainty, though she tries to smile when she sees me watching. Her effort shames me, and I look away.

All about me are beautiful, different, dismal girls. The cat-girl is in the far corner, thin and strong, with her back straight and her head high. She doesn't cry or stare into nothingness or hide her face like the rest. She looks straight ahead, but her hands are between her legs, fiddling endlessly with the knots. She is still fighting. When the man looks her way, her hands pause, but her face shows no recognition.

four

I wish I could count the hours that we travel. When the sun sets, the men light a lantern and share food between them. In the shadows, the eyes of the paler girls are dark holes in faces I can't make out, while those with darker skin blend in almost entirely. I watch the sky, mostly, and when the light is far enough gone that the air is muggy with the leftover heat, I start on the knots around my wrists again, under cover of evening.

The longer we go on, the more frantic I become.

The cord is tight, numbing my fingers as I try to work out the ridges where the knots start, my eyes closed and my head full of the books I've read on sailing. They were Tam's idea, in case we ever ran away and had to travel by ocean, he said. There were knots in those books, but practicing with pieces of twine didn't prepare me for freeing myself in the dark.

Suddenly, the cart stops. The horses nicker and the men

grumble to each other, climbing down from their seats. I sit still, rigid, listening. With a crash, the trap at the end of the cart comes down and the faces of two men appear, the lantern between them.

"On yer stomachs," grunts one, his voice like gravel. "An' be quick about it." *I missed my chance,* I think, frantic. *I was too slow.* There's a shout as the cart lurches and a girl climbs over the side. One of the men takes off after her—the cat-girl is missing, I notice—and I crane my neck to try to glimpse what's happening in the darkness. A second later, I hear a cry, cut short, and the man returns, coming into the lantern light with the girl over his shoulder like a rag doll. I assume she's unconscious since there wasn't a gunshot.

"I said on yer stomachs, didn't I?"

Everyone scrambles to obey as the girl's limp body is slung on top of us. "The next one that stupid gets worse," says the man. He slides his hand along his hip, where the pistol rests. "An' if I hear a sound from *any* of you, I'll kill the lot and the master'll get his money back, ay?"

I press my cheek flat against the grainy wood of the cart's bottom. I can feel splinters sliding against my skin, waiting to prick me if we're jostled at all.

If I'd run, too, would one of us have been shot and killed? Would he have run out of patience? Or would one of us have gotten away? Maybe trying to escape will only get me killed. Maybe it's not worth the risk. Maybe I should wait patiently for Tam.

There's hardly enough room in the cart for all of us;

sweaty, sticky skin presses against me on every side, smoth-
ering. Maybe if they'd fed us in the past day and a half, we
wouldn't have fit at all.

A noise like thunder or flapping wings makes me jump,
and something heavy falls on me; some of the girls shriek and
there's a shout to "shut up" as the heaviness—which must be
a tarp of some kind—is adjusted. Then comes a second cover,
hard and heavy, which might be wood. The sound is like
furniture being moved; the crates from the front of the cart,
maybe. I feel like my ribs are about to break, and it's all I
can do to breathe and not panic. *Worse than the elevator box*,
I think.

I hear the whip on the horses' backs and we start moving,
but we've been traveling for only a few moments when we
halt again. I can hear people talking: questions, demands.
The rough voices of the men who drive the cart answer in
what sound like casual tones, and eventually the people who
stopped us must be satisfied, because we begin to move
again. I wait and wait for the pressure to be lifted so that I
can breathe again. But we only keep driving.

By the time we jerk to a stop, I'm drowsy and achy. The
weight comes off, and then the tarp, and the air feels open
and enormous and cool. I suck it in, wishing my lungs could
hold more.

But then the back panel of the cart swings down, and
there are more men than just the drivers now: some who were
at the warehouse with their velvet-voiced master, and some

faces that are new but just as distasteful. In the wavering lantern light, the only thing the men have in common is the eagerness of their expressions. My heart thumps madly against my chest as they come forward to drag us out.

One of them takes hold of my leg to pull me forward, his greedy fingers moving eagerly up my thigh. I grit my teeth, drawing back, but he grins, liking that I squirm. I imagine swinging my tethered hands at him, spitting in his eyes, clawing at his face until he bleeds, and screaming at him to never touch me again. Instead I hold my arms close to me and press my eyes shut. *This is a dream,* I tell myself as he pulls me toward him, his hands fumbling over my hips, my breasts. *I'll wake up any moment.*

In a second it's over. He puts me on the ground, moving on to another girl as a couple of men take knives from their belts and cut the cords around our ankles and wrists. They pull us to our feet and my legs feel like they're about to buckle. I lock my knees and look down at my hand, where the X stands out against the rest of my palm. I can almost feel the iron pressed against it. *One day,* I tell myself, *the scar will soften. It will fade, and I will forget what my hand felt like without it. In a way, I can look forward to that.*

Beneath my feet are cobblestones. A courtyard, maybe. In the moonlight I can see snatches of stone walls on all sides, twice as tall as me. Behind me, what looks like a mansion rises up and away, a few of the windows lit merrily.

Greedy-looking men crowd around us, tall and strong.

They could do anything they wanted, I think, shuddering. And then I wonder if *this* could be our fate, bought to placate the rich man's workers. *No.* I tell myself to breathe. *He wouldn't have picked us so specifically.* It's no great comfort, but for a moment it's something.

We huddle together as the men surround us. In the moonlight, one girl's hair is so light that it looks like silver. Her eyes are wide and her cheeks shine, wet. Valentina is holding the hand of a smaller girl whose face I can't see. She strokes the girl's shoulder and looks nervously about us.

"Come on, then," says one of the men, gesturing begrudgingly. They herd us in the direction of the mansion, away from the gate. Before we reach the house, we come to a stone shed with a door in it, which one of the men unlocks and opens. Blackness stares out at us. My feet stop short, and someone behind me trips on my heels.

Rough hands shove us forward with sarcastic mutters of "Watch your step" and "Look where you're walking," and by the lantern's light I can see snatches of a dark set of stairs leading down, down, down.

The air is thick with a smell like mildew and refuse, wafting up at us as we move forward. The lantern at the front does little good, and my feet slide over the steps. Then a hand, small and soft and clammy, finds mine, and I reach about and find someone else's. When the floor flattens out, we fall into step as a tight group, holding strangers' hands and tied together by the same fears.

A new glow appears ahead of us, and then the face, arm, and chest of a man carrying a small lantern come into view. He moves with stumbling, half-drunken steps, and his hair drags across his face, stringy and shining with grease.

He sighs, a long, rattling sound. "Bout time 'e got a new load, ay?" he says with a laugh, looking us over with eyes that gleam in the lantern light. Then he beckons to us. "Welcome, welcome," he drawls, but I don't want to follow him. I don't even want to breathe the same air as he does. The girls at the back are prodded along, though, and we obey. The floor is sticky, every step bringing a new tug on my boots and more of the same smells. When we finally stop, the man holds out his lantern and points at what I gradually realize is a cell.

We're underground, in a prison. I let out a shuddering breath. "In there," says the man, leaning in close to one of the girls. "If ye don't lak it, ye can always stay out 'ere and keep me company." *And he is our jailer.* We obey, because there is no alternative. The door clicks closed behind us and a key turns loudly in the lock.

Our guard takes a seat at a crude little station with a chair and counter and sets his lantern down. By its light I take in the cell as best I can: There are a few cots hung from the two solid walls, but they are bare and hard, scarcely better than the floor. The iron grating that makes up the two remaining walls is thick and, I suspect, impossible to break through. The darkness is too deep to show me for certain if the cell beside ours is occupied, but it looks empty.

The jailer sits on his creaky chair and watches us, unblinking. He smiles, a twisted half smile that curls up my insides.

Someone is whispering, and I turn to see Valentina comforting one of the girls who has begun to cry again. I take a seat on the cold, slick ground and try not to think about what makes it slimy. One of the girls sits down beside me, and in the half-light I recognize her.

"Eugenia," I say, startled. She jolts, then studies my face.

"Isla," she says after a moment. "Isla Powe."

Seeing her feels like a piece of home, for a moment. But we look at each other, and there is nothing left to say. I saw her face most days at school; I recognize the pale complexion, long, black hair, and slight frame that made people confuse us. But I hardly know her.

I look down at my lap, and she turns away. *Should we comfort each other? Are there words we should say? If there are, I don't know them.*

One by one, each girl takes a seat on the ground or on one of the bunks, and we nearly fill all the gaps as we make an unofficial circle about the perimeter. There are more than a dozen of us. A dozen girls who should be at home in bed, dreaming of sweethearts.

I hope Tam is thinking about me right now, looking for a way to get to me. I hope he dreams about me when he sleeps. I wonder what he feels when he thinks about kissing me, if he regrets it now, or wishes he'd done it sooner. *The latter,* I think, hoping it's true. *Maybe he's already thinking about when he can kiss me again.* Through the lace of my blouse, I touch the necklace, pressing my eyes shut and telling myself again and again that he'll come. *He's the boy who breaks rules, the boy who stands up for the weak, the boy who wouldn't see me attacked and not find a way to save me. He's the boy who kissed me, the boy who loves me, I hope. He'll find me. He'll save me.*

At some point, Eugenia falls asleep against my shoulder, our backs to the iron bars of the cell beside ours. My body aches; I wish I could relax. The jailer's rumbling snore tells me that he has fallen asleep, but even that relief isn't much. Most of the girls drift off to sleep against one another, but across the cell, the cat-girl is still awake. I meet her eyes, and we stare at each other for a time.

"I'm Isla," I say finally.

She regards me coolly. "Phoebe," she says after a moment. Her voice is low and beautiful. It's full of strength and pain and waiting, but somewhere underneath, there's also fire.

I only know one tie that connects me to every girl here. "How did they take you?" I ask.

"It doesn't matter," she says, still cool. "None of that matters. Because I'm going to escape."

I believe her. "Will you take me with you, when you go?" I hold her gaze while I wait for her answer.

"You can follow me, but I won't wait for anyone."

I nod and we are quiet.

Has it been two days I've been in this nightmare of a reality?

A night on the train, and now a night in this cell? In my head, a lifetime has passed.

I close my eyes and lean back my head, letting it drop against Eugenia's. At least if I sleep, I might dream. And if I dream, I might see Tam.

five

A sound wakes me, jolting me into reality. The jailer is sitting upright, looking behind and above him. I follow his gaze up a set of stone stairs, different from the ones we came down, to an open door. Figures appear, illuminated by a lantern that one carries. I sit up straighter, alert.

There are three men, crowded precariously together on the narrow stairs. I can't see them well until they reach the bottom, but it's clear that the two on either side are guards of some sort. Their uniforms are a little like soldiers', crisp and simple, belted at the waist with a pistol, their boots tall and heavy.

The third man, the one in the middle, isn't as tall. There are chains about his wrists, and his clothes are torn and grungy. After some muttered words, the jailer gets grudgingly to his feet and fiddles with his keys to unlock the cell at my back.

The prisoner is thrown carelessly inside and the door is

bolted. I watch in amazement as he scrambles to the bars and, taking hold of them, calls, "Always a pleasure, gentlemen! I'll take my tea anytime after three, thank you!" In one swift movement, the nearer of the guards draws a small club from his belt and cracks it against the bars with a ringing crash.

"I'm afraid you missed me that time," calls the prisoner, jumping back. But his voice catches slightly. I think he's lying.

I turn to watch him through the grating as the guards pause a moment to speak with the jailer, blocking the light, so I can barely see the man's face. "Are you mad?" I whisper, sitting cross-legged.

"Perhaps a little," he says softly. I get the distinct impression he's grinning, even though I can't see him. "A couple o' years in this place will do all sorts of things to you."

I exhale. "Years?" I ask, wanting to ignore the despair that is nipping at me.

"Three, I think," he says resignedly. "I've lost count of the days, you see. You all must be the new load."

I won't cry. I won't.

The guards bid our jailer good day, and as they move toward the stairs, yellow lantern light floods our cells. The man lunges toward the bars, eyes wide, staring at me. "Lillian?" he says, sounding frantic.

I pull back slightly. "I—I'm not—" I start, alarmed.

"I'm sorry, no, I'm sorry." He sinks back, shaking his

head. "I thought . . ." He takes a deep breath and shakes himself, as if it was nothing. Everything is quiet. Finally he says, "Never mind," plastering on an unconvincing smile and sitting back a little farther, so part of his face is hidden by the shadows.

"I don't know who Lillian is," I say softly, drawing close to the bars again. "I'm Isla."

He watches me intently, the muscles in his arms taut, his neck strained. "I thought you were my sister," he says, his voice very quiet. "You look just like her."

I feel as if I should apologize, or console him somehow, but I don't know what to say. For a long minute I just stare back. He can't be more than twenty or twenty-one, but his eyes look older.

"I'm Des," he says, extending a loosely shackled hand through the bars.

"What kind of name is that?" I ask, shaking it.

He grins wryly. "No one in his right mind would let a pretty girl call him *Despard*." I like the way his eyebrow seems to crook of its own accord. I can feel the tension easing until he asks, "When did they bring you in?" I don't answer, and he goes on. "It must have been sometime last night, when I was working. Did you go straight to Curram, then? Nobody get at you first?" Finally he must notice that I'm upset. "I'm sorry," he apologizes, studying my face. "Fresh, then, huh?"

I nod. "I guess. I was free two days ago . . . or three. I don't know now."

His hand grazes my fingers where they rest on the bars. "I'm sorry," he says again. "The first few days are some of the worst. Everything lovely is still fresh in your memory. You're better off just trying to forget, Isla."

"I don't want to forget the lovely things. There's nothing here but horror." Des watches me and sighs.

"You'll learn to forget," he insists. "You'll want to. There's only darkness in here. Thinking about the light just makes the shadows seem deeper."

"Who is Curram?" I ask, desperate to change the subject.

"All silk and velvet, dark beard and darker eyes; he would have gone to pick you out." The man Des describes is still fresh behind my eyelids. "That's Zachariah Curram. He owns you now; he owns all of us." His insistence on spitting out the truth is grating on me.

"Are you bleeding?" I ask as he presses his knuckles to his ragged shirt.

"Not much. I'll be better by the next time he tries to smash me in." That grin again. The pain at the mention of his sister is gone, replaced by carelessness and joviality. His next question confuses me even more. "How do you like the food, then? As good as home, or better?"

"Food?"

"They haven't fed you yet?" His indignation is mocking. "Just wait, Isla. You're in for a real treat."

"I wasn't sure they planned on feeding us at all."

"Why else would they install that charming toilet in your cell? Don't be silly, my dear girl. There's a perfectly lovely hole in the ground in the far corner for your convenience once they've fed you. Curram doesn't want skeletons."

"There's a tunnel?" Phoebe's sharp voice interrupts our conversation. The cat-girl scrambles over to the bars and shoves her way in beside me.

"Pleasure to meet you. I'm Des." He grins, extending his hand again.

Phoebe takes no notice. "Does it lead to anywhere? Where does it come out?"

"She's Phoebe," I say, and Des nods his thanks. "She likes to eavesdrop," I continue, teasing. It's strange to joke here, when everything is wrong. My words echo back to me, scolding.

"The tunnel is only about a hand's breadth wide, but you're welcome to try it," Des says. "Don't eat anything for a few days and you should be fine."

"Don't mock me," Phoebe hisses, settling back in momentary defeat. "I'll be gone one morning and you'll wish you had listened to me."

"You wouldn't be the first one with grand schemes of escape," Des says quietly. He isn't smiling now, and I try to picture him, three years ago, as desperate to leave as we are now. *How can that go away? How can time make a place like this, a life like this, more bearable?* He turns away from the bars, and when I look up, I find Valentina's eyes on me. She makes a weak attempt at a smile, pulling her knees up to her chest, but there are tears on her cheeks.

"Are you all right?" I ask, and she nods, her eyes welling up again. I glance once more over my shoulder at Des before crawling to where Valentina is sitting against the back wall and settling next to her. She's shaking, trying so hard not to cry, her hands clasped in white fists at her sides. "You don't have to pretend," I say softly.

She fights it for another moment, but her next breath comes shuddering out, a dam breaking. "I don't want to forget," she sobs, her voice trembling. "I don't want to, but remembering hurts." She swipes at the tears streaming down her face, staring at her hands, shaking her head.

"What happened?" I ask, hoping it'll help her to talk it through. *Tam would have a handkerchief to offer her,* I think, momentarily distracted.

Valentina tries to take a deep breath, but she's still shaking, stammering through her words. "They must have thought I was—was alone in the garden," she gets out finally. "It's hardly a garden, really, just—just a pathetic square of grass in front of the house, with the peonies that I . . . it doesn't matter." She shakes her head like she's clearing it. "There were three of them, men like at the warehouse. They grabbed hold of me but my—my brother saw and came running into the yard, to stop them, you know? To help me. Davey." She exhales slowly, pressing her eyes shut. "One of them shot him. There was blood everywhere. He was thirteen. I'll never forget

him, and I don't want to—that he tried to help, that it was the
last time I'll ever see him. But, Isla, it's all there in my head,
whenever I close my eyes. The blood, on the house, on the
ground, coming out of his shirt. I can hear his gasping, and
the little ones screaming inside, the noise, and my own voice,
saying his name I think, over and over as they pulled me
away." She lifts her hands, looking at them hopelessly. "I
couldn't save him. I tried to fight them and I couldn't save
anyone, not even myself." When she stops talking, the silence
feels hollow.

"I'm so sorry," I hear myself saying once, twice, a dozen
times. "I'm so sorry."

It must be hours later that a pair of serving women come
with a pail of stew, spoons, and chipped bowls, and a loaf
of bread almost as hard as the stone we sit on. They set the
food down on the ground outside the cell, looking anywhere
but at our faces. There's also a jar of water to pass around,
but it tastes like rust.

One of the girls serves the stew. I'm too hungry to turn
my nose up, but it tastes like we're eating the burnt scrap-
ings of different pots all mixed together. There are shreds
of vegetables in the greasy broth, along with some indistin-
guishable meat. At the first bite, my stomach lurches, and
also at the second, but I force myself to eat. Slowly, so I
won't get sick. At least the stew is still warm. I've eaten half
before I notice that Des doesn't have anything. "Take the
rest," I say, moving closer and slipping the bowl underneath
the grating.

"Nah," he says nonchalantly. "I snatched a biscuit from Curram's study earlier."

"Des. Take it." My stomach growls, and I hope he can't hear it. Even as he picks up the bowl, he's still insisting he isn't hungry, but Pa pretended the same countless times, to make me eat when there wasn't much. Thinking about him hurts.

A moment later, the empty bowl clatters on the ground. "Thank you," Des says.

"Don't they feed you?" Valentina asks, leaning toward the bars.

"Not if Curram's cross, no." He watches her for a long minute. "Who's your friend?" he asks.

"I'm Valentina," she says, frowning.

"Lovely." Her frown deepens when he winks at her. "Well, Isla, Valentina, I'm going to get a few hours of sleep, but I'll see you in the morning. Or the evening. You never really know for sure down here." He grins once more and climbs onto the nearest bunk, and in seconds he's still.

Most of the other girls have begun whispering in their own tight clusters. Some still sit numbly without speaking. A few are asleep already, and one is still crying.

Valentina falls asleep against me as I sit and blankly watch the shadows cast by our jailer's movements. I hate the sickly yellow of oil light. *How long has it been since I saw real light? Just a day, since the cart?* It feels like longer. I miss the sun on hot shingles, the sun glinting off Industria's many machines. I miss Tam and his bronze arms, his golden head in my lap, his hastily spouted dreams sinking into my skin. *Why was I so certain I could keep him, when he was always telling me that he'd leave? Why did I think what we had was untouchable?*

Tucked into the corner of this cell, with the cold seeping into my bones, I feel nothing but fragile. Exposed, alone. I hate that I already don't notice the smell anymore. I'm scared to think what will happen next. But I'm tired, and slowly my eyelids start to droop, and the next thing I know, I'm waking up, with a dream somewhere in the back of my thoughts.

My neck aches from the stone, and my temples pound. A pillow should be the last thing I have time to wish for, but I can't help it. *At least I have a moment to myself,* I think, trying to be grateful for something. Then I catch sight of the jailer, watching our cell from his bench with his dark, beady eyes.

I shift slightly, willing him to fall asleep, or better yet, disappear entirely.

If it's morning now, then this is the fourth day, I decide, though it could be more or fewer; it's so hard to tell without sunlight. I trace four vertical lines on the floor with my finger, though it leaves no mark. *I've survived four days.*

Instead of giving me hope, the number makes me worry.

This won't last much longer. I'm sure Zachariah Curram did not spend his precious money only to leave us in a dingy hole and never . . . make use of us. I'm starting to guess what comes next.

This moment, this quiet, must be the calm before the storm, so to speak.

Still, I start when the door at the top of the stairs snaps open, and two men appear, silhouetted by the relative light outside. They descend the staircase, talking quietly and easily.

I hold my breath, heart pounding.

But it's only Des they want.

They unlock his cell and haul him out, up the stairs, and out of view. Des doesn't tease or cajole them this time. The door closes with a soft thud, and all is quiet again. My lungs collapse with relief, even though I know I shouldn't give in to it.

Around me, whispered conversations start as everyone wakes fully. Phoebe, of course, says and does nothing, and yet I can almost feel her mind working. I think about asking her what her plans are, but I don't. Instead I listen as Valentina tells me about the flowers she learned to grow, the seedlings that did poorly in the rainy months, the bulbs she found in the window boxes of an abandoned shop, and the care her brother Davey took to water them all when she was sick one summer.

"Around us, everything is ugly, even in the nicer months. It's just part of living there. But my boxes are like a little way out of that. A piece of prettiness in all the gray, even though Mama says I'm wasting my time. But I don't agree. My flowers give people a break from all of the plainness." I'm sure Valentina is wondering what will happen to them now, but neither of us says so.

The peace is broken suddenly by the door at the top of the stairs bursting open. We all start as one, and Valentina's flowers are forgotten. *Is it Des already? How long has it been, an hour? Two?* The silhouettes of three men appear: two soldiers, as always, and another. It isn't Des.

I catch my breath and watch as they descend the steps, the prison soundless but for the muffled thuds made by their boots. No one else speaks, moves, breathes.

The stranger is not a prisoner; if anything, he is leading the men. His clothes are fine, velvet and silk, but unflattering: his cravat tight but everything else ill-fitting; a black bombin hat perched awkwardly on his close-shaven head. He walks quickly with jagged steps toward the cell, and I recognize him: Curram's man, the one who handled the money at the warehouse.

He stops only inches from the bars and looks in at us, his face twisted into an ugly, condescending sneer.

We all shrink back at the same time, as far from the cell door as possible. Someone's hand clutches mine, small and cold as ice; Eugenia stares at me, trembling. I squeeze her fingers with my own, wishing I could tell her to be strong, that we'll be all right. But I'm sure we won't be.

The man is smiling now, his pale eyes raising gooseflesh on my arms. He puts a key in the cell's lock, turns it, and opens the door.

six

I can't back up any farther. The walls feel closer, the cell smaller. Someone starts to cry, and my pulse races in my ears. The man looks like a giant, towering over us with his arms crossed, amusement evident on his face.

He is still as stone except for his eyes, which flick from one of us to the next. I brace myself for him to move, but when he lunges forward, I jump anyway. It's Eugenia he grabs, yanking her to her feet, pulling her hand out of mine. I'm too startled to hold on, fixated as her hair tumbles forward to cover her face, and it's as if I'm seeing myself taken away, her skin as white as bone in the shadows.

He adjusts his grip on her arms as she screams for help and thrashes uselessly. He's bigger, stronger, and I'm frozen in horror.

I hear her cries, and they might as well be mine.

The man's hat is knocked off his head, and with a grunt he flings Eugenia out of the cell and to the ground outside.

The soldiers hoist her to her feet; she looks like a porcelain doll, pale and fragile, between them. They drag her up the stairs, weeping and still begging for help, and I sit, unable to move.

The fancy man is still standing in the entrance to the cell, but now he is watching us. He bends very deliberately to pick up his hat, his eyes running over us the entire time. When he places the hat slowly onto his head, he's smiling.

Then he backs out of the cell and shuts it behind him, turning the lock and hooking his cluttered ring of keys on his belt once more. He turns, climbs the stairs, and is gone.

Eugenia's screams echo off the walls, or perhaps only inside my head. Fear fills the air, pushing my heart faster and faster. I can't think about her. I don't want to imagine what comes next.

It sounds as if half of the girls in the cell are sobbing loud, ugly tears. I run over math problems and lists of principal cities in my head until I manage to drown out my imagination and at last feel numb. Someone begins to cough, and it seems to go on forever. Outside our cell, the jailer sits and watches us. Eventually he takes out a charcoal pencil and sketches on scraps of paper. I'm sure we're the subjects. Sometimes he drinks from a flask kept in his boot, and sometimes he tips his head back and snores. I stare at him until I forget that I'm staring, wishing he would drop dead.

Beside me, Valentina is trembling, trying not to cry. *Comfort is pointless here*, I think, but I bring her head down to rest in my lap and stroke the hair from her face, clasping Tam's locket in my free hand.

Eugenia had a brother the same year as Tam in school, I think.

We all jump when the door opens again. But it's a pair of sentries with a familiar figure between them, looking strong and confident, even in chains.

Des is tossed into his cell with no more gentleness than before and responds with familiar wit. When the sentries leave, he leans his face against the bars and studies us, one eyebrow cocked. "And how are you ladies faring this fine day?"

I have no patience for him this time. "You might have warned us how suddenly he'd come, or told us that he'd—that—something! You might have *tried* to prepare us!"

His face drops, looking ashen. "Boyne came? Today?" His voice is quiet as he looks over our number, taking a seat on the ground. "How many did he take?"

"One. Someone I knew from school." Some of my anger is siphoned away by his genuine sadness, but I wish I could hang on to it, as a sort of defense. "When will he come back?"

Des seems to sink lower. He glances around our cell, then back at me, closing his eyes and holding them shut for a moment. "It's impossible to say. It could be tomorrow, or tonight, or in a week or a month. I thought—I thought Curram was too busy—had too much—" He grasps at empty words.

"Apparently not," I murmur. Our jailer gets up and shuffles up the stairs, distracting me. "Will he be gone all night?" I ask, hopeful for a second.

"I couldn't say," Des answers, sounding tired. "He's allowed to leave, to eat and relieve himself and sleep. But I think he likes being down here, or he'd go more often. Doesn't miss the sun. He's made for the shadows, and the filth."

"I don't suppose he ever leaves the keys?" Phoebe's voice drifts across the cell, low and smooth. I wonder if she's always listening, or only when there might be an opportunity for escape.

"Never. And unless your arms are a lot longer than they look, it wouldn't do you any good besides."

Valentina is sitting up now, watching Des as well. "I don't understand you," I say, growing more frustrated. "Aren't you a slave here, too? Why would you mock her wanting to escape?"

He goes very still for a moment, holding her gaze. "You shouldn't ask questions," he says. "None of what goes on here is pretty."

I glance at Valentina. "We don't need pretty," I press.

There's a long silence and Des looks as if he's gearing up to make another joke, but his eyes are afraid. "I'm not a slave like you, no," he says finally. "I work for our dear Mister Curram. I'm a part of the reason you're here."

"What the hell?" hisses Phoebe, at my side in an instant, her face close to the bars.

I try to ignore her, holding Des's gaze. "What do you mean?" I say slowly. "The whole story."

He swallows hard. "I'm a thief," he states simply, the words heavy. "A good one, too. At least Curram thinks so." His voice becomes quieter. "When I was a kid, I lied my way into places, picked enough pockets to afford good clothes, and lied my way into better places from there. I wasn't hurting anyone. I only took from the ones rich enough not to miss it. Money, mostly; whatever was at the back of the vault, you know? I was always a good liar; it didn't take much to charm my way into a party at a great house or onto the arm of a woman with an invitation. I robbed at least a dozen fools in the first year." He takes a breath, glancing around as if to ask whether or not he should go on. Phoebe glowers at him, and his eyes drop to the ground.

"Early on I got books for my sister and me to educate ourselves, and with my pa not working, I was taking care of the three of us and it felt good, you know? Outsmarting all of these peacocks in their big houses? That was it. I was too confident. Me, cocky." There's a smirk at this, but it's gone in a second.

"Money wasn't enough. I told myself I needed to feel challenged. I was an idiot. By the time I worked my way up to stealing ledgers and family heirlooms for the thrill of it, I wasn't nearly as careful as I had been before. I didn't know who Curram was; just another rich face as far as I was concerned. I danced with his wife and took a bracelet right off her wrist, a whole string of sapphires. He was the first to ever notice. Had me followed home, and before I realized what was going on, I was out cold. I woke up tied to a chair in Curram's office."

He stops, and no one speaks for a long moment.

"But what do you do for him?" demands Phoebe, pressing in close again.

"I make him rich, simple as that. At parties, meetings. If he needs to blackmail someone, I get the dirt he needs."

"What else?"

Des scoffs. "Isn't that enough?"

"Then why not escape?" I ask. "You could think of a way. You have time we don't. Why aren't you trying to leave?"

"What does it matter *why*?" snaps Phoebe, glaring at him and gesturing around the cell. "Did you bring us here?" The other girls are looking over now. "If it's your fault that I'm sitting in this damned cell, I'll tear your head off—"

"Go for it," Des says, leaning back against the wall and closing his eyes. "We're back to your long arms, I see."

The cells grow quiet, and the stillness feels sad. A part of me wants to stand up and demand more answers, but it's clear that Des is done talking. Phoebe slinks back to the corner, her face contorted into an angry scowl, a promise that she won't let this go. I watch Des for a moment, running over his story in my head. *He's had three years. He could leave, I'm sure he could. When he's above ground, stealing something, he could find a way. He must have a connection to Curram that he's not telling us.*

Sitting in dismal silence, my thoughts turn to Eugenia. I

don't want to think about where she is. *Will I even see her again? What will Curram do with her after . . . after he's finished?* I could ask Des, but I don't. Whenever I glance over at him, he's staring into the shadows with a vacant look on his face.

When Tam told me stories, he knew how to make places sound familiar and thrilling at the same time, like the islands he longed to see were old but unpredictable friends. He'd manage just enough patience to finish a book written by a sea captain he thought very brave, and then come to my roof to list the number of times the man had beaten death.

"I could do that," he'd say, sprawled out across the shingles, squinting up at me.

And my heart would start to race at the idea that he'd go, and I'd think of an obstacle. "What if your sails had been torn in the storm, though? And they'd gone down with the ship? What would you do then?"

"I'd figure something out," he'd mumble, and I knew that I could keep him for at least as long as it took him to read another adventure story. He was the only person whose inability to read quickly never bothered me.

I wish I had a story to listen to now, instead of just my own thoughts. I wish I had Tam. *Hurry, my love. Fight the odds and find me quickly. Solve this problem like you solved all the others.*

seven

I wake up on the floor, achy and cold.

It was so hot in the city. How can it be so cold under-ground?

The jailer is back at his post, sketching something. He meets my eyes when I sit up, and I look away. I've only been awake a moment when the door at the top of the stairs clicks open.

All around me other girls wake up, rubbing sleep from their eyes and murmuring to each other. "Shh," I say, a finger against my lips. The door swings open, and I hold my breath. I look at Valentina; her mouth is set in a grim line, her eyes wide. She gives me a tight nod.

Wordlessly, everyone shrinks against the back of the cell.

Four figures this time: the man who came before, with the ill-fitting clothes and bowler hat, another pair of guards, and, held between them, the limp form of a girl. *Eugenia.* But it's the man who holds my attention. The hair on my

arms stands up; his eerie, intense strangeness makes me
feel almost sick.

When he reaches the bars of our cell, nobody breathes.
He puts the key into the lock and turns it creakily, enjoying
our fear. The door opens and he stands there a moment,
waiting to see if we'll react.

"There's no need for you to volunteer, ladies," he says,
smirking. "I'm only returning one of your own today. Don't
fret, I'll see you again soon enough." I look straight at him
and refuse to turn away. His gaze meets mine for the second
time, and he hesitates, smiling a little. Then he steps aside
and his soldiers toss Eugenia carelessly inside.

The cell door clangs shut, and in a moment the fancy
man—Boyne, Des called him—is gone, leaving the soldiers
in conversation with the jailer. None of us moves or speaks;
the soldiers' presence makes me uneasy, and when I steal a
glance at the other cell, Des only looks at the ground.

Eugenia is curled into an unmoving ball on the dirty
floor. At first I wonder if she might be unconscious, but
when I look closer, I can see that she's shaking with silent
tears. The frilly, revealing dress she was wearing when they
took her upstairs is gone, and in its place she wears the sort
of underclothes that I imagine are sold in the stores with
black curtains. Her corset, which has been laced up carelessly, barely covers her breasts, and her pantaloons are lacy
and revealing, almost transparent in the lantern light. Her
stockings droop unevenly, gathering around her knees, and

her hair is disheveled, spilling out of a ribbon that does little to hold it in place.

She seems unaware of her surroundings, crumpled on the floor, trembling but otherwise unmoving. I want to do something, but I don't know what, and Valentina acts first, taking quiet steps toward Eugenia and crouching at her side. When she puts out a hand to touch her shoulder, Eugenia jerks sharply, twisting away and scooting backward against the cell door. Her eyes are wide, red-rimmed, and startled; she looks from one face to the next, her knees held tightly to her chest.

"Don't touch me," she says in a shaky whisper.

"I want to help you," Valentina says, her eyes shining.

"D-don't!" Eugenia stutters. "Don't touch me."

"Please, let me—"

"I don't have to let you!" she shouts at Valentina, making us all jump. "I—I don't have to let you do anything. I don't belong to you, or to anybody. I don't. My name is Eugenia Margaret Rigney, and I belong—I belong to myself." Her voice catches on a hiccup, drops to a mumble. "My parents are Matthew and Veronica Rigney. I went to get a newspaper and tomatoes from the stand. I didn't mean to get lost . . . it wasn't my fault." She's stopped talking to Valentina at this point; her eyes stare off at nothing.

"They probably sent Jonah over to fetch them, when I didn't return. I meant to hurry back, but it wasn't my fault. I hope they looked for me. Maybe they're worrying now."

She goes on and on, as if the rest of us don't exist. There's bruising along her collarbone and arms, and a tear along the top of her corset. I feel like I'll be sick.

The guards finally turn to go upstairs, but one glances back at our crowded cell and sneers, looking pointedly at Eugenia. "Don't know why he wants that skinny creature back again," he says, spitting in her direction. "Why save her when you can have a new one any night?"

Before I can even take in what he's saying, Eugenia whirls around, scrambling to her feet and throwing herself against the bars. "He will never touch me again!" she shouts, her voice rough, hoarse. "I will never go back to him!"

But the man just chuckles, looking her up and down disdainfully. "You'll do whatever the master wants, whore."

"I am *not a whore!*" she cries, sobs racking her body. "I am *not!*" She continues to call after them, but they climb the stairs as if they don't hear her. "I am not a whore. My name is Eugenia Margaret Rigney!" She shouts the same string of words again and again as she rocks back and forth against the bars. The words pound into my head, sear themselves into my memory like the X on my hand: *"My name is Eugenia Margaret Rigney. My name is Eugenia Margaret Rigney. My name is Eugenia Margaret Rigney."*

She screams until her voice breaks, and still she repeats and repeats the same words.

I try to cover my ears, but it's useless.

It might be just minutes, or it might be an hour later that Eugenia finally wears herself out. She sinks to her knees, falling forward against the cold metal of the cell door, sobbing, pleading the words now, forcing them out with the last of her strength. I don't know why it's so important to her to say her name. Maybe she feels that it's all she has left.

How many others has he destroyed?

Eugenia knocks her head lightly against the door, then again. She finds a rhythm in it, clinging to the bars until her hands are white. The constant thudding is almost as bad as the screaming. I wrap my arms around my ears and press my eyes shut, picturing Tam and Pa and anything to distract me. Just when I think I'll go mad myself, I'm startled by a noise and the sight of the jailer lurching to his feet and bolting up the stairs with surprising speed.

With any luck his head will forever ring with the sound of her name.

I don't want to watch Eugenia, but I can't help it. *Is this the fate that awaits each of us? Taken one by one, used by Curram, and then returned to our holding place, miserable and tarnished? Driven mad because we are supposed to keep on living? Or is that only for the ones who amuse him? Will the rest of us be quietly disposed of? Maybe the unluckiest of us all will be resold, to a buyer who doesn't require, as Curram does, the "freshest meat."*

It all sounds feasible, making my stomach queasier with every second. I clutch my locket, wishing that Eugenia had something like it to ground her. I tell myself to be grateful that I was able to hold on to it. *Tam will come, Tam will come,*

Tam will come. I make it into my own sort of chant. *Against all the odds, he'll come.*

What calm we have is short-lived. The door opens abruptly to show the jailer with the bombin-wearing man at his side. Behind them is the tall figure of Zachariah Curram himself. Eugenia sees him and goes mad.

She lurches to her feet, gripping the iron bars with renewed fervor. *"Bastard!"* she screams at him, her face pressed against the grating. "I am *not* yours! I *do not* belong to you!" He reaches the foot of the stairs and comes toward the cell, and she spits in his face, throwing herself against the bars like an animal. "You cannot rob me of who I am. I am *not* yours. I am my own. My name is Eugenia Marg—"

He cuts her off coolly. "You know very well that I bought you, my dear. And I only part with my money for the most important objects. Objects I intend to hold on to, or make very good use of." He wipes the spittle from his face with an embroidered handkerchief and steps a little closer, his eyes darkening. "You're acting like a child, and your immaturity offends me. Will you behave, or will I have to punish you? I require good manners of my belongings."

She tries to laugh, but it comes out as a sob. "I will never obey you," she says, her whole body trembling.

Curram smiles an apologetic smile, shrugging a little. "You will, though."

She spits in his face again, swearing that she won't, that he can't have her again, that he'll burn in hell. He wipes his face once more and returns the handkerchief to his pocket.

And then there's something else in his hand, a pistol, only inches from Eugenia's head. I can't breathe.

"Shall I warn you again?" he says very quietly. He is perfectly calm, perfectly serious. *But he wants her*, I remind myself. *He saved her to have her again later, because he's selfish. He won't dispose of her. He won't waste his money.* I try to quiet my heart, but I can't stop shaking. I wait to see whether he'll replace the weapon with words of warning, or deliver an insult that will put her "in her place." Boyne's eyes flick between Curram and his latest trinket. He's timid in his master's presence, but he's enjoying the scene.

"My name," she says quietly, "is Eugenia Margaret Rigney. I am not yours." Curram's eyes widen, and his mouth quirks upward in what looks like an incredulous smile. His hand tightens on the gun. The barrel is only an inch from Eugenia's forehead, at the most. My panic resurfaces. *He won't. She's useful to him.* "My name," she says again, louder this time, "is Eugenia Mar—"

The deafening, splitting noise of the gunshot cracks the air. There's a terrible, slow moment as Eugenia drops to the ground, her hands falling away from the bars, a catch in my breath as I realize, *He actually did it. He killed her. . . . He killed her. . . . Someone I knew. She's dead.* I can't breathe, or move, or think.

This is not the world I knew.

Eugenia lies still on the cold ground, an arm thrown above her head, her dark blood pooling on the stones, seeping across her face, covering her eyes. I'm shaking, and my ears are ringing from the gunshot, from screams cut short, my own or those of the girls around me, I don't know.

I drag my eyes away from her mangled face and look instead at her murderer. Curram stands with his man beside him, unaffected. He pockets the gun as smoothly as he drew it, wiping his hands together as if to clean them. His face holds no emotion besides disdain.

"Dunbar," he says to the jailer, "make arrangements for someone to clean up the mess." He glances once through the bars to survey the rest of us. He must enjoy our distress, because he watches for a full minute more.

When Curram finally leaves, the jail fills with the sound of sobs. Even Phoebe tucks herself away so that her face is hidden by the shadows.

Eugenia's body lies where it fell. Every moment it seems more still, more lifeless. Even when I close my eyes, I can see, pressed into the backs of my eyelids, all that blood mingling with her hair, her legs twisted together as she crumpled to the ground.

In that other life, which seems so long ago, I saw her nearly every day, though I never thought much of it. In a class or across a street, people mixed us up, because we looked similar, though we were never really friends. Even if it was only a little, I knew her.

I knew her, and now she's dead.

This is real.

There is no hope, no silver lining. There is no use in waiting for Tam to arrive to free me. Tam will be too late. The only thing I have coming to me is defilement and misery.

My tears dry up as determination sets in.

I can't sit still any longer. I'm going to leave this place, or die trying.

eight

They don't bring us anything to eat, and the moments pass slowly. Not that we could eat anyway. Nobody tries to make conversation, and eventually the other girls drift off to sleep. But my mind is in a frenzy.

I need a plan. All the books tell me that a heroine has a plan.

But I have no idea how to get us all out of here. We could use the wire in our corsets to make a hook to snatch the keys, or maybe we can lure Dunbar to the bars somehow. We could use the water we're given with dinner to rust away the hinges of the cell door. It all feels far-fetched. Even after I decide to plan when I'm better rested, I can't sleep. Whenever I close my eyes, I see Eugenia clutching at the bars, screaming her name, dropping to the ground in a bloody mess.

What happens at home, when people are taken? I wonder. Do their families search and search for them? Does the newspaper warn of danger? Do the police post notes on street corners, asking for help? My thoughts turn darker and darker, but I don't know how to shut them off. *If a person is missing for long enough, does their family just try to forget? Will Pa try to forget me?* He hasn't forgotten Mum, but he doesn't speak of her often. He just gets a funny look on his face when I mention her.

Will he push back the memory of me when he realizes I'm not coming back? Will that be less painful than wondering where I've gone? What does he think happened to me? And maybe Tam didn't see me get taken. Maybe I've exaggerated everything to myself, that he could possibly find a way to save me, that he even loves me at all.

What if he kissed me only because he was leaving, and now he regrets it? What if it was just an impulse, and when he comes back someday he'll want to resume our friendship as it always has been? Or to ignore me so he won't feel awkward?

I don't need to worry about that. I need to worry about being there when he comes home.

I squeeze my eyes shut and try to stop. I have Tam's love here in my hand: I don't need to wonder if it's real. He loves me. With everything else in doubt and turmoil, *that*, at least, I can be certain of.

I don't remember falling asleep, but I wake with a start. *More nightmares,* I think, wishing I could somehow shake my head free of them. And it's not as if waking up is any better. It must still be night; most everyone appears to be sleeping.

"Des?" I say quietly, crawling over to the bars. The thin

lace of my stockings is wearing out already; my knees are nearly exposed, and tender from the rough floor of the cell. "Are you awake?"

"Yeah, sweetheart?" he answers quietly, his back to me against the grating. His voice is defeated, heavy.

"Will you talk to me?" He turns so I can see his face and raises an eyebrow.

"You think you want my stories of woe?" he says, shaking his head.

"Yes," I say. Beside me, Val nods, staring blankly at Eugenia's body across the cell. She's so still I didn't realize she was awake, her legs pulled up tightly to her chest.

"Anything but the silence," she whispers, her eyes wide, scared.

A corner of Des's mouth lifts, meant to be a reassuring smile. *How many smiles does he have?* Cocky and self-assured, either as a mask for his pain or a way to cope with it, or wry and rueful, his view on life so sarcastic. And then, at moments like this, kind and gentle.

"I have nothing to tell you but my own nightmares," he says, shrugging.

For a moment there's silence. I take a breath, hoping I don't scare him away. "Tell me why you stay, Des. You could find a way out if you wanted to. That's the story I want to hear."

When he finally looks up, I think he's going to cry. "I'm still here," he says finally, really open for the first time, "for Lillian, my sister. It wasn't just me they took that day." He almost chokes on the words. His eyes find mine and they are pleading. "He—Curram—took her. I'd have just let them kill me if it'd only been me, but . . . I couldn't . . . he said he'd hurt her if I didn't do as he said. There I was thinking I was king of the world and answering to nobody, and I couldn't even protect my own sister when it came to it." He runs a hand through his hair, looking frantic. "He had her tied to a chair, all bruised and bleeding about her face, and she was crying, though Boyne kept tellin' her to stop, like that'd help."

Now his tone turns hollow. "Curram said he'd keep her till he was done with me, and if I ever disobeyed him, I'd be responsible for her treatment. I've tried to learn where he keeps her. I can't roam free, but I've—I've tried." He's somewhere else now, his eyes vacant, and I try to picture a girl with a face like his, and hair as black as both of ours, her skin broken and bleeding.

"That's why—why I'm still here, why I can't help you, even why Curram is still alive. I'd have killed him three years ago if I thought I could find Lillian. He knows it, too, but he knows he's got me. I have to believe she's still alive, that I can find her somehow, that I can save her, even though I failed the first time." His eyes find mine again. "And then you showed up, and I thought he got messy or didn't care or—or I don't know. I thought you were her, right there in front of me."

"I'm sorry," I say, tired of apologizing for the evil on every side. I feel used up and tired, tired in my heart and down through my bones. I scoot backward to the wall, wrapping my arms around myself for comfort or warmth; neither comes.

"How old were you when you came here?" I hear Valentina say, her voice gentle and sympathetic as always.

"Sixteen, my pa said. That might not be true. He lost a lot of his wits after my"—he clears his throat, making light of his words with a halfhearted chuckle—"after my mum ran off. But I'd say he was probably about right." His voice is hoarse.

She asks more questions, but I don't hear them. When exhaustion pulls my eyes closed, I think of Tam. I remember the way my heart raced so hard I thought it would choke me, on a day just one summer before. Rain falling, and Tam and me running through the city's streets like children, laughing and pretending we could fly. The late-afternoon light seeped through a hole in the clouds and made the air yellow, and I was so sure everything was perfect and would stay that way. When the thunder began to crash, Tam pulled me under a peddler's awning for safety, his face glowing with life. He looked around us at the rain-soaked city, and I looked up at him.

I can see him behind my eyelids, opening his mouth like he'll say something, glancing down at me and grinning, catching himself and looking closer. I remember the way he leaned in so his face was close to mine with only inches between us. I thought I felt his breath on my cheek, and I thought he was going to kiss me. My stomach fluttered in panic, and I flushed with nervousness. But he didn't kiss me then. He just smiled again and told me in a curious voice that he'd never noticed just how odd my eyes were, with flecks of gold and brown in the green.

It didn't feel like a compliment then; the words stung because they weren't a kiss.

How different everything is now. I squeeze my eyes shut more tightly and try to remember the exact words Tam used, the pattern the raindrops followed as they rolled off his cheek, the number of times my heart thrummed against my ribs waiting for that almost-kiss. The harder I try, the further the memory slips away.

✦ ✦ ✦

When I wake, I'm clutching the locket to my throat. I look at my two hands beside each other, so different in the near darkness: one imprinted with the shape of the heart, the other mangled by the cruel, inflamed X of the brand. My life, summed up so neatly: on the right, my old self, my love, my memories; on my left, the harsh new reality from which I'm still trying to wake.

Eugenia's body, still lying where it fell by the grating, jars me every time my eyes fall on it. There's already an odor coming from her corpse, as if the toilet hole is overflowing. *How long will they leave it there to rot?*

I try to look elsewhere, but it's almost impossible.

The guards bring our stew and take Des upstairs in one occurrence, while we sit in tense clusters and wait to see if anyone else will be taken. When everything is quiet again,

Valentina brings a bowl to me. "Finish it all," she says, putting the dish into my hands. "Just don't look at the body and it's fine." *I could starve myself,* I think briefly. *That might be the least awful way out of here.*

No.

Escape will be the least awful way out of here. Taking the others with me, making my way home, finding Tam, upsetting Zachariah Curram and ruining his plans to keep us. That will be my story. Not wasting away in a hole in the ground, waiting for one of two fates.

In a few hasty mouthfuls, the stew is gone. A couple of the girls choke on it, or stare miserably into their dishes, and it dawns on me that some were probably raised on more delicate food.

I look around at them, all girls my age, but different in every other way. I wonder if I should learn their names, and then I wonder if I would be better off keeping my distance instead. If they become my friends, it will only get harder to see them taken. It could happen half a dozen more times before I think of a way out of here.

As if my fears had been broadcast aloud, the door at the top of the stairs bursts open. The noise is like a death sentence, but I don't look up this time. I leave my head on my knees, my arms wound around myself. *Why is it so cold?* I hate the cold. I hate being underground. I feel as if my head is filled with fog.

I hear footsteps, maybe two people; when I do raise my

head, two young men are approaching Dunbar. They wear
the sort of battered clothes that outdoor servants, grounds-
keepers or stable boys, might.

"Heard we're s'posed to 'elp you with removin' a body?"
one of them says, throwing a glance at Eugenia's form on
the ground. The other, younger man fidgets uneasily, looking at his feet.

"Help *me*?" Dunbar grunts.

"That's what I was told." The first one shrugs, refusing to
be put off. "Wanna unlock that door?" He crosses his arms
and Dunbar grumbles loudly, climbing to his feet and shuf-
fling toward the cell. After a moment of fiddling, the door
swings open, and I am suddenly filled with inexplicable panic
that it will be as if Eugenia were never here, that she will be
forgotten, that her life will truly be over.

I lunge forward, scrambling on my hands and knees
toward her body. I can't bring myself to touch her, so I pull
at the ribbon in her hair; it takes a second to come free, and
as I draw back with it clasped in my hand, someone grabs
my arm.

A strong hand hauls me to my feet, and I find myself only
inches from the face of the first servant. He looks me over,
grinning a little. I can feel his breath on my cheek, but I don't
risk trying to wriggle free. "Friend o' yours, was she?" he asks
me in a smooth whisper. I don't answer; it takes all my courage just to meet his gaze. His eyes stray from my face, down
the length of my neck, landing on the place where my

corset starts. He pulls me a little closer, and I brace myself
for a struggle if he tries anything. I can feel my pulse in my
fingers as they curl around the ribbon from Eugenia's hair.

"You been up to see the master yet?" he asks softly, meeting my gaze again for a second. When I don't answer, he
scans me and must realize that my clothes are wrong. "Maybe
not." He grins again and leans in, planting a hard, sharp kiss
on my mouth. I jerk away from him in surprise, anger making
my cheeks hot.

"Let me be!" I snap, throwing my hand out to smack him.
He catches it and slaps me hard. My ears ring, and my cheek
pulses with more warmth. His smile broadens.

"Nice spirit you've got there," he says, smirking. I'm shaking, but his grip on my arm is strong, bruising. "I see why
Mr. Curram likes to get you fresh. Wouldn't want 'is prod-
ucts spoiled by . . . damaging hands, now would 'e?" His free
hand trails along my cheek, then down my throat and over my
shoulder.

"L-l-leave her be," says someone behind him. The man
turns slightly, still holding on to me.

It's the other servant, looking nervous. He's got to be
younger than I am, maybe fifteen, and thin as a stick.
"Robbie, c'mon. Let her alone." I wish I could thank him,
but he avoids my eyes.

His companion sneers a little, glancing down my corset
again. Then he lets go abruptly, and I drop to the ground, surprised by the unexpected release. I clamber away from him,
toward the other girls, none of whom have made a sound.

Neither man pays any more attention to me as they unfold the tarp they brought, lay it out beside Eugenia's body, and take hold of her pale ankles and wrists. I turn away as they drop her onto it, and don't look up until they've left the cell. I'm grateful, in a way, when the bars clang shut behind them and there is a barrier between us again.

I wipe my mouth with the back of my hand, wishing I could undo the sharp kiss left there, so different from the nervous, candy-sweet one Tam gave me.

At the foot of the stairs, Dunbar is growling at the servants. "I'll say somethin' if ye try an' touch 'em agin, ye hear?" he says angrily. "They're not fer the likes o' you." Then he laughs in a scoffing way. "Bet ya couldn't bed a girl if you paid fer one, so leave the master's property alone 'fore you go damagin' it." The one who kissed me, Robbie, blushes fiercely, his hands curling at his sides. With controlled, stiff movements, he sets down the end of the tarp that he is carrying and crosses his arms over his chest.

"How'd ye like fer me to mention this to Mr. Boyne?" he hisses, looking like an angry boy whose teacher has shamed him in front of his friends. "You think it's funny to take a jab at me, huh, old man? I can tell 'im you were making friendly with the girls yerself when I spoke up 'bout it."

"Let's just hurry an' finish this, Robbie—" starts his helper.

"Go ahead and mention it," Dunbar jeers, cutting him off. "I've got my job, and I'll keep it. Now get on!" Grunting, he boxes Robbie's ears with his fists, but to my surprise the younger man does not retaliate. He just turns, slowly, and lifts his end of the tarp again. As they begin to make their way up the stairs, the boy struggles under Eugenia's weight, slow in his steps.

But Robbie scarcely notices; every step he takes, he's watching Dunbar, until he disappears through the door.

I start when someone touches my shoulder. "Are you all right?" Valentina asks softly, her hand fluttering to my face next, where it is still warm from being struck. I want to snap that I am, no thanks to anyone else. Instead I shrug.

"It could have been worse." *It will be worse, if nothing changes.*

A tear trickles from the corner of her eye, and she quickly wipes at it with the back of her hand. I know she's thinking the same thing, and there's silence for a moment. She looks as if she's drawing up all her courage, and says, "I just want someone to put a bullet in *my* head." Then her face drops into her hands and, leaning against my shoulder, she starts to sob. Slowly, awkwardly, I wrap an arm around her.

In my other hand is the ribbon from Eugenia's hair, coiled up and small, the only thing left of her. *Eugenia Margaret Rigney.* Now I'll never forget her. I won't let myself.

nine

I murmur what I hope are comforting things to Valentina and wrap the ribbon carefully around my wrist: once, twice, three times, tying the ends together in a tight knot. Of course it's black.

Valentina's tears stop eventually, but we stay where we are. "Do you have brothers or sisters?" she asks quietly, our shoulders touching, her head resting against mine. "Where did you go to school? Tell me something good."

"I haven't got brothers or sisters," I say quietly. "Or a mum. She died when I was young. It's just my pa and me now. . . ." My voice trails off. My throat is so tight I don't know how to breathe. I swallow and force myself to continue. "He must be worrying about me now. We're all each other has." Just the thought of his face makes me ache. "I started at the city school ten years ago, when I was six. I haven't finished yet." There's more I could say: that I love books, and meeting the people inside them who don't exist until you turn the page,

that I'm afraid of a lot, and that I usually watch other people
have adventures. Instead of any of this, I say the most important thing: "And I love a boy named Tam Lidwell."

"Who's that?" Valentina asks softly, turning to look up
at me.

"My best friend in the world," I answer, feeling as if
I'm somewhere else for a moment, somewhere I like for
once, with something beautiful to show off that no one
can take from me. "He's brave, and sure, and lovely. He's a
lot like the sun, bright and strong, nothing like me. All he
wants is to go on a proper adventure. I'd give anything to
have him back." My fingers stray to the locket around my
neck. I wonder if Tam has held on to his key as tightly as
I have my little heart. I wonder, too, if he uses the spyglass I
gave him, even though looking back with it won't let him see
me after all.

"Did something happen to him?"

"He joined the army. I went to say good-bye and they took
me. I should have told him how much I loved him, but . . . I
never did."

"He probably knows," Valentina whispers. "If you love
him that much, he must know."

"He gave this to me, before he left," I say, holding the
necklace away from myself so she can see it. "He's got the
matching key."

She sits up and looks at me, her eyes wide. "How did you
keep it?"

"I put it in my mouth when they took my clothes," I say. "It's the only thing I have from him. I couldn't lose it."

"You're very brave, Isla," she murmurs.

I want to ask her to tell me about herself, but I don't know how to phrase the question. Eventually I say haltingly, "Is there somebody at home that you love, Val?" I don't mention Davey.

She shrugs slightly. "No, I hardly know anyone—I didn't go to school for long. My pa died and Mama couldn't send me because she needed me to look after the little ones. She didn't tell us what she did and we didn't ask. She was gone most nights, so we guessed that . . . well. It doesn't matter. I taught my . . . my brother what I had learned, and we tried to take care of things as best we could. Even when Mama hit us or had fits, we managed fine." She sniffs and goes on. "Benedict and Cara are real little, though. They're sick a lot, so I . . . I don't know what Mama'll do now, without . . . without Davey and me."

I don't know what to say, so we sit together in silence, and I think about how beautiful my old life looks now, and my head swims with thoughts of Tam.

I can't remember the day I first saw him; he was just always there. Across the alley, in the flat that mirrored ours one building over, clambering along the railings that lined the tall complexes where we lived. I'd sit outside my window on the piece of roof that stuck out, wrapped in a patched coat with a book in my arms. Often enough I found myself watching him instead of reading, though. Even when he was young, he was stronger and taller than me, while all the other boys his age at school were waiting for their height. He was sure of himself, too; he never fell.

I knew he saw me, because sometimes he'd wave before doing something impressive, even though I rarely returned the gesture. We might have always been strangers, living parallel lives, but it happened that his pa and mine stopped in at the same pub sometimes, and our mums brought their washing to the same place.

We only started talking when his mum sent him over with messages or things for mine, to save herself the trip. He'd climb out of his window and to the ground, jog across the alley, and then make his way up three stories of rusty ladders to my roof. He'd ask what I was reading, and I'd start to tell him until he got excited and interrupted because I'd reminded him of something he wanted to tell me, even though he hardly knew me. It was hard to think he was rude when the things he'd tell me were so fascinating and he was so eager to share them.

During the winter that saw his family sick with a bad fever—the one that took his mum and sister Elsie—I was so afraid for him that I read every book and magazine at the library about illness and sent a hundred paper aeroplanes with suggestions for treatment through his window.

And when he came to see me at the end of it all, when my own mum had died, too, he wrapped his arms around me and held me for so long that I thought we might stay that way forever. He told me he'd always look out for me, and it was then that I decided that nothing would separate us. As if drifting apart was the worst thing that could happen.

Eugenia's blood on the stone floor is proof that there are worse evils in the world than disappointed hopes.

"It's hard, thinking about home," a girl I don't know says suddenly. Her voice is shaky, and she stares straight ahead, her eyes unfocused. "I don't know what my grandmother'll do without me. She can't walk much anymore and it was just the two of us." She looks lost, sitting in the corner of the cell, her thin face awash with freckles that stand out in the dimness.

"I wish someone'd miss me," murmurs another, looking at her hands.

The girl beside her scoffs. "No one even knows we're gone, Caddy. Even those missionaries with their soup pots an' words of blessin' don't recognize a face day to day. Where else were we goin', anyway? The orphanage wasn't gonna keep us any longer. Someplace like this was comin' to us all along." Her bitter tone is a poor mask for the pain seeping through her words. Pa and I sometimes served meals on Sunday afternoons to children who came from orphanages or lived on the streets, though we had little better to eat at home.

"I know," the quieter one responds. "I just wish is all."

Time doesn't feel real anymore. *Has it been nearly a week now? Five or six days, I think.* I've lost track of their beginnings and ends.

Opposite me, Phoebe opens her mouth to say something but snaps it shut when I look at her.

To my left, one of the girls sits with her legs crossed, her knees against the wall. Her eyes are closed, but her fingers, delicate and white, move across the stone like she's drawing something, twisting and turning, sweeping up and down.

"Are you an artist?" I ask, gesturing at the wall.

She nods. "I painted every day at home. I even convinced my parents to hire a tutor so I didn't have to go to school and could spend all my time with my canvases. There's a gallery joined to my bedroom." She looks like a fairy, graceful and lithe, her white-blond hair standing out in the dark.

"I was never a very good artist," I say quietly, imagining the grand house she must have lived in.

She just shrugs. "I'm Cecily," she says, extending a hand. When I shake it, even her fingers seem to teem with manners and good breeding. She glances at the wall, seeming shy. "I know I'm strange for pretending, but it's a kind of escape and I . . . I need to escape. At least if I close my eyes, I can imagine that I'm painting. It helps a little."

"I'm Isla." I smile as reassuringly as I can. "We all need a way to stay sane."

"It's my own fault that I'm here," she says, her eyes sad and lost. "I was stupid, I—"

With a bang, the door at the top of the stairs opens.

A pair of soldiers appears, but no one else; I hold my breath, and beside me, Cecily does the same.

The soldiers descend the stairs slowly, enjoying our

uncertainty. My heart drums faster and faster as Dunbar questions their demand that the cell be unlocked, and one of them sneers, "Mister Boyne is otherwise occupied. We're here to pick up tonight's order."

No, no, no.

Our jailer begrudgingly gets to his feet and fiddles with the lock, and all we can do is wait, afraid. There's nowhere to go, no corner I can press myself farther into. The door swings open, and the men stand side by side in the opening. One of them crosses his arms over his chest. "You'd pick a blonde, if it was you, right?" he asks. The other scans us, his lip curling with something between disgust and desire.

As he nods, I look from Cecily to Phoebe, the only fair-haired girls in the group. "That one," says one of them, and his partner lunges forward, grabbing hold of Cecily's arm.

"No!" I scream as he jerks her to her feet, dragging her out, away. Her eyes meet mine, wide and panicked; she struggles, but it's no good. "No, don't—" I lurch to my feet, my thoughts all in a jumble. Hands shove my chest and send me tumbling backward. I shoot to my feet again, lunging after them, but the door shuts and it's too late. *I'm* too late.

"I'm sorry," I say, my throat aching, my eyes filling with tears. "I'm sorry, I'm so sorry!" *What was I going to do, trade myself for her? How was I going to help?*

"No, please!" she shrieks as they lock the door and drag her toward the stairs. One of the men slaps her hard across the face and shouts at her to be quiet. She blinks away her shock, tears streaming down her face. Her eyes find mine.

"Find my family, please, tell them I love them, tell them what happened."

They get to the top, to the door, and she wrenches around one last time so I can see her face. Her eyes are full of fear. "Give him hell!" I shout. "Make the bastard pay."

"I will," she says, so quietly that I barely hear it.

Then she's gone.

ten

For a while I sit and wonder about the rest of Cecily's story. *Why did she think it was her fault she was taken? What did she do that was so stupid? How am I supposed to find her family and tell them what happened, when I have no idea who she is or where she came from?* I have fewer tears this time; maybe they're almost used up.

When Des returns, he's somber; he must know that someone was brought upstairs.

"Does it always go the same way?" I ask when he sits down at the bars.

"As the last one?"

I nod.

"Only every so often. Different words, of course . . ." His voice trails off. "Sometimes if he sends them back, they make a fuss, so usually they just . . . don't come back. I doubt you'll see her again, whoever she was this time."

I'm not going to say anything else, but the words come

out on their own somehow. "I'm going to get out of here."
Des looks up at me sharply, his eyes full of pity.

"Isla," he starts, but I already know what he's going to
say. He's going to tell me how many times he's heard girls
just like me on this side of the bars say the same thing. And
he's going to tell me how every one of them failed, how I'll
only be getting my hopes up, how it's a waste of time.

"Don't try to talk me out of it; my life is the one at stake
here. It's time someone fought for a way out and didn't
give up."

He flinches at this, but his eyes stay fixed on me, sad. "I
know what you probably think of me, that I've given up, but
if it weren't for Lillian, I'd have found a way out long ago. I
know I look like a coward . . . I don't know, maybe I am one.
But if Curram is still keeping her somewhere, how could I
take a chance?"

She's probably dead, I think.

Des goes on, letting his forehead fall against the bars that
separate us. "Maybe I've no heart left, you know? This . . .
every day . . . it's all been eaten away. Maybe that's why I'm
too selfish to help anyone get out."

Beside me, Valentina takes a shuddering breath. "It's
hardly selfish to stay here in this horrible place," she says quietly, "for the sake of a sister you've no proof is even alive."

Des looks up, meeting her eyes and holding them. "Thank
you."

"You're not helping," I snap, glaring at her.

From across the cell Phoebe meets my eyes. Her sharp,

serious face is lit up on one side by the glow of Dunbar's lantern. After staring back at me for a moment, she smiles a little; there is no pleasure in it, just a dysfunctional camaraderie of sorts.

I get up and take a seat in front of her, next to the bars. It seems that the only times Phoebe has moved since we were brought here are to berate Des or to use the makeshift toilet, and even then she always slips back to her place with her quick, catlike movements.

"We don't have to be friends, but we should work together to leave this place."

She studies my face. "I've learned," she begins, her voice husky with emotions I doubt she'll share, "that helping other people can be overrated. I'll work with you only if it benefits us mutually." I'm tempted to guffaw, but I hold it back.

"How does freedom not benefit us both?"

"I won't risk my life just so you can get away on your own in the end," she snaps.

"I would never do that," I respond evenly, fighting my temper. "No one is going to be cheated or left—"

"No one?" She's on her guard now, drawing away from me. "Since when is this a party?"

"It's my plan. I decide who comes," I say sharply, and she looks taken aback.

"'Your plan'? When did that happen?"

"I'm working on it. Will you help me or not?"

"I'll think about it," she says eventually.

✦ ✦ ✦

I return to my corner on edge, irritated by Valentina and Des's whispered conversation. I can't stop thinking about his sister, the only reason he won't risk an escape. It's hard for me to imagine that Curram would hold her for leverage and actually leave her alone. Maybe it's easier for Des to believe that Curram would keep his word for some reason, but to me it sounds too good to be true. If Lillian is here, I can't imagine where he would keep her. In a bedroom? Locked up in a pantry? More likely she's gone. If we do escape, and we free Des with us, I hope someone will know what's become of her.

Dunbar leaves for the night, and we settle into sleep in what is becoming an uneasy routine.

It seems like just moments later that the door at the top of the stairs opens loudly and we're all startled awake. It isn't our jailer, but it isn't the usual soldiers or servants with our meal, either. There are only two men this time, Boyne and a younger man, a servant, behind him. *Not enough to take one of us upstairs,* I think, though the sight of Curram's right-hand man still makes me sick with nerves.

After the men reach the bottom of the stairs, Boyne strides over to the bars, glances around at us, and then back at his companion. "You know the rules, then: no fraternizing, no inappropriate touching or talking. Always be ready to assist me with the keys when I arrive, or if there's trouble. Your meals will be ready with the other servants' at the appropriate hours. You're allowed to leave only then, to relieve yourself, and at the evening bell, to sleep. You'll be expected again at dawn, when the rest of the house wakes."

A new jailer.

The man taps a set of keys at his belt, and they jangle loudly. "Thank you, sir," he says quietly, and I start because I've heard his voice before.

Boyne looks at us once more, and then at the other cell. "I'll need him in a few hours," he says, pointing at Des. "Be ready when I come." The new jailer takes a seat on Dunbar's chair.

As soon as the door closes behind Boyne, he jumps to his feet, and suddenly his face is at the bars. I do know him: Robbie. No doubt he put in a word to get Dunbar dismissed the same day he kissed me and carried away Eugenia's body.

I wish he didn't have a set of keys. I have an idea that rules won't stop him if he thinks he might get away with breaking them. "Can't say I'll mind a job like this one," he says in a syrupy voice, like he's bringing us in on a secret. "I could be doin' a lot worse. Sittin' 'round all day watching pretty girls gossip? I *could* be movin' stone like my old man. It's all about grabbing yer chances, eh?" He continues to smile at us, and his eyes find me, snagging for only a second before they move on to sum up each girl in turn. In the poorly lit dungeon, his hands and face are ghost white; they look independent from his dark-clothed body.

Ghosts can walk through walls, I think, and then try to forget the thought.

His eyes are the worst: pale and wide, glued to us as he backs away and takes a seat again. He pulls something from his pocket; I don't know what it is until he flicks his hand and a blade slides out. There's a piece of wood, too: a long, thick stick about the length of his hand. With slow, deliberate movements, he slides the knife along the wood, peeling off sliver after sliver and letting them drift to the floor.

◆ ◆ ◆

I can hardly keep still all morning, with Robbie watching everything we do. Des gives me pointed looks to stop fidgeting, but I ignore him. When Boyne eventually does come to fetch Robbie, a servant brings our meal at the same time: the usual chipped pitcher of water, a few cups, and more than enough bowls with a bucket of stew.

Behind me, Jewel, the bolder, more snide of the two girls from the orphanage, opens the lid on the pot and laughs, a short, bark-like sound. "Feels like home after all," she says, smirking. Caddy, her shadow with darker skin and a quieter voice, comes closer to look. Even Phoebe inches forward to see.

I've never seen anything so ugly that's supposed to be food: something pale and twisted and slimy-looking that smells like the wharf on a hot day fills the bucket. Jewel slams the lid back on and glances around at us, grinning. "Pass me yer bowls," she says.

One of the girls raises her hand timidly. "What . . . what are they, exactly?"

"Never had a pickled whelk before?" Caddy looks genuinely surprised, but Jewel smiles knowingly.

"Course they ain't ever had a pickled whelk. This is just cheap leftovers from the kitchen. I bet none of 'em have had anything coarser than a plum duff in their lives." I don't ask what a duff is.

A couple of the girls look stricken. "I've just never eaten something that looks . . . well, or smells . . . ," says the timid girl again, unable to finish. She looks like she's about to be sick, and I almost laugh. It's not as if the food is the worst part of all of this.

"Are they any good?" I ask, deciding to be brave.

"You're not going to try one, Isla—" Valentina starts.

"Why not?" I snap, still irritated with her.

Jewel grins. "They're fine if you hold yer nose."

Just when I've chewed long enough to try to swallow, Jewel tells me about the snails they come from, and it's too much. I choke and spit the slimy substance back into my bowl, and both Caddy and Jewel laugh.

"They ain't *that* bad."

"I'll wait for tomorrow's dinner, I think." I'm not the only one.

✦ ✦ ✦

For the next hour or so, Caddy tells stories of their escapades at the orphanage, while Jewel embellishes them. We ignore Robbie's heavy gaze and the rumblings of our stomachs, and for a long, sweet moment, the horror of everything seems to pause.

But then the door, the awful door at the top of the stairs, opens. Soldiers appear, with Des between them. They throw him into his cell and remind him they'll be back in "just a bit," and Robbie smiles to himself as we grow quiet again, uneasy.

"What's going on?" I ask as Des dusts himself off and takes a seat near our cell. He looks puzzled.

"Curram's hosting a gala tonight; looks to be quite grand and important, and he wants me to join them. Officially I'll be staff, but really I'll be there to listen to secrets and wait on Curram's smoking room, where he means me to deal cards. Maybe he knows I used to set up games at school, when I was a kid."

"You seem worried," I say.

"Confused, more like. I don't know what his game is, with me or his guests. I wish I knew what's going on, is all."

Phoebe crawls over to the bars, shooting a glance at Robbie before whispering, "If they're distracted, we should make our escape tonight." She has reined in her fire this time, but it still smolders in her eyes. "The guards will be—"

"Everywhere, I'm afraid," Des interrupts her. "They've already brought in half an army in preparation for all the dolled-up guests Curram has invited. You'd think Nicholas Carr himself was expected. Sorry, love, tonight is less of a chance than ever." Phoebe frowns, sitting back on her knees. *Still*, I think, with a little comfort, *at least Curram will be busy tonight.*

Eventually the guards come again for Des. I find a

corner and curl up, waiting the day out and hoping to find sleep. Robbie stays at his post, watching us and whittling, and rest evades me long enough that my hunger grows until it's all I can think about. Despite the dampness of the air below ground, my lips are cracked and dry, and my head throbs. But somehow I do sleep, only to be troubled by dreams that make my ribs ache and my heart pound.

I wake to a scream and the sound of a dozen boots on the stairs. I shrink against the wall in a now-familiar way, trying to breathe, trying to think. Trying not to panic.

But why shouldn't I?

Soldiers pour down the stairs, Boyne leading them with his superior attitude, his fine clothes, his condescending sneer. Robbie lurches to his feet and hurries to unlock our cell, and I want to beg him not to, as if his disobedience could save us all, only because he has a key.

How many have they come to take? I can't move. Valentina is clutching my hand, trembling. The iron door swings open, and Boyne steps inside.

"That one," he says, pointing to a girl. The soldiers follow his finger and grab hold of someone I don't know. She begins to scream and thrash, and Boyne ignores her as she is dragged away. "And that one," he goes on, and this time his gaze falls on Winifred, a quiet girl with skin the rich color of mahogany. She begins weeping even before a hand has reached her, and as they pull her out of the cell, her body slackens. I think she has fainted.

"This one," continues Boyne, pointing down at the girl

with the freckles. She is sobbing and scarcely seems to register that she's being moved as hands take hold of her arms and drag her off. For an instant I find myself remembering her grandmother. *Who will take care of her now, since she is really gone forever?*

I'm trembling when I look up at Boyne again. *Anyone but me,* I pray silently, *anyone else.* I don't care about selfishness. But then I think, *Except for Valentina. Please, don't pick Valentina.*

And then he's pointing again, and he says, "This one, too. Then lock it up."

And it isn't until the soldiers worm their way past him and one yanks me forward by my arm that I realize he was pointing to me.

eleven

I can feel my head shaking back and forth, the word *no* pulsing on my lips, but everything feels slow. I hear chaos all around me, girls crying and struggling. My throat burns and something like indignation throbs at the back of my thoughts, but I can't make enough sense of anything to know how to react. All I can think is, *Eugenia Margaret Rigney,* as my heart tries to choke me. *Her fate will be mine.* The men holding my arms pull me past Boyne, and for a second I meet his eyes.

He's so content.

I hate him.

Suddenly I'm on fire. I writhe away from the soldiers so I'm facing him, holding his gaze, willing him to feel the anger that's coursing through me. *Don't forget me,* I think, hoping I'll haunt him when this is all over with. *That would be enough. That, and the hell I'll give Curram, until he's sorry he ever bought me.*

Boyne puts up a hand. "Wait," he says.

The soldiers pause. I hang between them, my shoulders aching, my arms numb.

Boyne watches me, searching for something. The cold, white hatred surging through me leaves no room for fear. I stare back at him, waiting to see him shrink. Instead, he seems pleased. He stands back, beginning to smile.

"Leave this one," he says to the soldiers, and then, leaning in toward me again, "We wouldn't want to waste you on one of the master's guests. Not with all that fight still in you." Before I know what's happening, I'm on the ground, my knees burning, and Boyne is saying, "That one will do instead." They grab someone else and pull her past me, screaming.

I lie on the ground, frozen and numb, while everything moves slowly around me. The girls are dragged upstairs and Robbie locks our cell. My hands and knees sting where I landed on them; I look down and see blood, but I can't remember if I should do anything about it. I close my eyes, my face against the cold, damp floor as I listen to the sounds of the other girls crying. I used to think trial and happiness balanced each other out, but that feels naive now. *Whoever the other girl was, she didn't deserve to be taken upstairs any more than I did.* Guilt tugs at me, but in the end it feels pointless.

Someone was going to be taken. This time it wasn't me.

But if we don't escape, the next time it could be.

✦ ✦ ✦

It's hours before Des returns, by which time I'm the only one in the jail besides Robbie who is still awake. I try to keep from glancing over at him too often, since he always meets my eyes when I do.

Des looks exhausted, his eyes rimmed in dark half circles and his shoulders heavy.

"Cards went well," he exhales as he slumps to the ground next to the bars. I nod, my throat tight. "How many did he take, Isla?"

I'm surprised he knows about it. "Four," I say quietly. I don't tell him the details.

"He brings them up for his guests, the ones who are staying the night. Filthy pigs."

His eyes move across the group, sad and resigned.

When Robbie eventually climbs the stairs and the cell is quiet, I clear my throat. We're as close to alone as we'll ever be.

"There are only seven of us left, Des. I'm *going* to get us out of here."

There is perfect silence for a moment. He doesn't chuckle like he does when Phoebe talks of escape. When he meets my eyes, he just looks like he's really sorry. "I told you to give up," he says.

"No," I say, pressing my eyes shut. "No, I don't care what you say. Haven't you ever considered making Curram pay for what he's done? Couldn't you find a weakness? A way to make him tell you where your sister is?"

Des shakes his head. "I take one step out of line and Curram'll have me beaten half to death. It's happened before."

"Could you bribe a servant, do you think?"

"Isla, listen to me—"

"Could you?"

"No. They hate him, sure, but they're all as terrified as rabbits when he's around. He pays them to inform on each other, so you can't trust anyone."

"Could you steal something, if I told you what I wanted?"

"Isla, forget about—"

"Don't tell me that!" I snap, slamming my hand against the bars. Des starts, and next to me, Valentina stirs in her sleep. "Don't. I'm the one who Curram's going to take to bed, Des. I'm the one he's going to rip open and then throw to the dogs when he's finished. As long as I've got a life to risk, I'm going to look for a way out of here. Just because you've seen girls like us come and go again and again does not mean we are less than people, that we aren't worth saving. If I have to find a way to save us without your help, then so be it. But *stop telling me to give up.*"

Tam would be proud of me, I think in the silence that follows, but I feel tired.

"How will you do it, then? Dunbar wasn't the brightest chap, but in three years even he wasn't stupid enough to get tricked out of his keys. That creep Josiah Boyne has the only other set, and he'll kill you if you try anything. Even if you did manage to get out of here, where would you go next? Those stairs take you into the house itself. It's a maze upstairs, even if you weren't spotted, and a trap downstairs. There's no way out."

"There's another door, though, to the courtyard; we came down those stairs the first time. If we left at night, we might not be—"

"That door's locked. And again, the keys aren't just lying around."

"If I *could* free us, would you come?" His expression turns to one of fear. "Des, you'll never find out what happened to your sister if you keep on doing the same thing day after day. You can't keep working for the man who took her and *hope* you'll learn the truth. Certainly not if you want a happy ending." I shouldn't promise anything, but I can't help myself. "If we get out, we'll look for Lillian. We can find out what happened once and for all. I'll help you."

He watches me for a long moment, his jaw set like he won't let himself hope.

"The day I was taken, Des, there were so many people that when the hands grabbed me and dragged me away, no one noticed." I'm there again in my head, on the platform in the hot sun. I can feel the fear again, the same as when they pulled me through the crowd. "How did no one notice?"

"I'm so sorry, Isla." Des's voice draws me out of my memory trap and I look down, realizing I'm clutching the bars between us. I release them, my fingers burning from holding on so tightly, and take a deep breath.

"I can't remember if I even kissed my pa when I left, Des. I was going to say good-bye to someone." I feel as if something is crushing my chest; the talking hurts, but keeping quiet is worse, with the words pulling at my tongue.

"His name is Tam and I love him. Everyone in this cell loves someone they're missing. Your sister, Val's family. We need to get home to them." For the longest time, everything is quiet, with only the breathing of the other girls stirring the air.

"You really do look so much like her, you know," he says quietly, his eyes far off. "And she could always twist my arm." He smiles ever so slightly, nodding. "Where was he going, your Tam?"

My Tam. "To join Nicholas Carr's army. I don't know where he is now."

"But you'll go and look for him?" I nod, hoping I look confident. "Maybe we can look together, after we find Lillian." I hiccup on a sob of relief. "Do you even have a plan?" Des says, shaking his head. "Nothing stupid, I hope."

"All my ideas are stupid."

"Well, so long as one of them works, then." He grins, running a hand through his dark hair, shaking his head like he can't believe he's agreeing. "But let's keep the plotting to ourselves for now. Better not get anyone's hopes up." His gaze flicks away from mine, and he sighs. "I must be the biggest fool," he says.

We scheme all night. Des shoots down most of my ideas, even though I don't see escaping the dungeon as the same problem that he does. As far as I'm concerned, we can leave at night as long as Robbie is unable to raise the alarm; Curram would hardly keep more than a few guards in the wee hours before dawn; we could fight our way out if necessary.

The real difficulty is getting the keys. Dunbar may have known better than to be lured to the bars, but Robbie might have a weakness we can exploit. I doubt we could overwhelm Boyne when he opens the door, not with our jailer behind him and at least two soldiers. We're all half starved and brittle-boned at this point, and Des would still be locked in the next cell.

"If we can get Robbie to come to the bars," I start, "then the battle is half won. We just have to bash his head against them or choke him or something before he can sound the alarm. We could be over the manor walls before anyone knew something was up. It can't be that difficult."

"We need to get upstairs, though," Des says. I give him a questioning look. "To find Lillian."

"I doubt Curram's keeping her here." I frown.

"Why not? He must have seen her recently, don't you think? I keep asking myself how he knew I was good at cards, and that's the only thing I've got—she must have told him, let it slip or something."

"Maybe," I say, still frowning. "But I think we'll have a better chance of finding your sister once we get out. If he was keeping her here, why wouldn't he just leave her locked up with us?" Des nods slowly, still looking unconvinced. "How long have we been here, do you know?"

"I'm not sure . . . maybe nine or ten days? At least a week."

"And how long does a . . . a group of us usually last?"

He looks at his lap. "A month, give or take."

I bite my lip and taste blood. "We can't waste time, then, can we?" There's silence for a moment. "Have you ever tried to pick the cell's lock?" Des gives me a condescending look. "Of course you have. Sorry."

"At the beginning, before I knew just how scared of Curram I should be. But it's no good; I'm a decent burglar, but these are the good locks. Boyne's not stupid." He must see that my spirits are dropping because his hand finds mine through the bars. "Isla." I look at him. "I said I'd help, didn't I? I'll find my sister, and you'll find your soldier. Happy endings all around, all right?"

✦ ✦ ✦

My jittery heart won't let me sleep, even when Des insists he's too tired to keep planning.

I lie down where I am, curling an arm beneath my head and bringing my knees close to my chest for warmth. But all I can think about is Tam—what it will be like to find him, the surprise on his face when I show up to whatever base he's stationed at. The days feel so much longer down here, it seems strange to think that he's most likely still in the beginning of his training.

I wonder if the army is hard on him, if he's miserable. I wonder again if he saw the hands take me, and if he's worried about me, or trying to find a way to get to me, even now. Or maybe he likes what he's doing, because he can finally see new places. Maybe he thought he would miss me, but he doesn't. Maybe he is free, and he likes it that way.

I hate that I don't know how he is, that I'm disconnected from him.

The first time we fought was the day he found a ship that needed a cabin boy, and he told me he was going to volunteer. He told me to cut my hair and borrow some of his clothes and come with him. I said he couldn't abandon his family like that, and he said I was too scared to go myself and didn't want him to leave me. He was right, of course, but I told him he was stupid, and he stuck out his tongue and said it was my fault if I never saw him again.

I didn't sleep at all that night, wondering if he'd actually gone and joined that ship, but I was too proud to go over to his family's flat and ask for him. I felt like the flow of blood to my heart had been cut off, not knowing what Tam was thinking or whether or not he hated me. I waited for hours on my roof, certain he was gone forever, cursing myself every minute. I even wished—a hundred times, but only for a second—that I had done what he'd suggested and gone with him.

And then Tam's head appeared at his window, bronze hair tousled by the wind, and I watched as he climbed out the window and across the rusty platform and down. In a moment he appeared before me, oblivious to the anxiety that had torn me apart and ready with a new plan about a man who built enormous balloons, who was hiring apprentices.

Our hearts are disconnected again, but this time there's no easy fix. I wonder if he feels the same loneliness that I do.

I dream that I'm the only one left. That all the other girls have been taken to Curram and that I sit alone in the corner of the cell for days, hoping Curram will forget I'm there, but knowing he won't. When I wake up, it's hard to convince myself that won't be my fate after all.

◆ ◆ ◆

There's no way to predict when we'll be fed; once or twice we've been forgotten altogether, and it's beginning to show: When the women at the warehouse laced me into my corset, it was snug across my waist, ribs, and breasts. No doubt it's stretched a little because I've been sleeping in it, but there's more than enough room to wiggle around now.

I suppose they don't bother to feed us much because nobody needs us to live very long.

When the soldiers arrive with our dinner, they bring the usual number of bowls, and I'm angry, suddenly. "There are only seven of us!" I shout impulsively as they climb the stairs. They laugh. Valentina is staring at me when I turn around, but she looks away when I meet her eyes.

The anger feels good in a way; hot and sharp. But it does me little good, with nothing to do but sit and wait all day. *All we have to do is lure Robbie to the bars at nightfall.* Only one thing between us and freedom, but not an easy thing. I look down at my hands. They're small, weak; I doubt they can overpower anyone. *What would Tam think of my unstable plan, if he were here? Would he think it was too risky, or would he be proud of me? I* convinced Des to help. *I'm the one who* is trying to save these girls. That's more than anyone else is doing.

Robbie continues to whittle, glancing our way every few seconds. I almost miss Dunbar's easily forgotten presence; I'm reluctant to say anything out loud now, when I know we'll be listened to.

Sometimes Robbie paces in front of our cells, watching us suspiciously. At one point Des leans over to tell me something, and Robbie smacks the bars, making us all jump. "Hey!" he shouts. "I seen the way you go whisperin' to each other about me. Yer not gonna get over on me like you did the other one. Enough of that, or I'll come in there and teach ya a lesson myself."

Des looks up and meets his eyes, then crosses his arms over his chest, despite the manacles. He smiles. "But if you open the door, what's to stop me from breaking your nose?" Robbie's mouth snaps shut, and he turns pink, grinding his teeth.

"A warning," he says, trying to look superior as he eases back into his chair.

"You know, you should join us for supper sometime," Des calls over to him, his tone laced with spite. He sneaks a glance at me. "There are more than enough bowls."

Robbie gets up again and saunters over to our cell. He stands close to the grating, watching us and pretending to ignore Des's taunts. Then, in one quick movement, his hand slides through the bars and snatches Phoebe's arm, hauling her to her feet. Valentina shrieks, I lurch forward, and Des starts to shout something as a distraction, but it doesn't help. Phoebe struggles, but Robbie is strong; his lingering purple handprint on my own arm is proof of that. "I can come in and visit anytime I want, actually," he says smoothly. "But thank you fer the offer. Some other time."

Phoebe spits at him, and he jerks back; he's just surprised enough for her to tear herself away. She shoots onto one of the bunks and draws her knees up to her chest, saying nothing, breathing heavily.

Even after Robbie finally leaves, the air is heavy and no one speaks above a whisper.

✦ ✦ ✦

Sleep evades me, and whenever I stir, I see that Des is still sitting against the wall, looking at the ceiling. When I've resigned myself to restlessness, I move closer to him. "Is something wrong?" I ask, resting the side of my head against the bars. He continues to stare upward.

"What if . . . what if you all go as we planned, and I . . . stay here?" My eyes widen, but he continues in a hurry. "To find Lillian, you know? I could . . . I could always find you later, after I get her out of here. . . ." His voice trails off. I think he's been crying. "What if, when we go . . . when I go, he hurts her? Or kills her?" Finally he looks at me. "It would be my fault. I can't do that to her." I wish I could take him by the shoulders, force him to face me squarely.

"Des, don't you think that if Curram had any intention of hurting Lillian, he would have done so already? You know

his character better than I do, and I think . . ." I don't want
to be harsh. "We'll find a way to learn what he's done with
her, all right? But you can't stay here. We'll find her when we
get out. We'll come back if we need to, but first we need to
save the other girls."

"What if I could find the information we needed though,
before we left?"

"Des, you said yourself Curram will have you beaten
senseless if he catches you. We can't risk snooping around."

After a pause, he shrugs ever so slightly, letting out a
long breath. "You're probably right. Of course you're right."
He looks away again.

"Do you want me to . . . ?" I motion like I'll leave him
alone, but he shakes his head.

"It's all right. I'll be fine."

"I doubt that," I whisper, and settle my back against the
bars so our shoulders touch in places.

"What's your friend's name again? The one you want to
find?"

"Tam," I say, and it's as if saying his name out loud lights
a match in the darkness: bright and warm, but only there
for a second, and then the cold surrounds us again.

"I suppose I have to come, then; I can't leave you to look
for him on your own."

twelve

When I wake, Robbie has returned to his place. Morning, then.

"Soon?" I ask quietly as Des stretches and yawns to muffle our conversation. "Tonight, maybe?"

"Maybe," he whispers. "We'll see."

Caddy and Jewel try to teach the other girls a hand game, but Robbie snaps at them to be quiet and the day drags by. I'm aching to do something, and I wonder if this is how Tam feels every day of his life, itching with the need to move.

I'd give anything to be able to run right now.

To strip off these boots and bloody, torn tights and run.

It's the only thing I'm better at than Tam that matters to him. He's never cared how many more facts I can recite, or how the books I've read can help me read the weather and make predictions, or how I've memorized the names and principal cities of every country in the world. The only thing I've ever been able to make him jealous with is running. I beat him in every race: down any street, up any hill, through the busiest market-day crowd.

That's the way I want to run now, with my hair streaming out behind me and my bare feet slapping against hot cobblestones. I want to close my eyes and imagine I'm taking flight, or to run so fast that tears slide out the sides of my eyes and my ribs ache and my heart is ready to burst.

Sometimes Robbie gets up from his chair and paces, still whittling. He finishes one stick and starts on another. I don't pay attention to what he makes. At times he stops in front of the cell and watches us, letting the wood shavings float down to the floor. His gaze sweeps back and forth, exploring whatever of our bodies is exposed. I try to remind myself that there are worse things in his power to do than to stare at us.

"Do you think you could stir him up, Des?" I ask. "Tonight, before he goes? Insult his manliness or something?" I shrug. "You'll have a better chance of overpowering him through the bars, or getting him angry enough to come in."

He smiles, a hint of the Des I first met who mocked the guards and made light of the shadows. "It would be my sincere pleasure to start some trouble," he says.

✦ ✦ ✦

The waiting is hard. I tell myself that it's not the worst thing, but it leaves me to the mercy of my memories, which hurt. I can't stop thinking about Pa, and what he must be wondering. I want to feel his arms around me, his rough fingers pushing my hair behind my ears, or to feel him planting a scratchy kiss on the top of my head. Even the little things—the puff of dust every time he came home from working and dropped into his usual chair, the way I teased him that he'd be so much handsomer without his mustache, even though I secretly liked it—seem sweet to me now.

Tam fills the other half of my thoughts: I miss him rolling his eyes at my books, the moments when he'd take my hand and drag me after him on some adventure, completely un-aware that he was making my heart race with every touch. I miss the way he always smelled like sunshine, sitting next to me on the shingles and dreaming out loud.

I wonder if he has written me any letters.

I was so certain I would flood him with my own, just as soon as he told me where to send them. *Does he think I've forgotten? Or does it only feel as if a long time has passed? Has he even noticed, the short time that he has been away?*

Occasionally, I walk about the cell, though my legs feel shriveled and my knees hardly feel as if they can hold me. *You'll need your strength when you escape,* I tell myself. *If you want to run, you need to make sure you can walk.*

I could swear the day is coming to an end when the door at the top of the stairs opens, but it's only two men coming for Des. "When you come back," I whisper as they approach the cell and remove him. He nods tightly.

I stand at the bars as they take him upstairs and only re-alize when they've disappeared that Robbie is watching me and smiling. "D'ye fancy 'im, sweetheart?" I draw back, but not quickly enough. His hand curls around my wrist, his grip as strong as Des's iron manacles. "What a shame there're bars between you, eh?"

You don't know anything, I want to say. But he's the last person I'd tell that I already have someone to love, someone to find. I want to laugh at him, spit in his face, and bite the hand that grips mine, all at once. I smile instead. "If you're so bored that you've turned to this sort of speculation, perhaps you should find other employment."

"Don't think ye can use fancy words with me, darlin'. I've got a key an' I can tell the master anything I like about what happened to ye if something goes . . . wrong." He smiles as he releases my hand, and I feel filthy. Two weeks with no way to clean myself and only a hole in the ground for a toilet, yet somehow Robbie's touch is the dirtiest part.

Valentina moves closer to me when I sit. "Des says you're planning an escape," she whispers, and I nod, surprised that he told her. "Of course you are, you're so brave. If you're going to take Robbie's keys, he's already in a bad humor. Maybe he'll be volatile and Des can provoke him tonight."

My heart starts to race. "That's what I'm hoping," I say, and Valentina starts to smile. "If we can incapacitate him and get the keys, the rest should be easy, right? We can leave by the same door we came in. And since it'll be dark, we can get over the wall if we help each other. Then we're free." The thought crosses my mind that the whole plan is almost too simple, but I fight that thought. *If I start to doubt it now, I might be tempted to give up.*

"Can you pass the word along, one at a time? Tell the

girls to be ready. I don't think they'll need to do anything."
She nods and turns to a girl with dark skin and close-cut
hair. Marion, I think she's called. As Valentina whispers
in the girl's ear, her eyes widen and she stares at me. Then
she nods and turns to her neighbor, and I watch as the
plan spreads around the cell.

Now I can't let them down, I think. Now they have hope.

My thoughts turn to Curram as the afternoon ticks by.
How many of us have there been? How many have lived in this
cell? What does he do with the ones he's finished with? Does he
kill them, or is that only if they give him trouble, like Eugenia
did? Maybe he sells them "secondhand."

I want to pretend that I don't feel like someone's property, but I do.

What if I had been in Eugenia's place? What if I had been
the first one chosen? Would someone else have plotted an escape? And what if I hadn't been kidnapped at all? Or if Curram had not chosen me at the warehouse? Would all these girls
be feeling hopeless?

I wish I had never come here. But I can't help but wonder if maybe this won't be only about me, in the end. Perhaps
it will be about saving lives besides my own.

Something like satisfaction lights up inside me. You haven't
done anything yet, I remind myself. Lives have been lost and
ravaged and I didn't save them. But still, I feel hopeful.

I don't have a guide to tell me what to do, moment by
moment. But every story I've ever read has some love and
some good and some evil. Bravery, selflessness, cunning. I

may not be quite as brave as Tam, or as kind as Valentina, or as clever as Des. But I have hope flooding my veins, and love pumping my heart with promise and strength. So if I am to be a heroine, to save the lives of these girls around me, perhaps I can bear what has happened.

I wish Tam were here, to be proud of me. *But I'll find him,* I reassure myself. *When I'm free, I'll find my love.*

For just a few moments, I forget to be nervous.

Then the door at the top of the stairs opens and Boyne appears. Behind him are four soldiers, clustered around a prisoner in shackles, who limps a little as he walks. *Des. Of course it's Des; I expected him. But why is everything wrong?*

The last figure to appear is the tallest and proudest of them all: Zachariah Curram.

I can't catch my breath. Questions pummel the inside of my head.

Breathe, I tell myself. I get shakily to my feet, my eyes following them down the stairs. *What did he do?* I think over and over. *What did he risk, what did he let slip?*

Boyne's shoulders hunch like they always do in his master's presence, his eyes darting here and there under the rim of his hat. Curram saunters casually toward our cell, running his eyes briefly over our group. I refuse to cower, but my hands tremble.

His gaze is careless, though; it lingers on us only a moment before he turns to the soldiers who surround Des. Valentina is beside me now at the bars. "Two of you, hold him," says Curram, and his men take Des's arms and force him to face their master. I watch the way Des glowers, his forehead shining with sweat, the muscles in his arms tensed for a fight. He's strong enough to take two or three of them if he weren't shackled. I pray he doesn't try.

Curram begins to remove the dark kid gloves he wears, pulling on one finger at a time, every movement deliberate and calm. It's hypnotizing. And then, when his hands are bare, he moves suddenly, punching Des hard in the gut.

I bite back a scream. Curram hits him again and again, every blow brutal, hard. I flinch at each, but I can't look away. Valentina's hand grips mine as one especially heavy blow hits Des's jaw loudly, knocking his head backward. Somehow he remains silent, pulling his head upright as his eyes struggle to focus. Blood streams from his mouth, his nose; there's so much that I can't tell where it's heaviest.

"Now," says Curram, taking a step back and holding up his clean hand. Boyne supplies him instantly with a handkerchief. "I've had my fun. I think it's time you really learned your lesson, young man." He cleans blood off his knuckles with slow, precise movements. "Secure him."

My mouth is dry and I can't stop shaking. Des's eyes are glazed over, uncomprehending. He's too strong to black out. The guards remove his manacles and shove his face against the bars to his cell, taking thin black cords from their belts. Two of them raise Des's arms over his head and tie his wrists to the bars; there's a loud tearing sound as one of them rips the back of his shirt open.

No, no.

Boyne pulls something from his belt, and I drop Valentina's hand and move closer to Des's cell to see better. Illustrations from a book flash through my memory, a book that I'd read in hopes of persuading Tam not to become a pirate, a book about punishment and torture methods used in prisons. A short rod with fraying strips of leather coming out of one end: the cat. *Originally used by sea captains to punish rebellious crew, or plantation owners their disobedient slaves.* I read the accounts, marked drawings to show to Tam, studied the materials used to make the devices. But to see one in Boyne's hand, to know that it's meant for Des . . . it seems surreal. The leather pieces are barbed with shiny metal spikes, glinting like Curram's smile.

"Would you like to do the honors?" he asks in a syrupy voice, taking the vicious instrument from Boyne and holding it out to Robbie, of all people. "We owe you something for the tip."

No.

I'm going to be sick.

Our jailer saunters forward, giving Curram a little bow and taking the outstretched weapon. His mouth twists into a crooked, awful smile, and he flashes me a pointed look. If I *were* in love with Des as he thinks, I couldn't hate him any more than I do now.

Robbie draws back the cat.

I close my eyes.

I hear the snapping sound anyway, the straps striking Des's bare skin, the cries he tries to keep to himself. I have to look, I have to see his face. But the angle is awkward; I can't find his eyes, and he doesn't look at me. He just puffs out his cheeks, gasping and writhing, trying not to cry out.

Another stroke. Another. Still Des won't scream. Tears stream down his cheeks and he holds his eyes shut, but the blows don't stop. The constant smack of the cat becomes a terrible rhythm, echoed each time by Des's moans. His back must be a bloody mess by now. Robbie pauses only to swipe the hair from his face with a sweaty hand, then he grits his teeth and goes again, and again. I turn to look at Curram instead. His face shows relaxed satisfaction, and my blood turns to fire. *I will kill him, I will kill him.* I only realize I'm gripping the bars when my hands feel like they're burning and the brand begins to throb.

I wish Curram would stand closer to the grating. I wish I were stronger.

I don't count the number of lashes. *Are they trying to kill him?* Des's body sags slightly; he's lost the strength to stand on his own, and he hangs by the straps about his wrists. Blood and saliva drip from his mouth, down his chin.

Beside me, Valentina is sobbing. The other girls wrap their arms around each other, and I'm vaguely aware of someone murmuring comfortingly as a few of them cry. I glance at Phoebe, but she stares at nothing, her expression empty, her eyes downcast. With each blow, we flinch as one.

The lashes finally cease. Robbie takes a step backward, wiping his mouth on his sleeve. "Will that be all, sir?" he asks his employer. Curram watches Des for a moment, then steps forward and peers at his face.

"He'll take a few more," he says dismissively.

"No!"

Valentina's voice is anguished and pitiful. It echoes off the stone walls and iron bars, and everyone turns to look at her. "Ple-ease," she sobs, wringing her hands against the grating. "J-j-just leave him, please." Curram takes a step toward her.

"No," rasps Des. He tries to look at Valentina, but his eyes won't focus. "Val, don't." He tries to shake his head at her and winces.

"Put him in his cell," Curram says suddenly, glancing between the two of them. The men obey, untying Des's wrists and unlocking the door. They thrust him inside, where he collapses, his back dark with blood.

I press myself close to his cell as if I can squeeze through the bars, wishing I could help, frantically trying to recall everything I know about medicine and nursing. There's nothing I can do for the pain. If he passes out, I could tear my skirt up to make bandages, but getting them around the wounds will be a feat.

"Unlock the door," says Curram, stealing my attention. He smiles slowly, glancing between his slave and his prisoner. Val doesn't move from where she stands trembling, and Curram's smile grows at Des's alarm. "I'll take this one to my room."

thirteen

Valentina shrieks. Des tries to get to his feet, with pitiful results. "No," he pleads, only increasing Curram's pleasure.

I can't move.

Boyne turns the key in the lock with a screech, and the door swings open. Valentina stumbles backward, and as the guards approach, something urgent and reckless and necessary swells up inside of me. *I can't lose any more. I'm supposed to get them all out.* I lurch to my feet.

"No!" I shout, shoving Valentina behind me and holding out a hand toward the men. "You can't take her." I could hardly make a stupider claim; blood rushes to my cheeks. But Boyne halts for a moment, surprised.

Curram is less taken aback. He strides forward, smiling curiously. "What's this, then? Loyalty? Self-sacrifice?" On his lips those traits sound like laughable ones. "How touching." I can feel Valentina behind me, trembling. "Come closer." I don't obey. Curram takes a breath, cocking his head to the side. "I *said*, come closer."

I choke back a sob that I wish he couldn't see. *I'm such a fool. What am I doing?* My eyes slide over to Des for a half second; he's managed to haul himself partway up against the bars, his chest heaving and his eyes darting between me and Curram as blood drips from his mouth onto the stone floor.

Curram takes a step toward me so that Boyne is behind him. He looks down, smiling without showing his teeth, his hand reaching slowly toward me. His fingers fondle a coil of my hair, move up to touch my cheek, and then trail downward, along my neck to the base of my throat, his thumb running across the top of my corset. My breathing comes in quick, painful gasps. *Escape, escape, escape* rings through my head. I can endure because I will escape. But I'm afraid I'll give him the satisfaction of seeing my fear. I try to hold my head higher, but tears are blurring everything.

I want him to shrivel up and die, like the spider he is.

His hand pauses suddenly at the top of my corset. Curram peers closer, beginning to smile, and my heart stops. Before I can move to snatch it, his fingers close around Tam's locket, and he tears it from my throat.

"No!" I scream, launching myself at him, at the hand that holds my necklace. He slaps me hard across my cheek and I hit the ground, ears ringing, face burning. I look up at him through blurry eyes, waiting for the next thing, waiting to see how this can possibly get worse, as I'm sure it must.

But Zachariah Curram steps back. He holds my gaze for a moment, looks down at the chain in his hand, and then backs out of the cell. The order is given and we are locked in again. I don't understand.

Curram's voice sounds like it's very far away. "I find that I've had enough entertainment for tonight after all," he says. "They won't be needing dinner, Boyne. Inform the kitchen." He turns to leave and then pauses. He pockets something— my locket—and takes something else out of his waistcoat. It looks like a cluster of papers, or a loosely bound book. "Remember the events of tonight, Despard. Things could have been much worse. I hope the scars on your back will remind you not to deceive me again." He turns and strides grandly up the stairs with the other men following closely behind.

I wait to feel relief but there's only despair. I stop trying to stifle my sobs and lower myself to the cold ground, fingering the burning ring around my neck left by the snapped chain. *I've lost Tam*, I think. *I've lost the one thing that bound me to him in this horrible place. It's gone now. Tam is gone.* I feel as if I've been smashed to pieces, and the pieces have been scattered in a thousand directions. I can forget Curram's hands sliding hideously along my skin, the way his eyes devoured my distress. I can pretend I dreamed it, or that he isn't real. None of that compares with the feeling that I've lost Tam.

I try to picture his face behind my closed eyelids—*Why does it seem harder now?* I'll find a way to hold on to him. I have to. I pull out my memories of all the little things that make him up: the messy blond hair, and how it made me shiver to run my fingers through it the day he came to me covered in burs, asking for my help. The journal he kept in his terrible handwriting of the places he would see one day. The dirt that was constantly under his fingernails, even before school.

I could swear he's already slipping away. I look at my hands, red from gripping the bars. The left one is bleeding where the tender skin of the X has cracked.

I have to leave this place. I have to find Tam, and touch him again and remember who I am.

A groan from Des makes me sit upright. He's lying on his stomach, his eyelids fluttering. Valentina sits at the grating, her hands reaching through the bars and fluttering nervously over his torn-up back. What's left of his shirt is soaked in blood. "Don't fight," I tell him, crawling closer and pushing my own troubles out of my head. "Let go. You were already strong enough for Curram." Des's brow tightens in pain with every quick exhale.

"It's all right to give in," Val says softly. Des shuts his eyes tightly, starting to cry, while she strokes the hair from his forehead until his body slackens and he finally passes out.

I dry my face with the backs of my hands and straighten my shoulders. Des's nose is probably broken, but it's hard to know with so much blood and the swelling. I tear a strip of cloth off the bottom of my petticoat and wind it around my finger, then reach through the bars and press the fabric against his split lip.

I hate imagining the pain he'll be in later.

Valentina sinks against the grating, breathing through her trembling. "What else can we do?" she asks, hiccuping.

"Nothing from over here," I say.

"I'm sorry," she says, her voice small and quiet. "Isla, I'm sorry."

I swallow hard. "Don't be," I choke. "You're all right, that's what matters."

"But . . . your necklace. Isla, I—"

"I can't talk about it right now." I nod, try to smile, then look away. If I could ignore the pain in my chest, it might be easier to pretend.

Before I realize what's happening, Robbie, resonating satisfaction, goes upstairs. *We've missed our chance*, I think, wishing for something I could hit or kick to exhaust my frustration. I watch the door, willing him to come back downstairs so I can take his keys somehow and make a fool of him.

For the first time I understand Tam's intense protectiveness. Earlier in the summer, when he and I were wandering through the marketplace and I stopped at a bookseller's stall, a beggar man snatched my satchel off my shoulder and ran with it. Tam chased after him without a word; I was too stunned to react. By the time Tam overtook the man and tackled him, I had caught up, and I watched as he wrested the bag from the beggar's hands and knocked him against the ground, punching him squarely in the nose. It seemed so brutal to me then. I told Tam to stop, that I had my bag back and it was fine. I didn't even thank him.

Now I look at Des and I understand.

Zachariah Curram has to pay, I think, watching Des's distorted face, finally peaceful in sleep. *For Eugenia, for Cecily, for the girls he gave to his guests at the party, for whatever he's done with Lillian, for every girl I'll never know the name of who came before us.*

"You should sleep, Isla," Valentina says quietly, touching my hand. "Tomorrow will have its own horrors."

"You're right." I stand, and she stares up at me, questioning. "Tomorrow we're going to leave this place forever," I say. "Des is not strong enough to overpower Robbie, and we cannot afford to wait until he heals. Our only chance is to lure Robbie close on our own and knock him out or hold him and grab the keys. He's shown attention to me before, and to you, Phoebe. One of us should do it."

Phoebe nods. "I'm strong," she says. "But someone else should be ready to snatch the keys. We can do it after supper tomorrow."

"I can do that," says Jewel, smiling a little. "Orphanage gives you quick hands."

"The rest of us need to be ready to help, if necessary. To grab an arm or a leg, to hold him still. Does everyone understand the plan? Once we get the keys and get out, we may need to carry Des. We can use the door we came in through to reach the courtyard."

Everyone nods, somber. For the first time I notice how much larger the cell seems with half of us gone already. *What were you thinking, Des?* I wonder, my eyes falling on him last. *What did you do?*

As everyone settles into sleep, one of the girls, Hanna, sings softly. Her voice is low and rich, and I don't understand the language of her song; she hardly ever speaks, and it's clear she doesn't understand most of our conversation day to day. But her song is easily felt, whether or not I know what the lyrics say. There's mourning in it, and anguish, a cry for the life that was. I wonder if she knows that I'm talking about escape. Or if she's resigned to this fate, and that grief is what feeds her song.

Before Hanna's song is finished, most of the girls have fallen asleep side by side on the grimy, hard floor.

I envy them; in the quiet, doubts attack me. They come in the memories of the small girl who clung to me in the warehouse, in her screams echoing in my head. She thought I could help her. They all think I can help them. *What if I can't? What if I fail and they're all taken one by one, until my nightmare comes true and I'm the only one left?*

I shut my eyes, but the sounds in my head won't leave me alone.

My neck stings with the memory of the chain that should hang there. I massage the skin dismally, wishing I could convince myself it was still there so that I could fall asleep.

"Do you think he'll be all right?" I turn at the sound of

Valentina's voice. She pulls her eyes away from Des's face to look at me. "Will he ever be?"

I nod. "Of course. If they'd wanted to kill him, they would have." I hope I'm right. Valentina turns back to stare at Des, stroking his forehead with her thumb, pushing the hair out of his eyes. I want to give her more reassurances, but they feel dishonest, even in my head.

Eventually she falls asleep facing the bars. I dream that I'm in the cargo car of a train again, choking my way through the stifling heat and the bodies all around me. When I wake to Robbie's arrival, my body is tense and the moments seem slow. My fingers repeatedly seek out the locket, restless.

Des sleeps late into what I presume is morning, and I grow more and more anxious. *When they bring our supper,* I think. *We'll wait for the door to close and we'll make our move.* A number of times, I glance over at Phoebe, who gives me tight smiles and curt nods but nothing more.

When Des does wake, his pain is evident. He holds on to Valentina's hand like it can save him, and if his grip is too tight, she says nothing. "We're doing it tonight," I whisper when talk among the other girls helps muffle my words. "We're getting out of here."

"You'll have to . . . go without me," he murmurs back, weak-voiced. "I'll slow you down."

"We would never leave you behind," Valentina says.

"We'll carry you," I tell Des. "We're not leaving without you." He closes his eyes, straining to breathe, and I know I should let him rest, but I have to know something. "What happened, Des? What did you do to make Curram so angry?"

He doesn't open his eyes. "I was trying to find something," he mumbles. "Something . . . that would help us . . . when we got out. Curram's plans. No good, I couldn't find them. Then he realized I was snooping." *What kind of plans? Maps? Records of our purchase?* He's asleep before I can ask more, and I know he needs to rest if he's going to make it out of here.

It takes all day for Des's swelling to go down enough that he looks like himself again, and even then he's far from pretty. When he wakes, though, his attitude has returned at least.

"Last night was a little showy," he calls weakly to Robbie from the floor, when our meal is brought. Our jailer doesn't get up, but his eyes flick over to Des. I try to catch Des's eye to shake my head at him not to anger Robbie, since we need him to go after Phoebe instead, but he won't look at me. "You're going about it all wrong, you're too obvious. I understand if you're overcompensating for . . . a particular lack of something? Is that it?"

"You think you're awfully funny," Robbie sneers, settling back into his seat. "Cracking jokes from behind bars. You'll sober up quick enough tonight." My heart begins to pound. *What this time?* I look at Des, but his face shows only confusion.

Robbie saunters toward the bars, looks Des up and down, then spits on the ground in front of him. *He's so close,* I think, easing my way toward him. *Maybe I can reach the keys while he's distracted.* But in a moment Robbie has turned on his heel and is striding back to his seat.

"*Not yet,*" I mouth to Phoebe, who nods.

"Saying your good-byes?" Robbie calls, and I realize with a start that he's looking at me.

"What—" I begin, forgetting to ignore him.

He grins. "Better start now."

fourteen

They're taking me tonight.

The realization sets my heart racing. *I can't be weak now. Curram occupied will give the others their best chance of escape. If he calls for me, I'll go, and I'll give him hell.*

Was it only a couple of weeks ago that the same knowledge would have destroyed me? Fire spreads through my veins; I'm not the same person anymore. I must have lost my mind down here in the darkness. I'm breakable and underfed, hardly in any condition to take on a man with five times my strength. But this may be my only chance to make Curram pay; I have to take it.

"Isla," Des calls quietly, sounding panicked. I pretend I don't hear him, and crawl instead to where Phoebe sits.

"Evidently I'm going to Curram tonight," I whisper. Her brow furrows; I can tell she understood Robbie as well as I did, but I don't think she expected my acceptance. "I'll fight him for all I'm worth, but if I don't make it back . . ." I swallow. "I'll try, but if I'm gone too long, if I don't come back, can I trust you to make sure they all leave?"

Phoebe watches me for a long minute. "It's stupid to think you can always help everyone," she says. I open my mouth to retort, but she goes on. "But I was wrong about you. It's not naïveté that makes you try." Her eyes hold something like respect. Then she looks wary. "Isla, our escape will be a victory. But Curram will just buy new girls. You have to stop him forever, or this will never end."

My heart lurches. *Does stopping him mean killing him?*

She nods like we've settled on a plan. "We'll leave if too much time passes. You have my word." I stand to go, but she grabs my hand. "And not before. We won't abandon you unless we have to."

Des continues to call to me until I join him. He whispers frantically, "Let's go now. Get Robbie to the bars and hurry. We can go before they take you. I won't let—"

I shush him, worried Robbie will hear, and shake my head. "I—"

"I'll tell them to take me instead," Valentina interjects suddenly from beside me. She grips my shoulder with white fingers. "I'll volunteer, and, and—" I try to cut her off and she snaps, "They need you, Isla!" She looks around at the other girls. "You need to get them away from here. You need to save them, you and Des. I'm nothing. I'll tell them to take me."

"No, we'll leave now," insists Des, trying to be commanding even though he looks like death. He tries to prop himself up on one elbow and collapses, clenching his teeth.

"Neither of you will risk your lives like that. I'll get Robbie to—"

"No." Valentina flinches at my tone. "No, if we go now, they'll be down in a moment, and we'll never make it out. When I'm gone, the plan will continue as before. Phoebe is going to take charge. I'll get away from Curram, all right? I'll put up a fight and be after you all in no time. It'll be good that he's distracted."

Valentina starts crying, her shoulders shaking pitifully. Des only looks angry. I think he's about to speak again when the door at the top of the stairs opens, and with the light comes Boyne, pompous as ever. Behind him are the usual two soldiers, and suddenly my heart is racing ahead of itself and I can't breathe. I pull away from Valentina and stand. *All I have to do is catch him off guard for a moment, long enough to find something to knock him out with. And when he wakes up, we'll be gone.*

As the three men descend the steps, I square my shoulders and take a deep breath. *This,* I decide with a momentary flicker of pride, *is the bravest thing I have ever done. It may also be the most foolish.*

"Don't," pleads Des, voice weak. "Isla, please, we can—" But there's nothing we can do; even if I tried to back out now, someone would get taken. I pry Valentina's fingers off my dress. Boyne reaches the cell.

"It's all right," I say with a small shrug at Des, whose eyes are wet. "It's all right." I glance at Phoebe, who watches me with a somber expression.

Boyne gives the order, and Robbie narrows his eyes at him as he unlocks the cell, no doubt eyeing the next job he'd like to have. As Boyne looks me up and down, I refuse to flinch. "You were the one he wanted," he says smugly. "I'm glad to see you've learned to behave since last night. Shall we?" He offers me his arm with sick pleasure.

I don't take it.

Swallowing hard, I take a step toward the cell door, and as I reach the threshold, the two guards fall into step on either side of me, seeming uneasy, maybe because I don't put up the usual fuss. I suppose they enjoy having to subdue the girls. My steps feel long and slow as I walk to the stairs and begin my ascent. I hear Valentina crying as the door is locked again, but I don't look back. Somehow that would feel like a good-bye. And I can't let anything feel final.

My legs ache and I'm out of breath when we reach the top and the door is opened. Lamplight spills through, almost blinding in comparison to the dimness behind me. I force myself to breathe as the guards take my arms and lead me into Curram's house.

It's a new world, different from the dungeon behind me, from anything I've ever seen before I was brought here. The walls are lit orange and yellow by oil lamps and the sunset that streams in the windows to my right. I feel a twinge of relief just from knowing what time of day it is.

A long corridor stretches ahead of me, its ceiling high and curved. The windows have pale-pink-tinted glass in them, changing the light where the sun streams through.

The colors are astounding, after a world of brown and gray and black, shadows and cobwebs, grief and fear. Up here, blue and white walls are carved into delicate patterns along the ceiling, vases of pink and yellow flowers on intricate tables line the hallway. The house reminds me of Industria's courthouse, but grander. The heels of my boots make gentle clacking sounds as I walk.

We turn onto the next hallway and suddenly I remember to be wary. My awe fades, and jitters replace it. *Details, details,* I tell myself. *Remember everything. You never know what could help.* I glance into every open door, try to memorize every turn we make. I tell myself to read the manor like a book, to feed my surroundings into my brain to be stored up for the moment I'll need them.

I try not to remember what I'm traveling toward.

Have they acted already downstairs? No, focus, I tell myself. *This is all that matters right now.*

I pass marble pillars opening onto a courtyard with a fountain and topiary. I hate Zachariah Curram and his black heart more and more as I see the extent of the beauty with which he surrounds himself. Occasionally we pass servants, who stare resolutely at the ground and hurry past.

We move quickly, past a set of doors that are wider than the rest, and I can see shelves lining the walls: the library. So many books, so many words. I could swear the books beg me to come to them, to open them and breathe them in and ingest the beautiful things they're filled with.

A moment later, we reach a grand staircase, the steps wide enough for a dozen people on each. Boyne casts an almost gleeful look over his shoulder at me and leads the way to the top. For a moment, I imagine this house abuzz with a gala; not one of Curram's parties, with his despicable political guests, but a really lovely one, with paper lanterns strung up in the courtyard, ladies wearing their grandmothers' jewelry, and mulled cider in delicate glasses on the servants' trays. *I'll bet he even has a ballroom,* I think as I make my way up the stairs. It must be beautiful.

There are two doors before me when I reach the landing. The stairs wrap around and continue to a third level, but we stop, and the guards lead me to the door on the left. Panic hits me out of nowhere and I freeze up, my shoes sliding on the shiny marble floor.

"Oh no, you don't," grunts one of the guards, grinning, as Boyne moves forward and knocks on the door. It opens immediately, and a woman appears, dressed in the simple blue attire that I've seen on the other servants. She looks me up and down vacantly, then motions to the guards to let me go, while I remind myself to stay rational, to breathe. *I'm not there yet. I have time to prepare myself to act.* I stumble forward, following the woman into a small, well-lit room with windows along the ceiling instead of at eye level.

There's a bathtub in the center of the room and wardrobes along the back. Three other serving women stand about, perfectly still and with downcast eyes. Boyne steps partway over the threshold. "Eight o'clock," he says pointedly. The first, older woman nods, rolling her eyes when he turns his back.

I stand where I am, trying not to shake.

The woman steps forward with her hands out to me, and I draw back a little, wary. The day in the warehouse comes to mind, the brusqueness, the heat, being stripped bare in front of too many eyes. "Your clothes, dear," she says plainly but not unkindly. She continues to hold out her hands, not touching me.

I bend slowly to unlace the boots I've been wearing ever since they were given to me. With no reason to take them off in the cell, my stockings underneath are brown with grime and sweat. My knees are caked with dried blood, and as I pull off my dress, petticoats, and underthings, the rest of me is revealed to be little better: bruised and filthy all over. At least the calendar has been kind to me, and I've not had to feel any less clean than I do already. I stand there totally naked, totally exposed. There's no way to wrap my arms around myself that makes me feel safer. It's impossible to hide.

This is not the end, I remind myself. *This will be nothing if I can free myself.* I can forget this humiliation later. The woman gestures to the tub, which is full of gently steaming water. Slowly, I climb over the side and slip into the delicious warmth. They must have given Eugenia, Cecily, and the others the same treatment. And dozens before us, as well. Cleaned up and readied for him like clams. The thought makes me sick.

There's soap and lavender oil to wash with, but no one tries to help me. I can't remember the last bath I had that wasn't cold; renting stalls once or twice a week at the bathhouses was the best Pa and I could afford, and the water temperature always depended on the weather. The rooms with heated baths cost more.

There's a rough brush that I scrub myself with until my skin is pink and feels like it's on fire. I hold my nose and slip below the surface, letting the warmth envelop me like sleep. Under the water, the world is silent, and the terror awaiting me when I resurface feels far-off and surreal.

But I don't feel at peace.

Doubts turn my stomach, and time refuses to slow down so I can think.

The water turns gray with grime, and I know I can't stall any longer. I stand, thoughts jumbled, hugging myself and letting the water tumble off my shoulders. One of the girls drapes a towel around me and rubs me up and down with it, while another wrings out my hair and combs lavender oil through it.

Again and again they steal glances at me, and then at one another.

"What is it?" I ask.

"Yer not upset, then?" asks one, wide-eyed. "It's just, everyone else is always throwin' a fit—"

"Enough conversation, Grace," says the woman in charge simply, a warning in her voice.

The girl nods. "You have beautiful hair," she whispers

hurriedly as a third girl opens one of the wardrobes and begins rifling through it. She comes back with a small pile of clothes, and between them all, I get dressed.

I shouldn't be surprised at the clothing: a lacy corset that ties up the front and short, frilly bloomers that leave my legs bare. I close my eyes as they fix me up, tying ribbons and fluffing ruffles. *I might as well be naked still,* I think, looking down at my bare legs and feet. *But none of this matters,* I remind myself. *My fate will never be what they assume. I will beat Curram. At the very least I will make him sorry he ever saw my face.*

But the moment is almost here and I'm not ready. I have no idea what comes next: Curram himself, or further preparation? I scan the room furiously.

This is his *bathroom as well,* I realize. There's a washbasin just a few feet from me, and beside it are the brush, pallet, and folded razor he must use to shave his face.

The girls fuss with my hair for a moment, tying part of it back with a pale ribbon and patting the ends dry. I start coughing and stumble forward, putting out a hand as if to steady myself on the counter. As they exclaim and help to right me, I snatch up the razor and, continuing to cough, slide it up the leg of my bloomers.

A second later, I recover, and the girls file silently out of the room, until only the older woman remains. She looks me up and down with a twinge of anger in her eyes, and then the emotion is gone. "Go in," she says, her words plain and resigned. She gestures to the door on the other wall. It must lead to an adjoining room.

"Thank you," I say, as if that will mean something. She doesn't respond, only opens the door and lets me through. The latch clicks behind me and I am alone.

fifteen

The room is large and dark, with tall, gloomy ceilings. There are windows on one wall, but even they are dark. Oil lamps hanging from the ceiling and set on shelves provide the only light, mellow and eerie. There's a desk to my right overflowing with books and papers and broken quill pens, and behind it are shelves with more books.

To my left is a grand canopy bed that sends a chill down my spine. *There is no way to turn back,* I remind myself. My toes curl on the cool stone floor. I'll need to find a way to take Curram by surprise, to subdue him. I need to knock him unconscious, if I can find a heavy enough object to smash over his head. Then I can tie him to something so he can't come after me when he wakes. *Maybe I can even find something here with a clue about Lillian.*

I'm a fool.

The realization shudders through me.

I'll never take control of Curram by myself. I'm small

and weak. I'm half starved and was puny even before all this. I don't have Tam to protect me, or iron bars to keep my enemies at bay; I don't even have the company of others to encourage me.

I'm doomed.

All of a sudden I can't hold on to a steady thought. *I could hide, and wait until he comes and then leaves again in search of me. Or I could look for a better weapon before he arrives. The latter,* I decide. *If Zachariah Curram is held up, I'll use the time to my own advantage.*

But the second I take a step toward his desk, the other door opens. Curram appears, filling the threshold, and my heartbeats blend together. I'm going to be sick.

His waistcoat is already unbuttoned, his loose cotton shirt half untucked.

"You may be surprised to know," he says, summing me up with a look that could not be more thorough, "that I've been looking forward to this."

He begins to smile, and I can't move. My nerve, so righteously built and fed, is snatched away. My knees tremble, my heart tries to burst. The only thing I can do is will myself to stand and face him.

Curram strides smoothly forward, his eyes exploring every crevice, every contour of my ill-clad body. *This is nakedness.* Not the day in the warehouse, not ten minutes ago in the bath. This. His hand hesitates against my arm, then slides up my neck to cradle the back of my head. All the while, his smile increases. He leans down, kissing me along my neck and shoulder and collarbone, taking long, deep breaths as I tremble and struggle not to cry. Every touch of his skin on mine sickens me.

After a moment, he draws back a little, seeking out my eyes for the first time. "No struggle?" he asks, taking delight in my discomfort. "I'm not sure whether to feel disappointed or strangely refreshed." He smiles. "I suppose I expected that your spirit would mean a good fight; I was looking forward to the challenge."

I stare straight into his eyes, hating my tears. *Just a moment longer, and I'll take out his eyeball,* I tell myself, my fingers inching surreptitiously up my leg to the concealed razor. Curram moves in again, his hot breath on my cheek before he buries his face in my shoulder and his hands move down my back. Finally my fingers feel the end of the razor through the fabric. I try to pull it out and suddenly he's pushing me backward, and I'm stumbling over my feet. I fall back against something soft—the bed, I realize—just as he comes down on me, pinning my arms at my sides.

My grip on the razor's handle is lost and I think, *I failed. I'll never get away. I'm as good as dead.* I hate the crushing weight of him on me, and I want to scream and I want to die. But then his greedy fingers move to the laces on my corset and for a moment my hand is free. I find the tiny weapon, pull it out, and flick it open, slashing his face with all the indignation and fury and hatred that have been building up inside of me.

There's a spray of blood, and Curram shouts, flying

backward off me. "You little bitch!" he shouts. He pulls his hand from his face, staring at the blood smeared everywhere, while his clear eye widens in pain and surprise. I scramble away from him, farther up the bed, grasping my small weapon and brandishing it as threateningly as I can. "She-devil," he spits, his expression turning to something like madness. "I swear you'll pay for that. And here I thought I wasn't going to get any fight from you. I'm almost glad I was wrong." He lets out a short laugh and suddenly I'm really terrified.

His hand drops and he launches toward me, across the bed, his face half covered in blood.

I can't move quickly enough. In a second he's on top of me, his strong, heavy hands wresting the little razor from my grasp and tossing it away with a clatter. He holds my arms down with brutal, bruising weight, smiling as my heart pumps so hard it aches and hot tears begin to slide out of the sides of my eyes. Struggling only leaves me breathless and weak, chest heaving. I spit up at his face in a last effort to distract him, but he just chuckles. "Now," he says, as blood trickles down his face and falls on my shoulder, "are you ready to pay for that little stunt? Hmm?"

I'm a fool, fool, fool.

I try to suck in the air to scream, but it won't come. He's too heavy on me, my throat is closed. I wish I were dead. I close my eyes, thrashing my legs and trying to wrench my arms from his grasp. *Useless. I'm useless. I'm weak and stupid.*

No, I swear to myself, time slowing down as my heart races faster. *I'll fight. Until the last second, I'll fight.*

I thrust my head against his and everything explodes in pain. But he falls backward, and I kick him, as hard as I can, shoving him off me. I can't see anything, though; my head is throbbing and the world is pulsing in pain. *Focus, focus,* I order myself, rolling off the bed and scrambling to my hands and knees. My vision clears in time to see Curram lunging across the bed toward me again. I get to my feet, unsteady, and bolt across the room to his desk.

Books, papers. None of this will help. He barrels toward me and I dart behind the desk so it's between us; I grab for anything I can, hurling the stone he uses to sharpen his letter opener at him as hard as I can. It misses, but he doesn't smile now.

"At least you're keeping things interesting," he says through bared teeth. His eyes are glowing with rage.

I'm the one who should be angry, I think, and then I am. I pick up one book and throw it at him, and then another. A third and a fourth and a fifth; he dodges or deflects each one, but with every hurled book I inch closer to the corner of the desk, where a marble bust peeks out from underneath a pile of papers.

Just as Curram raises his hand to knock aside the last book, I round the desk and my fingers curl around the side of the bust. "Still interesting?" I say, swinging it up at him.

The impact of the marble striking his head rings through my arms, and he crashes to the ground. I drop the sculpture, realizing with a dazed amusement that it depicts Curram's own head.

My legs feel like pudding and I sink, trembling, to the ground, casting about for the razor, just in case. Curram lies facedown on the floor, bleeding, I think. As it is, he'll have a bruise from where I struck him with my head, and a scar from the razor, I hope.

That's if he's even alive.

I inhale, raspy and still shaking, and crawl over to his body.

I don't want to touch him. The idea makes my head swim. But I hoist him onto his back and slowly lean down to listen for a heartbeat. At first I can hear nothing over my own short breath and hurried pulse, over the way I hate his smell and the way I still feel like I belong to him. But then, so faint, so quiet, I pick out the slow sound of his pumping heart.

He's alive. I feel a terrible mix of relief and disappointment.

At least I'm not a murderer.

His face is slick and red with his own blood; the razor cut is still bleeding. I turn my hand over, running a finger along the X, and I'm glad he'll have to think of me every time he looks in the mirror, glad he'll be forced to remember that I was more than he bargained for.

I pull myself to my feet and begin to search the room. The cords that hold back the curtains are the closest thing to rope I can find, so I turn Curram onto his stomach again and tie his hands behind his back. My fingers won't stop

shaking; even though I know the knots well, I can hardly
form them. My nose begins to run, and then I'm crying like
a baby, bent over his unconscious body.

Breathe, I tell myself, looking around the room. There's
a handkerchief peeking out of his pocket; I ball it up and
shove it into his mouth, just in case he wakes up. I wonder
why Boyne hasn't already come to check that his master is
all right, but maybe he's accustomed to the noise.

Standing in the middle of Curram's bedroom, I feel exposed in the skimpy clothes; my eyes fall on his dressing
gown, thrown across a chair. I don't want to touch anything
of his. My mind goes back again and again to his hand on
my arm, his hot breath on my neck, his greedy, heavy fingers working at the laces on my corset. I'm frozen again; my
hand goes to my throat automatically, searching for my
locket, for Tam's presence.

My locket.

I round Curram's desk again, pushing aside more papers,
opening drawers, frantic. And then I see it, tossed among
his seals and spare pens, a tangled pile of chain in the corner. It's broken, but just touching it is enough; I forget Curram for a second and remember only Tam. I wind the severed
chain around my wrist, with the heart dangling into my palm,
and shake my head free. *I have to get out of here.* I turn to go,
but remember Lillian. *Why would he keep records of her?* I
think, but I pause anyway, rifling through the remaining papers on the desk.

Bill of Sale reads one, catching my eye. The title is

followed by a list of five hundred rifles, one hundred pistols, and ammunition enough for them all. *Des said Curram is a politician, not a weapons dealer,* I think, skimming to the end of the list. His name is scrawled at the bottom as the seller, and beside it is the buyer's, one I've never heard before: "Alistair Swain." The army's seal is nowhere to be seen.

Slowly at first, and then in a hurry, I sift through the papers in front of me. They are piled in tall stacks all about the desk's surface: ledgers, expense reports, more sale lists. Most of them describe weapons. There's nothing to denote Curram's purchase from the warehouse, but that's hardly surprising.

I gather an armful of papers and the money purse from one of the drawers, stuffing the purse with any trinkets I see that look valuable: a compass, a watch. It's not until I start toward the door that leads to the bathroom that I remember Curram himself, still unconscious on the floor.

Phoebe's words come ringing back to me. *Am I supposed to kill him?*

This is *the best chance I'll get, and he deserves it. Another blow or two from the marble bust would do it. Or he must have a pistol stowed somewhere in the room.*

I look down at the bust and then back at Curram, and my heart beats faster than ever. *It would be quick, easy,* says a voice in my head. *Zachariah Curram, dead and gone forever.* I pick up the bust and take a deep breath, holding it above my head. He's lying right there. I should just do it.

But my hands shake and I put the bust back down. *I*

can't. I can't smash it against his skull and run, covered in his blood. I'm not a murderer. I'm a girl who escaped one, who's trying to get back to the people she loves. That's all I know how to be. That's all I want to be.

I slip through the door into the bathroom. The bathtub is empty now, and the room is silent. It's eerie. One of the wardrobes houses Curram's own clothes, and the next, frilly things like I'm dressed in. The last holds women's clothing too practical to have been meant for the girls he buys; I suspect they belong to his wife. I rifle through them and find a plain blue dress that is similar enough in color to what the servants wear to pass as a disguise if necessary. It fits me well enough to be unnerving; I hate to think that his wife and I are similar in size, and I wonder where she is. I tie my hair back into a neat bun and pull on the most sensible shoes to be found, plain brown leather with laces up the top.

Eugenia's ribbon, I realize with a pang, was taken with my old clothes.

Curram himself has plenty in the way of fine clothing; I force myself to sort through it until I find a coat that I think will fit Des. The corridor is quiet, but I feel in the bottom of my stomach that it will be now, when everything is going well, that I'll be discovered. I step haltingly toward the stairs, waiting for Boyne to appear, or a pair of guards, or the woman who was sorry but wouldn't say so.

But I reach the bottom unseen. The sky is fully dark, but it's still strange to find the house so quiet. *Have the servants all gone home, or to their quarters?* Perhaps the household staff know to keep to themselves on the nights that Curram is occupied.

My arms are quickly tired out, and I can't believe how weak I've become. But it's easier than I dared hope to find my way along the corridors I came through before. I pass the library and wonder how long it would take me to read all of the books inside, but it isn't books I want right now. And it certainly isn't Curram's books.

It's my freedom. It's reaching the door to the cellar and collecting my friends and stumbling our way out of here, away from this mansion and the vile people who inhabit it.

It's fresh air and the stars and the smell of summer sunlight in the afternoon, and the feeling of hot cobblestones under my feet.

And more than anything, it's Tam.

It's time to find him.

sixteen

I'm certain the corridor is longer this time. Was it only an hour ago that I walked it first? Two? The door at the end is not locked; I assume Robbie is supposed to see to that when he leaves for the night.

But the second after I cross the threshold onto the landing that overlooks our cells, I back against the wall, my breathing ragged. Directly beneath me is the bench where Dunbar and Robbie sat, empty now. Half a dozen feet in front of it, the grating of the first cell is visible. *I don't want to go down. I don't want to go back to the darkness.* The smell of mildew and refuse snake upward and around me, choking me. My body locks up. *If I go down, will I ever come up again?* Escape through the house sounds better all of a sudden. I need to get back out.

Tam. It's a step toward Tam, I tell myself. I close my eyes and step onto the first stair. Another shaky step and then another, until I reach the ground. It's dark down here;

Robbie's lantern is gone, and maybe he is, too. Maybe they did it, beat him and got out. I take a breath and choke on the smell, and suddenly someone jostles into me, making me cry out.

"Oh, is that you?" snaps a sharp voice. *Phoebe.*

I exhale. "Yes. Don't—" She steps on my foot, hard. "Careful, Phoebe! What are you trying to do?"

She doesn't apologize. "I thought I heard someone. The others are just at the door now; they've got the lantern. I've got Robbie's knife and the pointy things he was always carving." She guffaws. "Haven't had to run anyone through yet. I knocked the hell outta Robbie, though. That was a good time. He's in Des's cell now." I imagine her eyes glowing at the thought of stabbing an intruder.

"I can't believe it was so easy," I say, my voice trembling. *The razor, the blood, his weight on top of me, the heavy, insistent despair that it was all over. Easy* is relative. But I know it could have been so much worse.

"We're not out of the woods yet," Phoebe says. My eyes are adjusting to the darkness, and I can see that she's grinning, her teeth standing out in the shadows.

The blackness becomes total as we go on. My arms are still full, so I have no means of feeling my way along the corridor as I follow Phoebe toward the others. Finally we turn and I see a pinprick of light ahead of us. "Valentina? It's safe!" Phoebe calls softly, and the glow explodes into brightness as a lantern is uncovered. I see the five other girls huddled together at the bottom of a worn set of stairs, Des crumpled up on the bottom step, and, beside him, Val with a lantern in her lap. Her face lights up when she sees us; she lurches to her feet and throws her arms around me, the lantern's light bouncing here and there as it swings in her hand.

My achy body protests, but there's something wonderful about being held. "What happened?" Valentina asks. Some of the others stand and we form a little group.

Phoebe crosses her arms over her chest. "Is the bastard dead, then?"

I shake my head, and she starts to protest. "I'll explain it all once we're out, all right?" I say. "It's complicated." Her mouth closes quickly, and I see her eyes flicking back the way we came, as if she'll go back and slit his throat herself.

"Let's leave this place," says one of the girls, Marion, I think. I meet her eyes, dark and serious, and nod as we move toward the stairs. Jewel and Val carry Des between them, his arms wrapped about their shoulders. He seems only half conscious, and his back is still dark with dried blood.

Phoebe goes ahead with Robbie's keys. At the top of the stairs, she fiddles with the lock. I'm tempted to sit on the ground while we wait, but I force myself to stand, to push my thoughts ahead of the situation. *What if we're caught now, so close to the end? What if someone finds Curram? How long does he usually spend with a girl? When will Boyne return for me?* Finally the right key turns in the lock, the handle moves, and the door swings gently open. We all spill out the door, into the darkness, and for a second I forget to worry.

The dense, delicious air of summer nighttime surrounds

and fills me. I've never tasted anything so wonderful, or seen anything as beautiful as the sky above me, rich and endless, full of too many stars to count. I'm vaguely aware of the other girls filing out behind me, of Val covering the lantern with something, of Phoebe standing beside me. We're at the edge of the courtyard, in plain view if anyone happens to look.

But for a reckless moment I hardly care.

I tip my head back and turn around and around, trying to memorize the stars and count the number of crickets that are chirping, and wishing my lungs could take in more air. *Did I take this all for granted, lying on my rooftop with Tam, laughing and thinking nothing of the sky except to sometimes search for constellations?* He could never see them, no matter how many times I traced them with my fingers.

"How can you tell one from another?" he always asked with a scowl. And when I tried to explain that they were in patterns and some were brighter than others and that they told stories, he'd stare at me and then laugh in a bewildered sort of way and tell me I wasn't like other girls.

I close my eyes and imagine that I'm stargazing now, with Tam; it's easier to pretend he's beside me when I'm not in a dungeon, with the threat of Zachariah Curram looming over me at every breath. The cobblestones are cold now, but I imagine how they were hot from the summer sun all day, just like the roof's shingles were the last time I saw Tam. *Was that only weeks ago?*

"Isla," says a voice, and it's not Tam's, and I have to wake up. All about me, the faces of my friends are ghostly in the moonlight. I remind myself that we could still lose our lives if we don't make it out of the courtyard, and I feel foolish. "Are we going to climb the wall?" Phoebe asks quietly. I look about us, and my hopes fall. The wall reaches too high for us to climb, I think, and it's too sheer. Phoebe continues. "Maybe we could steal a wagon and just ride out?"

Marion looks between us. "And tell them what, that we enjoyed our stay but we'd like to go now? He must have guards posted."

"Just one." Des's voice comes out sounding strained. "I can do the talking." I steal a worried glance at Phoebe, but she looks excited.

"Pretend to be drunk," she whispers. "You know what to say to get through?"

I see a hint of a smile on his face. "Certainly."

"Bring him somewhere dark," I tell Caddy and Jewel, motioning to a corner that's even more deeply shadowed than the rest of the courtyard. I pass the satchel I took from Curram's room to Val, and the coat I found to Marion. "Put this on him. Phoebe and I will see about a wagon."

They slip into the darkness, and the two of us creep along the courtyard wall, our footsteps as soft as possible. When we reach the next wall, we pause, and I hold my breath. I don't feel very free, crouched in the shadows with baited breath. I can make out the gate just down the wall from us, and the chair where the guard is sitting. Behind us are the double doors of the garage, standing open just enough for us to squeeze inside one at a time.

While most people in the city travel on foot or by way of the cable trams, Curram has vehicles of every sort in his garage: a cart, a barouche, and even a pair of motorcars like I've seen in the newspapers. Pa told me that Nicholas Carr had been commissioning his own versions for years, though the man at the library desk said they couldn't last the journey from one city to another. No one could tell me anything about how they worked.

I trail my fingers along the smooth metal side of one motorcar, pulling back the tarp and wishing I had time to study the machines and their mysteries for hours. If only this were another time, another place. If only they didn't belong to Zachariah Curram.

"Looks like the stable is through there. You get the others, I'll find a horse," Phoebe says when we settle on a cart that will be large enough to hold all of us. It might be the same one in which we arrived.

I slip back outside and inch my way along the wall until I reach Valentina. We move in a slow line back to the garage, being especially careful with Des, who can hardly keep his head up.

When we're all inside the garage, a few of us help Des onto the driver's bench while Marion shows Phoebe how to harness the horse she found. The crates in the cart are empty, no doubt for show so Curram's men can bring their special cargo in without too many questions. We arrange the crates randomly, more toward the front, and drape tarps over them as casually as we can manage, with enough space between that we'll be able to hide beneath.

I'm anxious to move, afraid that we're wasting seconds. When the horse is ready, I usher the other girls under the tarps. One by one we crawl into the tiny spaces, curling up to make room for each other. I quiet my breathing, pulling myself into a corner so that Caddy can press against me. Des sets the lantern on the bench next to him and Phoebe hauls open one of the garage doors before racing back to climb in with the rest of us.

Don't let Boyne hear us, I pray silently as the cart rolls forward.

I'm jostled against the other girls, sweaty arms and legs pressed together like the first horrible night we were brought here. *But this time we're leaving.* After a moment, I hear a confused-sounding voice asking what Des's business is, leaving at such a time.

"Boyne—sorry, *Mister Boyne,*" Des drawls, while I imagine his head lolling to one side, "said I'm to head to the checkpoint"—he hiccups convincingly—"and wait for the next group. S'posed ta teach me a lesson, I'll bet, since he says I've bin drinking, but"—another hiccup—"he's full of shit, I'm sober as a straight . . . a straight . . ."

"Line," finishes the guard, sounding irritated. "He sure he wants you seen like this?"

"Don't know. Why don't ya ask 'im yerself?"

"You turn that cart over on the side of the street and it's not my fault," says the guard. I hear the gate opening. *Don't let Boyne hear us, don't let Boyne hear us.* The thought falls into a rhythm with my breathing. "Just be careful with that horse, ya hear?"

"Course," grunts Des as the cart begins to move again. Sweat clings to my forehead, sticks behind my ears. I don't move. It feels so familiar, lying cramped in the bottom of this cart, even with half as many of us now. This time we stay quiet of our own accord, a different kind of fight to stay alive.

The clopping of the horse's hooves on the cobblestone road seems slow beside my racing heart. I hear the gate shut behind us, but I can't relax. *Are we really free? Safe?*

Someone will come, I'm sure. Boyne will sound the alarm just now, and guards will pour through the entryway and stop us. The sentry will suddenly recognize Des and realize his mistake. At any moment, everything will fall apart. Panic pushes at my insides.

Still, the horse's hooves clack on.

"Val, Isla," Des moans as the cart slows to a stop. I push the tarp off my head and see him slumped in the seat. Valentina and I climb forward to help him, pulling him up by either arm.

"You need to lie down," she says. "I can't believe you've made it this far." I glance over my shoulder as we heft Des into the back of the cart, but I can't see Curram's manor. *I never have to see it again.*

When we've got Des laid out on top of the tarp, I strip off my shoes and jump to the ground, my toes curling against the cool stones of the street. The sky seems blacker, and the buildings that rise on both sides of the street where we've stopped stretch up to touch it, every window dark.

I'm really free. I want to believe it, but I still feel as if I'm surrounded by fog.

Phoebe stands beside me, staring at the sky, at the houses, at the ground. "I never want to stop moving again," she says with a sigh, and I meet her gaze. Her eyes hold the same restlessness I feel. Without speaking, we agree, and then we're running.

Bare feet slapping, pounding the cool ground, laughter tearing from our throats, though we know we should be quiet. My heart swells, my lungs stretch to bursting; we run, and we run, always at the same pace, so close our shoulders almost brush.

At the end of the block of houses, we stop, turn around, and glance at each other. And then she laughs and we surge forward again, and this time it's like I'm flying. I could leave the ground behind; I could spread my arms and lift off. I'm running toward Tam, away from Curram. Toward freedom and independence and an exciting unknown. My ribs are as tight as a corset and my knees shake like jelly. But I'm alive.

I reach the place where the others stand by the cart and this time Phoebe is a moment behind me. When she stops and looks me over, her eyes are wide: surprised but approving. I can't even choke out a word; my heart thunders against

my ribs and my back is slick with sweat. I just laugh, a distorted, breathless sound, spinning around with my eyes on
the stars above.

"You want to get us all killed?" Des groans from the cart,
but he's smiling.

Around me, everyone takes it in: Caddy clutches Jewel's
hand and Valentina cries giddy, happy tears of disbelief.
Hanna sits in the back of the cart watching us all, beaming.
Whatever little she knows of our speech, she understands
freedom.

"I can find home," she says in a thick, determined accent, sliding to the ground. "Home is here, I can find."

"You live in this city?" I ask, and she nods. "And you can
find your way?" She seems smaller than ever, standing on the
cobblestones in the little lace dress that still looks white in
the deceptive moonlight.

"Will you be all right?" Valentina looks worried, but
Hanna shrugs.

"Yes. Now I go home, I go to work. Not far." She takes
a step backward, looking between us and settling on me.
"Thank you," she says as she continues to walk backward.
"Thank you for saving." Finally she turns and disappears
into the darkness. *Is there anywhere safe in the city? I can't
trust anything anymore.*

"Does anyone else want to go now?" I ask.

"But where are we going?" Marion looks between us.
"No one's said."

Everyone is quiet a moment.

"Where are *you* planning to go?" Val asks me.

"I have to find someone. A soldier, he's with the army. And I told Des I'd help him find his sister." I sigh. "I had hoped something in his study would be helpful, but it's mostly lists of arms deals that Curram made with someone called Alistair Swain. Doesn't sound like anything that—"

"Alistair Swain?" Marion interrupts. In the dimness, her skin is so dark and smooth that it almost blends into the shadows. Her lacy blouse makes a stark contrast to the brown of her shoulders and throat, forming a pattern like an optical illusion from a magazine. "Are you sure? Curram sells weapons to Alistair Swain?"

"I don't know who that is, but yes."

She sits up straighter, her eyes wide. "But that's where I'm going. To Eisendrath. That's the rebellion."

seventeen

R ebellion?" several of us say at once. Des stirs.
"Have none of you heard?" Marion looks around
at us. "Well, I guess that makes sense. I don't know how
much you know about Nicholas, but it all starts with him."

"Nicholas? As in—"

"Commander Nicholas Carr. The 'Supreme Governor of
the People,' or whatever his pamphlets are calling him today.
He's always propagated himself as a hero, the voice of the
people, rubbish like that. But he's just greedy, and it's blinding him to the enemies he's making. His own people are
rebelling, and Alistair Swain is leading us."

"Oh," I breathe.

Valentina gasps. "When?"

"It's already begun. Preparations started over a year
ago." Marion's eyes shine with pride. *She said* us. . . .

"And you live with the rebels?"

She's beaming again. "My father is one of their suppliers. He farms for one of the camps; there are three. It's two days' ride from here."

"But who's Alistair Swain, then? If he's working with Curram—"

"Swain couldn't be working with him," Marion snaps, bristling. "Not if he knows what Curram does. He's not like city politicians, making deals and compromising. He's a visionary. If we tell him what's happening, he'll make Curram pay, I know he will."

Phoebe glares at me. "If Curram wasn't still alive, that wouldn't be a problem."

"Swain can help us," Marion insists.

"First, I have to find someone," I try to argue, but Phoebe cuts me off, pulling me aside.

"Can I talk to you?" she whispers, looking displeased.

"What?"

"Do you think Curram will just let us go? He'll be awake soon. He'll scream bloody murder, take out his anger on the servants, no doubt. Maybe he'll shoot Robbie, who knows?" Everything she says is calm and pointed, but my heart starts to race. "For all we know, the first thing he'll do is make another order, for more girls just like us. We haven't solved anything yet."

I swallow. "So I should have killed him," I say quietly.

She nods. "You might be the first girl he's ever lost." She shrugs. "And you took half of his 'shipment' with you. You took his pride, too. I certainly hope you hurt him." She looks at me long and hard. "Isla, that man is going to hunt us—hunt *you*—down. None of us are free until he's no longer a threat."

I feel cold, suddenly. It was my choice not to kill Curram, but with that decision, I let him go on killing other girls just like me. *If I don't stop him, am I responsible for them?* A nagging voice in the back of my head says yes.

"What should we do?"

"We can hardly march back in there on our own, not like this. We should go to Marion's rebel friends and persuade them to help us. If they're as noble as she says, they won't want to be in business with Curram once we expose what he's doing. We just need to convince them that he's as corrupt and wicked as the others they're targeting, and they'll do the job for us."

I crook an eyebrow at Phoebe. "Revenge?"

But she looks very serious. "Justice, Isla."

Maybe defeating Curram will mean finding out more about the people who sold us to him in the first place. Maybe we can stop them as well.

"Can you bring us to the camp? To meet this Alistair Swain?" I ask after Phoebe and I walk back to Marion and the others.

"Well, I'm not going back to school," she guffaws.

"Phoebe and I are coming," I say, and Marion grins. "We can take Des, too. He needs a place to recover before we can look for his sister. Val? Jewel? Caddy?" Time is slipping away; every tiny sound could be our captors in pursuit.

"I'll come," says Valentina very quietly.

The other two converse for a second in whispers and then nod. "For now," says Jewel, with Caddy's silent agreement. In the dark she really does look like her friend's shadow. "Until it's safer."

"The north gate," says Marion, climbing onto the driver's bench and motioning for me to join her.

We ride for a little while through the narrow city streets, with only the occasional yowling of a dog or scuttling of rats in the alleys to draw our attention. Everything else is silent, eerie. It's hard for me to imagine the city alive and bustling in the middle of the day, but when I try to, the day on the platform comes rushing back to me and it's hard to breathe.

When we near the gate, everyone hides again, except for Des, slumped along the side of the cart, and Val, cradling him to cover her suspicious attire. Soon a voice more bored than the last asks our business as a sentry steps into view, eyeing me warily. "It's late," he says. "Not a good time for honest people to be about."

"My friend is very sick," I plead, gesturing to Des. "We need to get him back to his family. They live along the merchant road."

"The gate will open at dawn." His tone is not unfriendly, but it is firm.

"Please," I beg, wringing my hands. "None of the hospitals will take him; they're afraid it'll spread, that the whole city—"

Instantly, he's on his guard, taking hasty steps backward

and coughing nervously, as if he might already be exposed
to whatever malady Des is spreading. "Go ahead," he says,
calling to another sentry to let us through. The other man's
protests are dismissed and the gates are opened. A moment
later, the creaking sounds as they close behind us tell us we're
finally free.

"We've really done it now," Jewel crows triumphantly,
eyes gleaming in the darkness.

Marion climbs up beside me again, offering to show the
way since she knows the merchant road well. As the others
drift to sleep behind us, my mind teems with questions.

A few years back, when Nicholas Carr went from having
high standing in the Assembly House to suddenly declaring
himself its head, very little changed for me or my pa. The details of Carr's quick rise to power were never broadcast, and
our days felt much the same, except that we were instructed
to recite, at the start of each school day, a pledge of obedi-
ence to Carr and his laws. Tam said he wanted to refuse, for
no real reason, but the teachers had been instructed to take
down names of anyone who didn't obey, and Tam wouldn't
endanger his family. He told me that sometimes he said the
wrong words on purpose, even though no one could tell. I
never told him about my own small rebellion, how I stole the
old newspapers from the library's trash pile, before they could
burn everything that had been written about Carr from a
negative perspective.

"Tell me about the rebellion," I say, watching the gray
road pass swiftly beneath us.

Marion sits up straighter. "It's been brewing for a long time. Carr makes private deals to provide weapons to uprisings in neighboring countries. Just enough to cost the existing government, so things become unstable. He makes a profit on the deals and then, while the countries are weak, he takes advantage of them; they'll sell land to him for any price because they need the money to rebuild their governments. He's smart enough to keep his own name clear; he has men who get their hands dirty for him." *The confiscated newspapers never told me any of this.* "But people are catching on. Some of Carr's own men are skimming off his profits to line their pockets, and selling his secrets to other parties who want to unseat him."

"And that's where the rebellion comes in. How did you join them?"

"My father's been there since the start. We've been farming land up north all my life, and when everything was starting, he kept the rebels fed."

"If your father sides with the rebellion, why did he send you to school in Verity?"

"Not just any school, the *best*. The kind of place important men send their daughters. He hoped I'd befriend the girls from influential families, but I was there for only a week, to settle in for the summer when . . ." Her voice falters, and for the first time since she began talking, she seems nervous. "Well, since I found myself in a dark train car. You know. I thought it was something to do with school at first. Everyone there was wealthy; I thought maybe I'd been kidnapped

for ransom money since no one knew my father was a farmer."
Her voice is quiet now, uncertain. "I've always been able to
take care of myself, you know? In the dark there, I don't know,
I froze up. I could never have left if not for you."

"I'm sure you would have found a way out," I say, but I
don't mean it anymore. Maybe they all *would* have died without me, or been sold off to the next buyer. Maybe everyone
needs saving sometimes.

There's silence for a long minute. "The rebellion, are they
winning?" I ask.

Marion looks puzzled by my question. "Well, the fighting hasn't started," she says slowly. "But our numbers are
growing."

"So Carr's army, you don't know if many of the men are
killed?" *Could Tam have already seen battle since I left?*

"I don't really know about that," she says like she's sorry.
"Why?"

"My friend, the one I need to find, he joined the army."
I'm not sure how much I want to tell; it's as if telling too
many people about Tam will cheapen him somehow.

Marion shrugs. "He may already be there by now."

My heart catches. "What do you mean? Be where?"

"Eisendrath, the camp we're headed for. Before I left for
school, it was filling up with deserters. My father says that
the rebellion gives the soldiers their honor back, since Carr
is so corrupt. Maybe your friend has joined." She settles
back against the side of the cart, crossing her arms.

Tam could be there. He's more impetuous than he is loyal. If he thought a rebellion would offer him a better chance for adventure, he might take it. No, he would *take it. I'm sure he would.*

"Just wait until you see it, Isla," Marion goes on, oblivious. "Everyone's equal in Eisendrath. Alistair Swain makes sure of that. He's the leader, of course, but he cares about the people, all of them. He'll help us."

"You said there are three camps?" I ask, still thinking about Tam. *What if he joined the rebellion but went to one of the other bases?*

"Eisendrath, Adderly, Kingston. They're spread out for safety."

I nod. *That's fine. If Tam isn't at one, I'll make my way to the next. I'll find him, no matter what, and we'll go home together.*

Home.

Pa.

If I'm not going right home, he at least needs to know that I'm alive.

I fish around in the satchel for a sheet of paper that's mostly blank, tearing off the end that's written on. There's a charcoal pencil in the mess, so I hold my face close to the paper and write as well as I can in the darkness.

My dearest Pa,
First, I am alive, and well. I never meant to leave
you, and I'll come back to you as soon as I can.
When I went to say good-bye to Tam that day

I pause, unsure what comes next.

I was taken captive by terrible people. I eventually escaped, along with several other girls. Nothing has been done to me. We are still seeking safety and this is the first chance I've had to get word to you. But I've thought about you every day, and wanted you to know I am safe and that I miss you. I know this all sounds unbelievable, but it is the truth. I will come back to you as soon as I can. I love you with all my heart.

~Isla

I read a book once that showed me the patterns for folding a letter into its own envelope. I'd forgotten about it, but my hands remember the movements. I write the address of our flat clearly on the back and find myself wondering if Pa is eating enough, even with only himself to feed. I wonder if he remembers to straighten his suspenders so they're not all twisted at the back. I wonder if he has stopped hoping I'll come home.

Behind me, the city is no more than a shadowy mass and a couple of pinpricks of light. It's too late to find a place to post the letter. *Maybe we'll come across a merchant caravan on its way to the city,* I think. But I also know that might be dangerous.

Pa told me it would take four or five days to walk from Industria, where so many of the laborers, schoolteachers,

seamstresses, and soldiers live, to Verity. I wonder where the
warehouse that we were first taken to before Curram purchased us is located. Somewhere not far from here, judging
by our journey. Away from prying eyes, lawmen with con-
sciences, and all human decency.

I remember Pa telling me that Industria's walls were even
stronger than those that surrounded Verity, that they were
built to protect us, to keep out the danger. But the sickness
that took my mum started up not three streets from our
home. The poverty that pulls my pa to work every day of his
life is the pulse of the city. And the hands that took me
sought me out within those walls. I can hardly believe there
could be worse evils in the wilder land beyond.

"You should sleep, Isla," Marion says finally. "I'm awake
for now. I'll stop when I can't keep my eyes open."

I nod, climbing into the back of the cart and sitting
across from Valentina and Des, who is asleep with his head
in Val's lap. She stirs when I sit down, opening her eyes
slightly. "You did it, Isla," she whispers, groggy.

*Am I really as strong as they all believe? No. Maybe? I don't
know.* A part of me wants to believe that heroism has always
been hiding inside of me. The thought settles in the bottom
of my stomach, heavy, but not comforting. *Was I content to
let my strength sleep as long as I had Tam to protect us both?
Will I shrink back into my quiet self when I find him again?*

Impossible, I decide. I'm not the same as I used to be. I
fiddle with the locket wound around my wrist, and I feel

strong. *I got away from Curram. Maybe I was the first. I showed him that he can't do whatever he wants with us. That was me.*

"I did, didn't I?" *Who would have thought I could be the strong one?*

We rock a little with the cart's movement over the ruts in the road, and my eyelids start to flutter and my thoughts slow. It feels like days ago that I did battle with the man who owned me. *Does Curram still own me?* I wonder. *Did he ever, really?* I still have the mark on my hand that claims he does. I'll have that forever, no matter how far I run. It's hard to believe I bathed only a matter of hours ago; I feel dirty again, tainted by Curram's touch. The skin on my hands is taut with the blood that sprayed me from the razor cut. It's dry now, but not gone. I wish it would fade, and that the memory would as well.

The stars have doubled in number now that we've left the city, ill-lit as it was. Through bleary eyes, I try to pick out the constellations that I know.

It's strange to think I looked at the same patterns with Tam only a month ago, when we thought nothing in our lives would change. Most of our troubles sorted themselves out back then; if we skipped supper one day, we usually had it the next.

I have no more reassurances now.

I don't know whether I'll make it out of Curram's grasp, really; he could catch us even now. For all we know, Marion is wrong and he might have Eisendrath under his thumb;

we could be turned in the moment we reach it. I don't even know if I'll find Tam.

At some point, as I drift in and out of sleep, I'm vaguely aware that Marion pulls the cart off the road, under the cover of trees, though I don't remember entering a forest.

"I just need a rest," she says with a yawn. Her voice sounds like it's coming from another room. "I think we're far enough from the city for the moment." The night air has turned cool, but we have the tarp spread over us for warmth.

I must sleep immediately, because all I remember is a breeze fluttering on my eyelids and then Tam's arms wrapped around me and his chin on my shoulder as he murmurs something that I can't make out. When I open my eyes, a grin still plastered to my face, and I realize slowly and sinkingly that I only dreamed he was with me, it is morning.

eighteen

I t's hard to shake off the disappointment, even with a
new world to take in around me. The trees are massive;
the city's spindly saplings could not have prepared me for
the majesty of these with their trunks as wide as my arms can
reach and their long, dark needles blotting out the sky. I climb
to the ground and turn around and around until my head
swims. Just knowing that I could walk for days and never
leave the trees behind is staggering. A part of me finally
understands why Tam cannot be content to stay still.

Around me, the others knead sleep from their eyes and
blink in the morning sunlight.

We find the road again and Jewel takes a turn driving,
with Caddy at her side, both speechless with awe. I sit on
the end of the wagon near Valentina, my legs dangling off
the back, trying to note any greenery we pass, in case I recognize something edible. But all I see are ferns and pine needles
that are brown from the summer heat. My books would say

that it's a good time of year for berries, but I don't trust myself to tell a harmless plant from a poisonous one.

The more I look for food, the hungrier I get, until I feel hollow all the way up to my throat. I can't stop thinking about thick beef stew and warm cider and the sticky date rolls Pa and I bought on holidays. *I've done this before,* I tell myself. *When Pa had to pay for the doctor to see Mum and we didn't eat, or when something broke and fixing it meant skipping a few meals. I won't starve. It's only been a day so far.*

Somehow even the cover of the pines does little to hold off the brutal heat. Sweat plasters my hair to my forehead, and my temples throb. Still, we drive on. Des wakes sometimes and asks questions about where we are, but Valentina mostly shushes him and tries to make him sleep, insisting it will help him heal faster. For hours there is no change in the scenery and no sight of anything to eat.

Eventually, I jump off the wagon and walk along the road, keeping pretty well paced since the horse moves slowly. After a moment, Phoebe joins me.

"It makes me restless," she says, shrugging. Her soft blond hair sweeps along her shoulders, and she looks cool, somehow refreshed. The frilly dress she wears is no longer than the ones we were all given, but hers suits her somehow, brushing the tops of her knees and swinging a little as she walks. Even in all the lace she looks tough and compact.

"At first," she says quietly, "back in that cell, I didn't care what happened to the rest of you." I wait for her to continue, and there's silence for a long time. When she does speak, she won't look at me. "I had a twin. Her name was Ever, and I loved her, more than myself if that's possible. She was so good, more than anyone should be. I wanted to be more like her, but I was always the selfish one. As much as she'd have liked to change that about me, she never could. We'd stand next to each other, though, and you could hardly say who was who."

She's quiet again, and we walk more slowly, letting the cart drift ahead.

"My ma said she could always tell us apart because my eyes were sharp, and Ever's were kind." Phoebe shrugs. "She said a lot about us, about how different we were. She said that I was the survivor, that I'd been born small and fought to stay alive, and that I'd do whatever I had to as long as I won. I wanted her to be wrong, but it was like a curse, I guess, hearing it all the time. It was true before I even meant it to be. There was nothing about Ever that was selfish. When we all got sick one winter, she gave everything she had to the little ones and ate nothing herself. I tried to make her take some of my food, but she wouldn't and I . . ." Phoebe pauses, squinting upward and around, swallowing hard. "I knew it was wrong, but I was so glad when she wouldn't. I was so hungry and we were all pretty bad off, and I was horrible for being glad, I know. It was the first time I'd forgotten to love her. Anyway, she grew weaker and weaker, and I was fine."

She still won't look at me. "She's gone. She wouldn't even

fight for herself. It only took a couple of weeks. Only Ma and Peter and I survived; the baby died before we'd even named her. Anyway, we lost four in all. Ma said it was a mercy; she didn't even cry. Probably welcomed the space in the flat." Phoebe scoffs, but it sounds more like she's choking.

When she finally looks at me, her eyes are red-rimmed but dry. "Valentina is good like Ever was, always taking care of other people. I wondered if you were the same, at first. I knew if I didn't let myself get involved, I wouldn't be responsible for anyone's fate but my own. It hurts to care about people, especially if they aren't going to help themselves."

We walk in silence for a while. I remember days spent at the library, sitting at long tables made of knotted wood, enjoying the unspoken company of other readers. I've missed the kind of silence that came with the right people. Tam always said that silence was awkward, but there were times when we'd lie side by side on my roof and watch the sky and say nothing, and he seemed happy then, with our hands next to each other's, just barely touching.

"There's a village just up ahead," Marion calls back to us. "We can buy food there."

Phoebe and I jog to catch up to the cart, which leaves me winded. We ride a little ways longer, until we see a shed through the trees and then, shortly after, a house. Slowly, a few more houses appear—farmsteads, mostly—peeking between the tall trees. *People,* I think. *People who might be suspicious of us. People who might somehow know we are running. People who might be as evil as so much of the world has proved itself to be.*

The X on my hand is mostly soft and pale now, the skin tight. It might not be the first thing someone will notice about me, but I don't know how I would explain it away if they do.

"We can't walk in like this," I say, gesturing at our clothes. "Someone will ask questions, or at the very least remember us later if anyone comes looking."

Marion nods, furrowing her brow. "Your clothes won't draw attention, Isla. You should buy something to eat and we'll meet you on the other side."

"Of course," I say, but my heart is racing. I grab the money purse I took from Curram's study and jump to the ground as Marion pulls the cart away from the road. *Just walk*, I tell myself.

House by house, a town takes shape around me. A street of hard-packed dirt, lined on both sides with mismatching houses, some of which have been transformed into quaint shops. What might be hundreds of people wander here and there between carts and stalls, calling greetings to each other and bargaining for better prices on the wares they're seeking. It should be charming, but I can't shake the memories of the last time I found myself in a crowd. I jump at every sudden sound, draw back every time someone jostles me. I turn around and around, half expecting to see hands reaching for me out of the corner of my eye.

Nothing has changed, I tell myself, not since the last time
Tam and I went to the market, not since I last walked to the
library alone. But everything feels unreliable. The world is
no longer trustworthy.

"New to town?" asks someone, startling me. A man just
at the edge of the road, standing in front of what must be
his stall, where baskets and finespun fabrics are on display
for market.

"Uh," I say, staring at him in confusion. He looks expec-
tant and I manage, "Just passing through," easing my way
past him and his wares. *He doesn't mean any harm,* I tell
myself, but my heart's racing. *There are too many people.*

And then I see a man moving through the crowd, striding with determination from one stall to the next. He's wearing a green jacket I've seen before, on Curram's guards. I
hold perfectly still, but everything around me moves twice
as fast as before.

There's another man, behind him. Across the little market square, I see a third. A fourth emerges from between
two stalls, where he had been hidden from view.

"He'll hunt you down," Phoebe had said.

I keep my head down and back slowly toward the edge of
the marketplace as more guards appear. When I reach the
first opening between buildings, I bolt into the trees and run
until I catch up to the cart.

"What's wrong?" Caddy gasps when I reach them, my
breathing ragged.

"Curram's men, in the village. Half a dozen of them,

maybe more. They must be looking for us." Phoebe nods; the others are wide-eyed. "He's looking for us. I was foolish to think we were safe."

"Get in, Isla, quick," says Marion, snapping the reins on the horse's back as I clamber into the cart. She steers us farther into the trees until we're a safe distance from the road. "They can spot us by the brands; I'll bet they're asking anyone they don't know. Curram must suspect we'd take this road out of the city. We'll have to get food at the next village." On cue, my stomach growls at the thought of another day of driving before we eat. But risking the marketplace is out of the question.

"He'll have men there, too," says Phoebe, rolling her eyes. "Curram doesn't know where we'd go, he probably just sent them in every direction, and if they passed us while we slept, they'll beat us to the next place as well."

Valentina crosses her arms. "Then what do you suggest we do? We need water, at least, and not only for drinking: Des's back is only going to get worse if I can't clean it properly."

Jewel raises her hand. "Let us get the food." She gestures to Caddy, who sits up straighter, her eyes twinkling.

"They'll see your hands or ask you who—"

"Not if they never see us at all," she argues.

"We shouldn't steal," pleads Valentina, looking alarmed.

"Bring the money," I say, "and, wherever you get the food from, leave a coin where it'll look like it fell out of a purse." Jewel's expression turns sour, as if we've taken all the fun out of her task. But Caddy grabs a couple of coins out of the purse and follows her friend through the trees.

It seems a long time that they're gone. Every few seconds I'm certain they've been caught. When they do finally appear, with grins on their faces, I let out a breath I didn't realize I was holding. They empty their bunched-up skirts into the wagon bed, revealing late-summer fruit, fresh bread, dried venison strips, and onions; it's a feast. Caddy is particularly proud of the melon she snatched, which Phoebe cuts with Robbie's knife, while Jewel takes on the task of rationing.

The melon's soft orange flesh is the most marvelous thing I've ever tasted; I try to savor it, but in seconds only the sticky rind is left. Even though I know it'll make me sick, I eat as much as Jewel will give me, until my tongue is heavy.

Valentina wakes Des and makes him drink out of the waterskin the girls took, before forcing him to turn over so she can see to his back. The coat has protected his back from too much dirt, but when she takes it off, I cover my mouth at the sight of the gashes in his skin. All the food I just ate threatens to come up again, but I force myself to breathe and help Valentina cut the bottom of the coat into strips that we can wash and then use as bandages.

For the rest of the day we drive on, parallel to the road in case we're overtaken. While she drives, Marion tells us more about Eisendrath, and how they gave it a foreign name so no one would suspect it was nearby if they heard rumors. She says that the people there come from so many places and backgrounds that it's impossible to feel like an outsider.

"And you won't be nervous, going back to your family?" Valentina asks quietly, her knees tucked up to her chest.

Marion turns to look at her. "Nervous?"

"After what happened. What if they look at you differently?"

"Why would they—I mean, nothing happened." Marion frowns at the path ahead of us. "We got out, didn't we?" I'd hardly say "nothing happened," but I don't argue; next to Eugenia's fate, it's hard to complain about my own.

When we stop for the night, I can't sleep. The air is still heavy with heat, even in the darkness. The sounds of owls and crickets fill the air, louder than the noises of the city ever were at night.

My eyes wander from face to face in the darkness. Asleep, everyone looks so peaceful. Asleep, I can't see their fears and insecurities. I can't see their histories, or their broken families. I can't see the brands on their hands.

For a second I feel safe, in a way. Even under an open sky, in a world of uncertainty.

But what must my pa be thinking? What torture has he been through since I've been gone? My eyes fill with tears, and what stars I can see swim together overhead.

"Are you asleep, Isla?" comes Des's quiet voice.

"I can't," I say, swallowing the knot in my throat. "Too hot. And too much to think about."

"Val says we're headed to Eisendrath." He doesn't sound happy.

I ease my way between the sleeping forms of the other

girls, taking a seat on the end of the cart next to him. "Do you know it?"

"Curram does."

"We're going to tell them what he's doing," I say. "That he's double-crossing them, working for Nicholas *and* with the rebels. If they know he's not to be trusted—"

"Of course they know he's not to be trusted. Everyone knows he works for Carr, Isla. He's one of their biggest suppliers, their ears inside the government. They're not going to pick our side over his. We might as well be walking into a trap when they find out he wants our heads."

"If the rebels want to end the corruption in the government, they'll want to know what kind of a man Curram is—"

"You mean the stuff with the girls? I hardly think that'll be their first concern."

Des doesn't know this Alistair Swain, who's in command at Eisendrath. Marion does. I change the subject before I get angry. "Why is Curram so concerned with the rebellion anyway? Does he think a successful revolution would look to him as its leader later on?"

"I doubt it. He's not *so* involved as all that; the only thing Zachariah Curram cares enough about to entangle himself in a messy rebellion is money. And he's smart enough to get it from both sides. As long as he supplies weapons and secrets to the rebels and keeps working for Carr, he's made himself useful to both parties, and no matter the outcome, he'll have friends in power." We're both quiet for a minute. "I wish you'd woken me up when you decided to go to Eisendrath," Des says quietly. "You know I can't waste time, that I've got to find my sister."

"You can hardly walk," I say, scowling. "You need to heal first, no matter what. We're kidnapping you until you're strong enough for your own mission."

He's not amused. "Isla, if Curram is looking for us, do you know who will suffer when he comes up empty-handed?" *More guilt. Phoebe was right; if Curram were dead, we wouldn't have to worry about any of this.*

"As soon as you're better, then," I say, but now I don't know if that will be soon enough. *Where could Curram be keeping Des's sister?* "I hoped the papers I took would say something about Lillian, but there was nothing. I'm sorry, Des. I don't know where to look."

"He must have *some* record," Des mumbles, and something dawns on me.

"*That's* what got you whipped, isn't it? You were looking for something about Lillian before we left." When he doesn't answer, I know I've guessed correctly. "Des, you risked our plan, all of our *lives* that day! I told you I'd help you find her, but that was reckless!" *You'd do the same for Tam,* says a voice in my head, but I ignore it.

"I'm sorry," he says, in almost a whisper. "I just needed to know."

"What will you do after you find her?"

"I don't know. I'd like to get as far away from scheming

and warmongering as possible." There's silence again for a few moments. When he speaks again, his voice sounds weak. "What will you do when you find Tam?"

Hearing his name makes my heart jump. "I don't know." I tip my head back and try to pick out more stars through the trees. Everything looks exactly as the encyclopedias led me to expect: trees everywhere, too wide to wrap my arms around and a hundred feet tall, craggy with knots and chasms in the bark, or pin-straight and sticky with sap. I used to know all of their names, but they don't matter now.

Instead, I think about the future. I'll get to Eisendrath and tell the leaders about Curram's treachery. With their resources, we'll find a way to ruin him, once and for all. Maybe that will mean killing him. And Tam must have joined the rebels; between Nicholas Carr's corruption and a thrilling revolution, there would be no other choice for him. I know his adventurous heart. If he's not at Eisendrath already, then he must be on his way, or he has found another base, and I will find him. I'll find him and make my own happy ending.

Maybe we could join the rebels together. Maybe I'd like to be a part of something noble and big. They might need scholars, or copiers. I close my eyes and imagine finding Tam, and telling him that I'm ready for an adventure. I can picture his confused smile, the way he'll ask what's gotten into me, or who I really am.

"I hope he's good enough for you," Des says.

I hold back my laugh so I won't wake anyone. "Maybe you'll meet him. He's perfect."

"Of course he is." I can hear the sarcastic smile in Des's voice. "Good night, Isla."

"Good night, *Despard*."

He chuckles. "Don't," he says.

nineteen

Phoebe and I walk behind the cart on and off all morning, and I can feel the life returning slowly to my legs, even when using them wears me out. Des, too, is getting his strength back little by little. He sits up in the back of the wagon, helped by the ever-faithful Valentina.

When Marion draws the cart to a halt at the morning's end, the only change in the scenery is a mossy cairn in the middle of our path. The rocks are piled as high as the wagon and as wide as any of the tree trunks around us, but there's room to go around.

"We're here," Marion announces proudly, crossing her arms in what's becoming a familiar stance.

"Here, as in . . . ?" Valentina looks nervous.

I walk in a circle around the cairn, then come back to the front of the wagon. "Are you sure?" Besides the structure itself, nothing looks out of place: There's the usual scattering of trees, spread over a hilly area, and some shrubberies along the ground.

"Wait a moment," Marion says, smirking.

Movement catches my eye, and I turn to see a man standing beside a tree who certainly wasn't there a moment before. One of his hands rests casually on the hilt of a knife in his belt, and the other holds a pistol. He's dressed in the colors of the forest and has a kind of relaxed way about him that suggests he's at home.

More movement calls my attention to another figure, a woman this time, also dressed to blend in. She leans against a tree, a rifle propped on her shoulder. "Got business here on our property?" she asks, scanning our group. I back up until my shoulder knocks into the side of the cart, and before I know it, half a dozen men and women make a clumsy circle around us. Their faces are weathered and they're well armed.

Most of them are watching Marion, who looks like the obvious leader from her perch at the front of the wagon, but a couple of the younger men seem to be staring at the other girls. Out of the corner of my eye, I see Val pull her skirt down across her knees, though it barely reaches.

"Business with Abraham," Marion says, still confident.

One of the women whistles loudly, a short melody that must be a signal. My heart races, fear mingling with excitement. Another man appears from between the trees, tall and thin, with a haggard face and gray stubble on his chin. *Where do they come from, rabbit holes in the ground?*

"Marion!" he exclaims, happiness transforming his gruff face. "What are you doing back so soon?" The others lower their weapons slightly but remain on guard.

"Fell into some trouble that wasn't my fault for a change." She smiles good-naturedly. "These are my friends. We barely got out alive and had to leave the city." The man's eyes widen.

"Well, if you can vouch for them, then. Feel free to signal me if they've got a gun to your back. This trouble, does it have anything to do with the way you're dressed?" Marion's skin is too dark for me to tell if she's blushing, but I'm grateful again for the dress from Curram's wife's things.

"Disguises," she says smoothly.

The man—Abraham, evidently—takes hold of our horse's bridle and leads the cart past the guards and over the crest of the hill. I climb onto the back, realizing too late that the other rebels have disappeared again, and I didn't see where they went.

The ride seems to take only a moment, my heart racing in my ears the whole time. When the ground levels out and Abraham brings the horse to a stop, the rebel camp is there, right in front of us and real. A steep hill slopes upward and away through the trees, while all about its base, where the land is flat, are campfires and tents. Farther out, to our right and partially hidden by trees, are clusters of stone buildings with patched-up walls. No doubt a village abandoned years ago, before the rebels came to reclaim it.

There are people everywhere, talking in groups, washing

clothes in barrels that have been sawed in half, herding flocks of sheep past the place we've stopped. *Tam could be here. Tam could be* here.

"Find your father," Abraham says, giving Marion a stern look. "If you've been in trouble, better he hear it from you straight off. I'll get your friends settled." He surveys us again and narrows his eyes. "And get them some new clothes as well."

"We need to see Swain. Is he here?"

"He is, but I don't know when he'll see you."

"Tell him it's urgent."

"I'll do that," Abraham says with a chuckle, and Marion looks stonily at him.

"Take care of them," she says, jumping to the ground. She gestures to Des. "He'll need medical attention. I'll be back soon."

"There's a stream through the trees just over there," Abraham says, taking care not to look at the exposed knees of most of the girls. We're already beginning to draw stares from the people passing by. "You can get fresh clothes from the supply hut, there. Just tell them I sent you."

He calls two other men over to help Des to whatever their version of a hospital is, and we walk as a tight group in the direction he indicated. Two men step into our path, their heads cocked curiously to the side.

"Our prayers are answered," says one, brushing his hands off on his smelting chaps. "Food, shelter, work, and now the company we've been missing so much out here."

His companion laughs loudly. "What more could a man ask for?"

Val hangs her head, grinding her teeth, but Phoebe just rolls her eyes. "Oh, look," she says, pointing, "there's a tree to screw yourself behind." I laugh, slapping a hand over my mouth as the men's expressions fill with offense. Phoebe marches us past before they can think of something to say.

When we do find the supply hut, the woman tending it looks suspiciously at our clothing. At least mine look normal, but she must suspect that the other girls are prostitutes come to join the revolution. *I'm sick of wearing things that came from Curram, whatever they look like.* I wonder what Marion's family will think when they see her. I wonder what they'll think when they hear her story.

"See if these work," the woman says, handing out bundles of fabric after glancing at us a few times. "We don't have much for choice here. They may not hold up well, but if you need anything else, just ask." We thank her and shuffle outside.

My eyes roam here and there, distracted. *Don't get your hopes up,* I tell myself, but everywhere I look, I hope for the familiar blond hair, the broad shoulders, and the confident grin that are always at the back of my thoughts. Every so often, I catch sight of a brown uniform and I start, but it's never Tam. *I'll have time to search after,* I scold myself, but my fingers itch to have him close again.

It's not difficult to find the stream—it runs along the base of the hill where most of the camp is settled, just where the ground levels out and the trees become more dense. I make my way upstream from the others for privacy—the first time I've truly been alone and at ease in weeks—and undress.

I hardly recognize my body.

I run my hands over my ribs—one, two, three, four, sticking out like fingers—to my hips, my bony knees and wrists and elbows. I've been small all my life, and we never had much food. But I was never this thin. *Are my cheeks sunken also? Do my eyes stand out? Do I look like that little girl from the warehouse, a lifetime ago?* I try to remember what I saw of myself in the mirrors in Curram's washroom and bedchamber, but all I can see is the skin-and-bones face I'm imagining for myself. And on my hand is the brand, as terrible as always.

I slip into the stream, which is cold despite the summer heat, and let the water rush inside my ears and block out the sounds of all my doubts and misgivings. My hair flows with the current, and when I resurface, I watch the birds above me flutter from one tree to the next.

When I'm clean, I dry myself off with my old dress and don the new clothes; the shift and underthings are soft from age, but clean. The dress fits me well; it's made of light, creamy linen with sleeves that reach my elbows and delicate, faded embroidery throughout the neckline, bodice, and hem. It's the sort of dress I always wanted for school: pretty, a little flouncy below the knees when I walk, the kind I hoped would make Tam notice me differently.

If I go home, I'll have a year left in school.

The thought hits me, unsettling. People I saw every day are now so far removed from me; I try to picture my classmates and the schoolrooms, but school is like a fuzzy dream. That was a different world. I was a different person.

The other girls are finishing dressing when I rejoin them. Our dresses vary from each other's in style, color, and fit, but the strangest thing is seeing how the girls are changed. Caddy looks more confident in the simple beige dress that stands out so starkly against her dark skin, while Jewel looks unassuming in blue, less brash. Valentina's eyes are the same kind eyes as always, but as she braids her wild orange-red hair tightly back to make it stay put, she looks more serious and grown-up than ever. Phoebe's dress is the most worn of all, faded white cotton with pale blue-and-gray stripes that almost blend together. Her hair hangs in long, wet streaks down her shoulders, but somehow she looks beautiful, her eyes sharp and bright. Barefoot and bone-skinny like the rest of us, she looks truly free.

"You look so pretty, Isla," Caddy says, coming toward me. "Could I . . . ?" She gestures to my hair. Before I can respond, she eases me to sit on the ground and begins running her fingers through my wet hair, twisting pieces of it together into a complicated plait that almost reaches the bottom of my ribs. When she's finished, she tears a thin strip of cloth from the hem of one of our discarded dresses and secures the braid. "Perfect," she says, turning me around with a grin. "You look perfect." I run my hands over the braid, wondering how long it will take for me to feel pretty again. The new clothes help. The bones almost poking through my skin do not.

The horse and cart are gone when we go back to find them, and Marion is nowhere to be seen. When we bring our old clothes to the supply hut, the woman directs us to the hospital, which turns out to be the remains of a small stone house with tents and tarps stretching off it as additional "wards." Des is sitting on a cot and grimacing when we find him.

"Stuff hurts like hell," he says, wincing whenever he moves.

"The salve will speed the healing along," says a young woman passing by. She puts her hands on her hips and looks at the rest of us, suspicious. "You're his friends?" We all nod. "Don't let him do anything too strenuous. It'll be a couple of weeks before that flesh will be fully healed, all right? He should probably stay here." We nod again, and Des rolls his eyes. The girl only grins, shaking her head at him and moving along.

Val looks between them, frowning.

"I hope you're not playing up your injuries to spend more time with pretty nurses," I say, crossing my arms. Des shakes his head vehemently, and then winces again.

"You all look nice," he says, maybe changing the subject on purpose. "New clothes?"

"You should find Marion," Valentina says to me, not

looking at Des. "I'll find him some decent clothes." She slips outside and I start to follow, but Des catches my hand.

"We're not free yet," he says, suddenly very serious. "Be careful."

I nod and leave, my head aching. *But we will be soon,* I tell myself, though it feels more like a question. *As soon as we talk to Alistair Swain and he takes our side. And as soon as I find Tam, and everything is better.* I twist the locket between my fingers, wishing the chain weren't broken so it could hang about my neck again.

A cluster of brown uniforms catches my attention and I take off toward them, forgetting about Marion. "Excuse me," I say when I get close, tapping the nearest soldier on the shoulder, suddenly nervous. The entire group turns. They're all Tam's age. Does Nicholas Carr look for the fresh and disposable? "I'm looking for a friend of mine. He enlisted recently and I was wondering if he might be here." My cheeks flood with warmth; the question sounds ridiculous, now that I've said it out loud.

The young men glance at each other, waiting for me to continue, as Phoebe catches up to me.

"He got a name?" asks the soldier whose shoulder I tapped.

"Tam Lidwell," I say, my confidence draining.

"Never heard of 'im," replies the soldier, and I shake my head.

"Thank you," I say.

One of the other soldiers pipes up. "You know what regiment he's in? That'd make him easier to find."

I shake my head again. "Thank you anyway," I say, knowing I probably look like an idiot.

*Was I a fool to think it could be this easy? Was I stupid to be
so certain?* My need for Tam is different now; I don't feel broken without him, incapable. It's his arm through mine that I
want, his confidence that I can find a way to defeat Curram.
*Together we could do anything. He'd probably lead the charge
if I let him.*

"That wasn't exactly what I had in mind," Phoebe says,
touching my arm. "Why should they know anything? We can
ask someone at this fortress *after* we find Marion and she
takes us there. Come on."

It was a long shot, I tell myself. *I'll get real answers from
someone who knows what they're talking about. I'll find him.* I
try to keep my head up as Caddy and Jewel reach us and we
go in search of Marion. My eyes drift over every face, hoping against hope that I'll bump into Tam somehow.

The fourth or fifth person we ask knows Marion and her
family, and directs us across the camp to the farms and
granaries. The houses here are still small, but at least they're
more permanent than the tents. The first children I've seen
since we arrived chase each other around the smoldering
remains of cook fires and the troughs where cows and
goats are drinking in turns. Beyond all this, stretching past
where the trees have been cleared, are long rectangles of
land tilled into rows for planting or fenced off for keeping
animals.

These people have built a whole world here in these woods,

I think, wondering how long they expect the rebellion to last.

"Marion!" I hear someone shout, sounding angry, and I see her making her way toward us with her head held high, still wearing the short, childlike dress she arrived in. Someone is coming out of the house behind her, probably her father, still shouting her name, but she doesn't turn around. "Come back this instant!" the man yells as she reaches us.

"Let's go," Marion says, swallowing, then setting her jaw. Her eyes look like she's about to cry. "We can wait for Swain to see us at the fortress." She brushes past us, and as we turn to follow, a woman comes out of the house as well, clinging to the man's arm. She looks like a scared rabbit, eyes wide, hands trembling, tears streaming down her face. Marion doesn't turn around, and none of us risk asking her what happened.

The way to what Marion calls the fortress is up the steep hill that stretches along one corner of the camp, and the climb leaves us winded. It's not long before the muscles in my legs are screaming at me, tying themselves in knots and threatening to collapse. I blink sweat out of my eyes and glance up from my feet, for the first time seeing our destination: At the top of the hill, hidden until now by the trees, is a castle.

It must be a century old. The stone is gray and weather-beaten, no doubt by the harsh winds at the crest of the hill where the earth is treeless. Many of what might have been a dozen turrets have crumbled, and doors have been made here and there in the walls for easier entry. As we clear the trees, a salty breeze smacks me in the face, pulls at my hair, and swirls over the other side of the hill.

The ocean. Memories flood my mind. Pa took me to the ocean after Mum died. He bought me a piece of taffy off the puller and we climbed the rocks, and I went too fast for him. I had to keep doubling back, and he was always wiping his face and saying how the salt made his eyes water. But I knew he was crying because of Mum; I didn't say anything so he wouldn't feel worse. Then we sat on the sand and I told him all about the books I'd read that week, and neither of us mentioned how we felt.

It was the only time I went to the ocean, though Tam talked about making trips there often enough. There was always the salty river that slid alongside the city, taking the boats into and out of the open seas, but it was a whole day's trip in the trolley to the actual seaside, and it cost as much as a day's meals.

Have we really reached the sea? As this is obviously far from a port city, we must be farther up or down the coast, but still. *The ocean. We've come so far.*

Marion doesn't pause once in her trek to the top. When we've reached the fortress, we pass under a rust-eaten gateway and then through a door beyond it that must have been beautifully carved before the harsh weather turned the wood soft and green.

It's darker inside, and my feet pick up dust and cobwebs

as I walk. There's nothing to suggest this place isn't still abandoned; the only sound as we make our way along one wide hallway after another is our ragged breathing. When we reach a large, hall-like room at the end of a corridor, Marion finally stops in front of a wide set of doors, each with a rusty coat of arms on it. There's a man sitting at a desk outside, looking bored, but he frowns when he sees us.

"Would you tell Mister Swain that Marion Colter is here to see him with important information?" Marion says, and the man gives us a curious look, aimed mostly at her attire.

"Do you have an appointment, *Marion Colter*?"

She bristles at his condescending tone. "I live here. He'll know my name if you tell him I need to see him." The man does not appear convinced. "Look, he'll know my father, Reuben Colter—"

"I'm sorry, Miss Colter, but you'll have to return another time."

"We need a moment, no more." Marion sounds desperate as she glances around at us.

"And you'll have that moment. Just not today."

We came too far to be turned away right at Swain's door. "Tomorrow, then," I say. Everyone looks at me, including the secretary, who is growing more annoyed. "We're not looking for a social call," I go on. "We have time-sensitive information that Alistair Swain will want to hear. It concerns the safety of this camp."

The man grinds his teeth, looking between me and Marion like he's deciding whether it's worth it to just give in. "Very well, tomorrow. Come in the morning and we'll fit you in." He smiles at us with pursed lips and Marion turns in a huff.

"I'm sorry," she says, shaking her head. "It shouldn't be this difficult, and I promise he'll be interested in what we have to say. He doesn't take injustice lightly. When we tell him what Curram's *really* up to, and about the girls he buys, he'll rally to our cause, I know he will."

The light in Marion's eyes increases my hope. Des has never met Alistair Swain. Just because Swain does business with Zachariah Curram does not mean he's anything like him; maybe he's simply been duped like so many others. Maybe Swain is using Curram, and Curram has no idea.

We're halfway down the corridor when I tell the girls not to wait, and I double back.

The secretary looks exasperated when he sees me, so I hurry through my question. "I'm looking for a soldier here, a deserter," I start, and he puts up a hand to stop me.

"Find Harlen. He's in command. He'll know your soldier."

"And where's he?"

"Well, *I* don't know."

When it's clear he doesn't mean to be more helpful, I thank him and return to the others, my heart racing. They're waiting just outside the fortress, and Marion is explaining how Swain helped break wrongly accused convicts out of prisons to give them a chance at a new life with the rebellion.

"I'm going to look around here for a bit," I say, earning questioning glances from the others. "Swain's secretary said someone here might know where to find my friend. I'll look for you later." Phoebe gives me an encouraging nod, and they turn to make their way back down the hill.

Maybe this Harlen has an office in one of the rooms here, I think, turning down a new corridor and looking into each doorway I pass. Most of the rooms are empty and quiet; those that look lived in have only dusty furniture and the occasional remains of a fire in the hearth.

My footsteps echo grandly as I wander until I find a set of half-crumbled stairs covered in spiderwebs. I trail my fingers along the railing and they come away covered in dust. For a moment I'm grateful for the loneliness: everything in gray and white, even the old tapestries hanging on the wall so moth-eaten and dusty that I can't tell what they picture. The floor is covered with crumbled pieces of stone and the occasional half-burned torch, and one door I come to is so rotted that it hangs crookedly on just one hinge.

I tentatively push open the door and step inside, only to find the walls are covered in shelves.

A library.

There are hardly a dozen books between all four walls, but I feel instantly at home. Some of the shelves have doors to protect the contents, but these have swung open and the glass in them has been smashed. *How long has it been since someone set foot in this room?*

There's a wide window in the far wall with a bench beneath it, and beyond it, a view that catches my eye from all the way across the room: a thin piece of turf that breaks off suddenly, and then, far below, beyond where I can see from here, the ocean. Even through the dirty-orange glass of the old window, the view is awe-inspiring. To me, the sea has always meant that I'd reached my limit, though Tam said it held the greatest adventures of all.

Tam, I think, shaking my head clear. *I need to find Tam. Books can wait.*

✦ ✦ ✦

Once I'm satisfied that Harlen is nowhere to be found in the fortress, I make my way back downhill, toward the rest of the camp. *Does Alistair Swain keep that whole place for himself? Or is it unsafe to live in?*

I spy Phoebe sitting cross-legged against a tree, but she jumps to her feet when she sees me. "Marion's getting some new clothes," she says, coming toward me. "The others are going to find some food. Any luck?"

"Not yet. I have to find someone called Harlen. I met a woman who told me where the barracks have been set up, so I'm going there now."

"I'll come with you," Phoebe says, falling into step beside me. I'm too nervous to talk as we make our way through the camp, past the farms, and deeper into the woods, to a place where more trees have been cleared and simple pavilions have been constructed. Hundreds of young men in brick-brown uniforms run laps or practice formations to shouted orders.

We approach the nearest pavilion, where a burly, stressed-looking man sits at a table talking to a handful of soldiers.

Their once-sharp uniforms are stained with mud and sweat; recent deserters, I'd guess. Tam isn't among them.

While we wait our turn, Phoebe shoots cryptic glances at me and I chew on my lip until I taste blood.

"Looking to enlist?" drawls the man I assume to be Harlen with obvious annoyance when we approach.

"Hardly," Phoebe says curtly. "We're looking for a soldier who may have joined your ranks." She gives me a pointed look and I take a step closer.

"Tam Lidwell?" My voice cracks a little. Harlen's expression says I'm wasting both of our time, but he begins rifling through his papers, puffing out his cheeks in irritation.

"I—I just want to be sure," I say, and he crosses his arms, dismissing us.

"Second unit, training far end of the field now," he growls.

"E-excuse me?" I stammer, blinking.

"Thank you so much," Phoebe says loudly, grabbing my arm and pulling me sideways.

"Did he—"

"Far end of the field," she says, grinning. I hardly know how to walk; I feel like I've just been spinning in circles and the dizziness is twisting the world around under my feet. Phoebe pulls me after her along the side of the field, demanding to know if I'll become one of "those giggly girls" when I find Tam. But I hardly hear her. I move faster and faster until I'm racing ahead. An ache begins under my ribs, but giddy certainty fuels me.

At first there's nothing different about the last group of soldiers on the field from any of the others; I'm too far away to see their faces, and they all move in synchronized steps. There must be thirty of them, mostly tall and broad-shouldered. But then I see him.

I know his squared-off jaw, his perfect ears, the way his hands twitch a little with nervous energy even though he's marching. *It's him. It's really him. I can't believe he's here.*

"Well, which one is he?" asks Phoebe, nudging me in the ribs.

"There," I say, stretching on my toes and pointing. "One row in, third row back."

The man shouting orders calls for a halt, and the men shuffle into slightly uneven lines. I don't take my eyes off Tam, standing with his head held high, his rifle against one shoulder. When his commander turns away for a moment, he quickly shoos the hair out of his eyes and then resumes his stance. The officer in charge is giving some sort of instruction for the use of the rifles, which he's saying load differently from the type used by Nicholas Carr's army, and I see Tam's eyes wander aimlessly.

I know he sees me because his eyes widen and he drops his gun.

"Lidwell!" shouts the officer, and Tam fumbles to right his weapon. He stands straight again and looks back at me with his mouth open, blinking, while I stand perfectly still, grinning like a fool. "Once around, Lidwell," snaps the officer, and Tam breaks away from the group, jogging toward me.

Toward me. He's coming over here. My heartbeat gets faster and faster, but then my gaze falls on his legs; he's limping, favoring his right leg, though he's trying to hide it.

And then he's in front of me, tall and real and sunny, the same as always.

"Isla," he says, his mouth still hanging open like a fish's. The rifle slips in his hands again, and he scrambles to keep hold of it. "Wh-what—"

"That's not a lap, Lidwell!" comes the shout of his commander, but Tam just keeps staring at me.

I don't know what to say.

"I have to go." He casts a glance behind him and takes a step backward.

"We need to talk!" My voice comes out higher than I expect.

"Yeah," he says with a laugh, shaking his head at me. "Yeah, we do."

He's getting farther away from me. "There's a library in the fortress; find me there, all right?" The words come out in a rush, but he's nodding even as he jogs backward, away from me. As he starts his lap around the field, he grins over his shoulder.

My cheeks are sore from smiling when Phoebe clears her throat and I remember she's there. "Sorry," I say, blushing, but I'm not. I'm giddy. *Is he real? Is he really here? How did I ever take him for granted, all those years?*

I watch as Tam makes his way to the far side of the field, still glancing over at me every few seconds. His limp bothers me; the longer he jogs, the more pronounced it becomes. He slows down for a moment, and I notice the officer shaking his head before he looks my way disapprovingly. Phoebe grabs my hand and pulls me back the way we came.

"Library?" she says. "You're meeting him in a *library*?" I raise my chin. "That's the least romantic thing I've heard in my life."

twenty

Back at the infirmary, Des is sitting up, but he's still pale. Valentina passes around bowls filled with stew that looks at least a little better than what Curram had to offer. "There's a common fire," she says by way of explanation. "And the nurse told me where we can stay tonight."

We eat in silence for a moment, but I can't stop smiling. *Tam's here.* The words ring over and over through my head. *I wish I'd touched him,* I think, replaying the moment he came toward me. *Then I could be sure, absolutely sure, that he's real and I'm not imagining him.*

"Are you all right?" I hear Valentina ask, and I look up to see that Marion is staring at her bowl, not eating.

"I'm fine," Marion snaps. She goes on in a quieter voice. "I knew I'd need time to adjust, but I didn't figure they'd . . . my mother just cried when she saw me, and my father wouldn't even look at me. They didn't believe me that nothing happened. I told them I'm no different, but they wouldn't even listen to what I was saying."

Valentina touches her knee. "I'm sorry," she says. "I know that must be hard."

"Actually, you don't know," Marion says sharply, getting to her feet and thrusting her bowl into Phoebe's hands. "I'm not hungry. I need to clear my head."

She leaves behind awkward silence, and Valentina looks at her lap. I'm about to say that Marion didn't mean to be harsh, when Valentina speaks first.

"In a way, we're not *really* the same," she says softly. "If I go back, I'm not telling anyone what happened. I don't want them to look at me like damaged goods." Before I know it, I'm tracing the X on my hand with one finger. *Damaged goods.* That isn't what we are. We fought, we survived. We won.

But there are violations I can't forget, no matter how small they might be in comparison to others' fates. I can't shake Robbie's rough kiss, or Eugenia's bloody death in front of me. It's impossible to forget Curram's greedy glances, his hands slithering along my body, his weight on top of me.

Even if I *could* forget, my hand is a constant reminder of everything that happened. The ugly, fleshy X, forcing me to accept the reality of what was done to me. In some ways I'll never be the same again, never be able to go back. The person I was before that hot day in the crowded city, that person is gone.

"We're trying to think of an exciting story for when

people ask about the brand marks," Jewel says, trying to lighten the mood.

Phoebe ignores her, turning to me. "Was it hard, to see Tam after everything?"

The others stare. "You found him?" Des demands.

I nod, grinning despite the tension. "Actually it was perfect."

Val looks unconvinced. "And he didn't act . . . strangely?"

"Why would he?"

"When you told him what happened, I mean."

"I didn't have the chance. We barely spoke."

Phoebe stares me down. "But you will?"

"Of course," I say, nodding. *We tell each other everything.* But Valentina won't look at me. "I actually have to go," I say, shoveling the last bites of stew into my mouth. "We're supposed to meet."

"And you don't think you need a chaperone for that?" Des teases, but he looks strained, even just sitting up slightly in his bed.

"I'll see you all in the morning. Don't forget that we've got to see—"

"Got to see Swain first thing," Phoebe cuts me off. "I'll fill them in. They gave us a couple of tents by the common fire. You and I can share."

I nod and slip outside, heading uphill. *When do the soldiers finish their drills?* I wonder. *Is he already there waiting for me? How long since I saw him, an hour?*

The fortress looks more dramatic than ever, framed by

the afternoon sun. As I crest the hill, the wind picks up suddenly, climbing the cliffs behind the castle and pulling warm,
briny air down the hill to weave between trees and toss my
hair in my face. I smell the salt again and close my eyes, imagining I'm sitting on the pier with a paper bag of fried onions
and clam bellies, with Tam next to me and the harbor before
us. He would be naming the ships and their captains on their
way to the sea, and I'd be telling him the names of the best
knots and how rudder systems worked.

Not long now, I tell myself. *He'll be with me soon.*

I take care not to go by way of the corridor where Alistair
Swain's secretary is stationed, and when I reach the library,
it looks the same as I left it. I gather an armload of books
and carry them to the bench beneath the window.

The covers are coming unstitched, and the pages are yel-
lowed with age and mildew, but most are still clear enough to
read. *Cultivation of Rocky and Difficult Soil* reads the title of
one, and another, *The Language of the Fan; for Society's Edu-
cated Woman.* Though I'd never have chosen these at home,
in this wilderness, written words are like gold. Still, I wish the
books told tales of battles or espionage, instead of fans and
farming. *The old Isla mightn't have minded,* I think. But the
new Isla is more easily bored. There's a mathematics primer
too; *The—of Fishing in—Regions,* some of the title rubbed
away; and an eerie-looking gothic novel, by an author whose
name I don't recognize. Some of the books are so fragile
they fall apart in my hands.

I stack them in order of most interesting to least, and

start with the novel, settling into the position that I've missed so much: my legs curled up to my chest, my arms tucked in tightly, and my head bent, letting the words suck me in as I read them.

But the story that might have once held me captive with its twists and turns feels predictable now. *The heroine's unfeeling parents, arranging her marriage to a nobleman whose name is connected to a murder from years ago. Her chance meeting with a wounded knight in the woods, the screams she hears at night, and the secret compartment in a back room of her fiancé's palace.*

I can't focus. I stare out the window at the ocean, as gray as the day Pa and I saw it, though it looks colder here, and wonder when Tam will arrive. I pace back and forth, blowing dust off the windowpanes, straightening crooked shelves to little avail, fiddling with my hair and wishing I'd thought to have Caddy fix it again. *At least my dress is clean. Mostly. The dust can't be helped. I hope I don't look too skinny, or that he doesn't notice if I do. I hope I don't act strangely around him. I probably will. No, I know I will.*

Eventually the sky begins to darken, orange on one side, and rich, deep blue on the other. I'm hungry again, but I ignore it, and the room grows cool.

When I finally hear footsteps in the hall, I stop breathing.

"Isla?" his voice calls softly.

"In here!" I shout back, and then he's there in the door-way, real as I am and squinting into the sunset behind me.

He coughs nervously, rubs the back of his neck. "That is you, right?"

I tear from the window seat and across the room to him, burying my face in his coat and breathing in the smell of him, my heartbeat pounding in my ears. *Not a dream!* my thoughts scream at me. *Not a dream, not a dream.* I feel him laugh, slowly, and his arms slide around my back and hold me, like they should, like they always did, like they'll never let go.

He's warm and broad and solid; something real to make up for the memories I've had to content myself with. I feel his long exhale of breath on the top of my head, shuddering a little through his chest as I hold on to him. I feel so small again, tucked into his shoulder where I belong.

When he pulls back a little, I look up at him. "Did you miss me, then?" he says, pushing my hair out of my face, grinning in what's still a confused way. I missed that. I missed his hands, which are so much bigger than mine and so gentle as he wipes a tear off my cheek that I didn't realize had fallen. I missed the roundness of his voice, and the hint of a joke laced through all of his words, and the smile that makes me forget we're supposed to be growing up now, because it's still boyish.

"So much," I whisper, not sure I can manage anything else.

When he lets me go, I feel exposed, cold again. "You seem different," he says, like a question. Then amusement spreads across his features. "How'd you come to join a rebellion, Isla?"

I love the sound of my name in his mouth; I hang on to it for a second.

He's here.

But he asked a question. *How did I come to be here?*

Memories come flooding in, in flashes of pictures and the sounds of screams. The hot, crowded city, the red panic as I was dragged away, the blackness of the confinement when I woke, the dankness of the cell. Do the smells still cling to me? The mildew of Curram's prison, the stench of the hole that served as our toilet, and before that, burning flesh and the agony of the brand against my palm.

I curl my fingers into a fist so Tam won't see the X imprinted in my skin.

"It's too long a story for now," I say, though the words crowd together in my mouth and want to escape. "I'll explain, I promise."

Tam gives me a funny look, letting silence stretch between us. And then, "You look cold," he says, like a reprimand. He sheds his coat and drapes it about my shoulders in one smooth gesture, and it's heavy and still warm from his own body, and smells familiar.

I want to ask how he came here himself, but when I meet his eyes, he's watching me, and my thoughts stagger. He breaks into a grin again, slowly, and shakes his head. "Tell me what happened," I finally manage, shaking my head back at him, my tongue heavy with disbelief.

"Mine's a long story, too," he says. Watching his mouth

makes me want to jump up on my toes and kiss it, so I look at my feet instead, trying to will my heart to calm down. "I've only been *here* a few days. I shouldn't be surprised you found a library in the middle of a rebellion. You're predictable, dear." That word sounds as casual as it ever has, and the smallest of doubts pricks at my heart: Will everything be the same between us? Was the kiss an affectionate farewell, and not a mark of something more than friendship? I knock the thoughts aside. They don't matter right now. There is no disappointment today.

"There isn't much here at all, though," I say, smiling. "Books about soils and herbs and how to use a fan properly. Mostly boring."

"Exactly the sort of book I let you read for me," he agrees, nodding deeply. Then he pauses, watching me again. The watching happens every few seconds, like he can't place me here. Like I don't fit, or he doesn't fit, or we don't fit, together. "I'm sure you have a lot to tell me," he says eventually. "And I've missed your rambling. Can we find something to eat while we talk?"

I nod, slipping past him. I feel as if I have a prize to show off, and a beautiful secret that I want to keep all to myself, both at the same time.

Tam.

Tam is here.

I found him.

"How long has it been, since you left?" I ask when we

reach the bottom of the stairs. He scans the ceiling for a moment, thinking. There are spiderwebs in the corners, and broken plaster lines the walls along the ground.

"Almost a month, I guess?" He whistles through his teeth. "Seems longer." I nod, my head spinning. *So much longer.* I don't know how to begin.

"When you left, I thought maybe I'd just sit around all summer with nothing to do but talk my pa's ears off—"

"Is he here? Did he come with you?" Tam looks around, as if my pa might come around the corner or appear behind me.

"N-no—"

He's disappointed. "How is he? When did you leave? Did you see my family before you left? I don't know how they're doing, because nobody wrote back to me."

"You wrote?"

He frowns. "Twice. I sent your letters with ones to my brothers so the postage wouldn't be double. I thought you'd answer." There's a hint of hurt in his eyes that cuts me.

"I—I never got them," I stammer, feeling overwhelmed.

"Don't worry about it." He touches my shoulder, casually, wonderfully. "I didn't expect to see anyone from home for a while yet. How was my family, when you last saw them?"

The hallway is empty, but I feel stifled.

"The same as when you left," I squeak. I can feel the words—about the kidnapping, the dark train car, the brand, the prison—trying to push their way past my lips. I bite them back, suddenly trepidatious.

"Please tell me," he goes on, rocking back on his heels,

"how in the world Isla Powe, of all people, came to join a rebellion, so far from home and all alone?"

I don't know how to say that I was hurt. The weight of the story crushes my chest; I want it off, but somehow I can't answer him. I can't. Not yet, at least. I choke back the reason I never wrote. Instead, all I say is, "Not alone, exactly," which makes him give me a funny look.

"What's wrong with you, Isla? So cryptic all of a sudden. I suppose I can't leave and then expect the same girl to be waiting when I get home, huh?" He's teasing, but my stomach turns.

"I'm the same," I insist, trying not to panic.

"The Isla I knew would never have lived in the woods with rebels." My mind turns to turmoil. *Will he want somebody different? If he doesn't want me to change, should I go back to the person I was before?* I hate myself for thinking that way. *Why should I try to be only what he wants?* But I can't help it.

"What happened to *you*?" I ask, eager to change the subject so I can breathe. "When you left, you didn't know where they'd take you, or what you'd do. Tell me about it." I expect Tam to light up and bubble over with stories, but his eyes darken suddenly, his face turning ashen.

"Nothing good," he says seriously.

"Tam?"

He doesn't answer at first. The corridor is bleak, and his silence makes it more so. "It wasn't so bad at first, the training, I mean. A lot of exercise and early mornings. Not much food. We got our orders to march right away." I reach over and take his hand while he struggles to cough up the words. He looks down at our fingers and takes a breath.

"Our first orders brought us toward the border, east of the principal city. We made camp during the day and waited for commands. When they came, they . . . Well, there was this town, a country village, really, right nearby. We were told that when the rebels began to gather, they'd cleared it out and were using the barns and buildings to store weapons and food. They told us to burn it.

"Seemed stupid to waste the supplies, but we had already learned that questioning orders got you flogged." He grinds his teeth and his eyes flicker with a painful memory, but he's not done. "So I obeyed. We all did.

"When night fell, we surrounded the village and began to start the fires. It was so dry and hot, the flames caught easily, and the heat pushed us back. I stood with the other men and we watched walls crumbling. The roar of the flames was deafening. It took me a moment to recognize the sound of screams."

A chill ripples through me. "There were people inside? Oh, Tam. Did you help them?"

"I couldn't even get near the buildings, Isla. I tried, a bunch of us did. It was too late." I realize that I'm squeezing his hand too tightly, so I drop it.

"What horrible people," I whisper, shaking my head. *Like Curram, and Boyne, and Robbie, and everyone they work for and with. There is too much evil.*

"That wasn't the only thing we did," Tam says.

Indignation rises up in me. "But why did you obey them?" I demand, taking a step backward. "Why did it take you so long to leave?"

His eyes turn angry, but not at me. "We thought it had been a mistake, that our officers didn't know there were people hiding there. The next night they sent us to another village, same orders. I suggested we check for inhabitants first, and the officer in charge told me that the first unit had already done so, after what had happened the night before. I was stupid to trust him.

"We started the fires, and it wasn't long before we heard the screams. Isla, I didn't know what to do." He looks frantic. "They turned us into murderers. I was so stupid. The next morning, I didn't report for duty. I stayed in my tent, waiting for punishment. Most of us did." He flashes me the smallest, briefest of smiles. "I wrote to you while we waited. Talking to you always helped before, and I needed to sort out everything in my head, you know? My letter was rubbish, though. You must—well, if you didn't get it, I guess it doesn't matter anyway. They had us flogged, and forced us into a line, to stand for hours, until our next orders."

His eyes look hollow as he talks, like he's somewhere else. "That night was the same as the others, but without any of the pretenses. When we reached our new target, I refused to act and so did half of my unit. The officers screamed at us and beat us with their fists, but we remained still, until they drew their guns on us. Then we pretended to obey.

"One of my buddies signaled, and when we got close to

the buildings, we started yelling, shouting to warn the people, to help them escape. That was when the officers started shooting." I flinch. "They were aiming for our legs; when we fell, they left us in the dirt, close enough to the fire that the heat burned us while we couldn't move."

He shrugs. *As if he's fine. As if it doesn't matter what he suffered.* For the first time, I notice that his temple is marked with uneven, pink flesh. The scarring runs down as far as his jawline, faint but definitely noticeable now. I take a step closer, running my finger from one end of the patchy skin to the other; Tam closes his eyes and sets his mouth in a tight line, breathing through his nose.

"They left us on the ground until they were finished," he goes on as I take his hand again. "But before morning they dragged us back to the camp, to the infirmary tent, the dozen or so who were still alive. They should have killed us that night"—I flinch again—"but I guess they thought we'd learned our lesson.

"We had a week to recover, but they found work for us around the camp, so we never got much of a chance to heal properly." *His limp. Of course.* "I thought about deserting; a buddy of mine, Esau, did, and they found him, brought him back, and shot him half a dozen times while we had to watch." He takes my other hand, drawing my gaze up to his.

"I—I just want you to know that I wasn't a coward," he says. "I wanted to fight, to protect my country. I didn't want to burn families alive inside their houses." I nod, wishing my throat weren't so tight so that I could reassure him with words. "A man approached me after that with questions about my feelings on the army, what I thought of Nicholas Carr. I found out he'd also been talking to the other guys who'd rebelled with me. Eventually he told us he was from the rebellion, the very people we'd been attacking. He wanted us to join him, and said he'd help us get out if we would swear our service to the rebels instead. We all agreed.

"The next night we ran. It took three days to get here, three days of sprinting and hiding like hunted animals. But we made it." He smiles a little, with one side of his mouth. "And then you found me."

twenty-one

H is words echo around in my head, heavy in the air.
But then I remember my branded hand. I jerk away
without thinking, and Tam takes a step back, looking upset.
"I'm sorry," he starts saying, almost frantically. "I should have
warned you, it's just I forget sometimes because it doesn't
hurt anymore, but I don't mean to upset you." He's cupping
his right hand around the left one, hiding it from me.

"What?" I sputter, confused.

"It's not so terrible, really. I wasn't scarred as badly as
some. I'm sorry."

"Tam," I say, realizing he thinks that his burn marks
have repulsed me. "Let me see. I want to."

He tries to look nonchalant. "Don't be nice for my sake,
Isla. It's really—"

"Tam. When you scraped half the skin off your leg trying
to ride that rusty bicycle, who read about sterilizing bandages

and homemade salves and didn't care about the blood?" He looks wary. "Show me. Please?"

He holds his left hand out unsteadily. The back and side of it are sleek with pink flesh, the scars a little shiny, not fully healed. He has such lovely hands, firm and strong. They could never be ugly, even now that they're imperfect. I smooth my fingers over the burned skin, then bring his hand up to my lips and kiss it. "It must have hurt," I say, meeting his eyes. "But you've always planned to collect scars, Tam." I watch his face until he finally smiles.

"Well. You're perfect," he says, "so I'll take the cuts and bruises for both of us." I glance down again at his marred hand. He isn't the only one whose skin tells a story.

He'll have to see eventually. "You know, I've got scars of my own," I say unsteadily. *Can he hear my voice trembling?*

"Let's get out of here," he suggests, oblivious to the story I'm trying to tell. He starts down the corridor, looking over his shoulder at me. "What did you mean about not coming alone? Did you bring friends here with you?"

"I did," I say, smiling despite myself as we leave the fortress and make our way down the hill.

"Anyone I know?"

"No. New friends."

"Do you think they'll mind if I share their supper? I don't really want to go all the way back to the barracks."

"Of course not," I say, imagining showing Tam off to the other girls. But with my next step, panic hits. *He'll ask how we met, or what brought them here. I told them I was going to tell him about Curram.* "Actually," I say, grabbing his arm, "let's not find them yet. One of the girls is in a pretty bad mood; I wouldn't want to bother them."

He looks deflated. "All right," he says, clearly disappointed. "Do you want me to go? If you'd rather I didn't come with you or something."

"No, it isn't that. Maybe we could go somewhere to talk on our own first?"

He nods. "I've got somewhere to show you anyway," he says. His grin makes my stomach clench with nerves. He takes my hand and pulls me after him in the near dark. We weave between the trees where they're dense until finally Tam stops, and the moon is straight ahead of us, glowing white and sitting just above the ocean horizon.

We're right at the cliffs. The air tastes clearer here, and the wind feels stronger, taunting me with a fall to my death in the icy water a hundred feet below. Tam lets go of my hand, jogging out onto the rocks until he's only a foot or so from the horrible drop, lit up in silver, moonlit clarity. "Tam," I start.

"I know you don't want to come out here, don't worry. I just wanted to see the view." His words sound like a challenge, and something besides nervousness stirs in me. Before he can finish saying that he's been wanting to come out here at night, I run nimbly across the cliff to him, stopping only a few steps before the edge, putting my hands proudly on my hips to hide their shaking. Tam's mouth drops open in surprise, while my heart pounds against my ribs.

Next to me, the cliff cuts off and the drop is straight and terrifying, dark and unsurvivable. The crash of every salty wave echoes against the rock face. I feel unsteady even with my feet spread wide, like I'm already starting to fall, or like the ground is moving out from under me.

But it's worth it for Tam's look of amazement.

It's hard to tell now if the dizziness comes from the drop or from the fact that he is looking at me and only me, and smiling like that.

It's a few seconds before he clears his throat, breaking eye contact. "Should we sit? Less chance of falling that way, you know?" He's trying to be funny, but I'm still too shaky to laugh. We walk a couple of steps away from the edge, to a place where the rocks flatten out and moss makes the ground softer.

The stars are out in their full splendor. I curl my fingers into an O and stretch my hand out, trying to count the twinkling dots of light that fit inside the O, but there are too many even then. "The city has nothing on this," Tam breathes, and I catch a hint of the same wistfulness that always clung to his words back home. *At least the army hasn't stamped that out of him,* I think, and I'm glad. I nod, moving closer to him and watching his movements in case he doesn't like it.

"Show me a constellation," I prompt, setting him up.

He laughs quietly. "I know one this time," he says, sitting up straighter. "It's a tiger, right? That clump there, where four stars are bunched together and then there's that one that looks like it could be a tail."

"That's not the tiger at all. She's right there." I point in a
different direction and he sighs.

"But isn't that something? It's not a camel or something?
Or a hero?" I shake my head, trying not to laugh at him. "I
don't know how you can keep them all apart in your head."

"Books," I chirp, moving another inch closer.

"I'll just let you be the astronomer, then," Tam says with
another sigh, before wrapping one arm around me.

I don't speak. I hardly breathe. A small part of me wishes
that he'd never kissed me that day, because it's so much harder
to be relaxed with him now. I always knew I loved him, but it
didn't matter. Now I'm second-guessing every move he makes,
every word spoken in my direction.

We watch the stars in silence for a while. The moon rises
slowly, turning the ocean silver and giving us enough light
to see each other. I like watching the moon's wobbly reflection
stretch toward us without ever getting anywhere. More than
that, I like sitting at Tam's side, with his arm around me, feeling the gentle rise and fall of his chest with every breath,
and letting his warmth lull me into drowsy thought.

Maybe, I think, *this is the moment to be vulnerable and
tell him*. Or it could be a terribly important moment that I
shouldn't ruin. *I'll wait*, I decide. *Just for now.*

"I might be leaving again," he says quietly, making me
start. "If they'll let me, I mean. Harlen told the men to
be ready; they're going to move on Verity soon. Could be
any day."

"Oh." The information hits me like a sucker punch. "What do you mean 'if they'll let me'? Because of your leg?" He nods.

"I don't know why it's such an issue," he goes on, while I try to persuade myself to cheer him on. "Most of the combat will be within the city, at close quarters, sneaking around and the like. It's only with those damn formations I have trouble keeping up." There's a long moment of silence. "Anyway, they're trying to pull me out for a while. I didn't join the rebellion to sit around and do nothing."

I don't know what he wants me to say to this. It's like we're back on my rooftop again and he's full of an idea for an adventure that will take him away from me. But this time there's a part of me that understands the pull. I can hardly hate that he's found a cause to care about, an evil he wants to fight. For the first time I know what that feels like.

"Maybe I'll come with you," I say, but my head echoes with all the promises I've already made. *I need to bring Curram to justice. I need to help Des find Lillian.*

"We'll figure it out," Tam says. And then, "Can you believe that somehow, in this great, big, confusing world, we found each other again?" I don't answer. I don't know how to. Instead, I close my eyes and hold on to his words as tightly as I can, wishing the moment would last forever.

For the first time since I woke in that hot, filthy train car, I think I could forget what happened to me. Bundled up in Tam's coat, with the stars above me and Tam at my side, I could almost convince myself that none of it ever happened, that it was nothing more than a nightmare. I could almost be all right.

✦ ✦ ✦

When I wake, my feet are cold and I'm vaguely aware that someone is calling my name. I turn a little, attempting to burrow deeper into the warmth, and suddenly I remember where I am: still on the cliff, curled up on my side, with Tam's arm under my head like a pillow. I twist about so I'm facing him—the sky is pale pink with dawn—and he's already awake, watching me.

He must have been cold all night, I think, feeling guilty for wearing his coat.

Tam smiles with one side of his mouth. "I didn't want to move you once you fell asleep," he says, his voice just a whisper, as if there's someone else whom he might wake. I don't want to say anything. I just want to keep the moment frozen.

But someone was calling me. I sit up slowly, hoping I didn't crush Tam's arm, and he scrambles to his feet.

He offers me his hand, and I give him my unbranded one to pull me upright. The ocean, stretching endlessly away from us, is draped in thick, chilly fog. I push the hair out of my eyes, only to find it's damp with dew. *I probably look terrible.*

"Isla!" comes the voice again, and this time I recognize it: Des.

I look around and see him standing against a tree—no, gripping it for support. *What does he think he's doing?*

"Who's that?" Tam asks, squinting at him.

"A friend," I say, taking a step toward Des. Tam moves to follow and I put out a hand to stop him. "I should talk to him alone; I forgot we have a meeting this morning at the fortress." Tam looks surprised, and his gaze flicks back to Des.

"I guess I should be getting back anyway," Tam says. "They'll miss me soon, and since they're already trying to say I'm not fit for duty, I'd rather they didn't have a reason to get on my back, you know?" He throws one last glance at Des, who is watching us innocently. "I'll find you later, all right?"

"Yeah," I say, smiling briefly. "I've got to go." I jog toward Des, feeling my anger mounting. "What are you thinking?" I demand when I reach him. "You are *not* strong enough to be here, like this. Did you walk all the way over on your own?"

"So that's Tam?" He peers around me, and I snap my fingers in his face.

"Hey," I say, slipping one arm around Des's back and urging him in the direction of camp. "Don't be stupid, all right? You probably shouldn't even be walking."

He looks very serious all of a sudden. "I'm fine, Isla. Whatever happens up there in that fortress, I intend to be a part of it. Lillian's fate is tied to Curram's, remember?" He stops, tipping his head to the side slightly. "Now that you found Tam, will you forget all about me and our adventure? Will you still help me find her?"

"Of course."

"Which part were you answering?"

"Figure it out," I say, smirking.

"I never heard you come to bed last night," Phoebe says, appearing in front of us.

"I slept outside," I say, and Des gives me a pointed look.

"So romantic," he croons.

"Nothing happened," I say, but the blush I feel spreading across my face probably doesn't help my story. Phoebe looks between us and rolls her eyes.

"Ready?" she asks, skimming my appearance. *I'm still wearing Tam's coat,* I realize. I nod, and she calls to the others to join us.

Half of our trek up the hill is filled by Val berating Des for venturing out without help, while he argues that her fussing is exactly the reason he had to do it. But he seems to be getting slower with every step, fatigued after only ten minutes on his feet, even with his arms around Phoebe's and my shoulders.

When we reach Alistair Swain's office, the secretary looks unhappier than he did yesterday. "You're early," he says with exasperation.

"It's Marion Colter," Marion says quickly, and the man nods before disappearing behind the door. "Finally," she says, bouncing slightly on the balls of her feet.

When the man reappears, he groans and opens the door for us. "Mister Swain will see you now, but only for a moment." A little nervously, we shuffle inside.

The room is vast—a feasting hall or ballroom, no doubt, when this castle was first built. The ceilings rise dozens of feet above us, the walls made up of tall, cobweb-covered windows or hidden by hole-riddled tapestries. A hundred years of mice and negligence.

Movement across the room draws our attention.

Two guards are stationed at the back corners of the room, watching us carefully, and between them, a man stands in front of a desk by one of the windows, regarding us coolly. He's tall, lanky even, but his clothes are well fitted, and his self-assurance makes him imposing. His arms are crossed over his chest, his eyes drifting over our group, falling on each of us one at a time, as if he knows all our secrets and is only waiting to see what we'll confess on our own. Despite a quizzical, almost crooked mouth, there's something startlingly attractive about him. I think it's his eyes, his blue, blue eyes. Their icy confidence makes me nervous. "What's all this, Miss Colter?" he asks, his voice mellow and careful, his accent lifting the ends of his words.

"We have valuable information for you," I say, my voice coming out louder than I meant it to. The man's mouth turns up in a smirk.

"School friends of yours?" he asks Marion, but his eyes are on me.

I hear her take a breath. "Fellow sex slaves, actually." The man, Alistair Swain, turns to Marion sharply. "All property of Zachariah Curram."

twenty-two

I know you work with him," she goes on, "because we found receipts among his things. Isla brought some of his papers and your name was on them. But he works for Nicholas Carr as well."

"I know," Alistair interrupts, nodding. "That's why he's been so valuable to our cause. It isn't just the weapons."

There's silence for a moment. Marion looks confused. "Did you—"

"Did you know about the girls he was buying?" I demand. "Girls like us?"

He looks straight at me with his piercing eyes. "I did not," he says. "Can you tell me anything specific about his practices? Do you know whom he deals with?"

My chest is tight. "I don't. They took us from different places, shipped us by train to a warehouse and—and branded us." I hold out my hand and he takes a step closer. Around me, the other girls hold their hands out, too, and Alistair's brows come together in what might be anger. "He came and chose a dozen of us. Then that group was brought to Curram's manor and kept in his cellar."

"You weren't the only ones, then?"

"At least one of them died," says Valentina quietly from behind me.

"We don't know what happened to the others," adds Phoebe.

"But we are the ones who escaped," I say. The words taste of that first night of victory, of the starry sky, my feet on the lamplit pavement, my heart pounding in my chest.

"And how did you manage that?"

"You were there," Des says suddenly from the back of our group, where Valentina supports him. Alistair Swain seems to notice him for the first time.

"I don't know what you mean," Alistair says evenly, his eyes narrowed.

"You were a guest of Curram's. I saw you at his house. There was a gala."

Recognition comes over Alistair's face. "You deal cards," he says slowly.

"But . . . ," I start as the implications of this dawn on me. "But Curram gave some of the girls to his guests that night." I glance at Marion, my anger building, but she just looks stricken.

"Not to me," Alistair insists, catching my gaze and holding it. "I had no part in that. I give you my word."

"You just said," Phoebe starts, standing next to me with

her fists clenched tight at her sides, "that you didn't know what was going on. Why should we believe anything you say now?"

Alistair sighs, and I can see the gears turning in his head. "I did know, to an extent. Perhaps I shouldn't have pretended otherwise. But I never accepted Curram's . . . *generosity* in that regard. The simple answer is that Zachariah Curram and his excessive habits are a symptom of the very corruption we're trying to put an end to. As long as Nicholas Carr remains in control, and Curram proves himself useful to Carr, there is nothing I, or anyone else, can do to stop him. With his money and connections, Curram will always be in a position to use others. The best I can do is to use him to get to Carr. Once he's out of the way, we can put an end to Zachariah Curram's atrocious ways. Unfortunately, we need him for now."

The room feels like it has doubled in size. "So you won't do anything to stop him from buying and raping and killing more girls like us." My words echo off the ceiling and come back to cloud around me, putting me once more in the moment when I thought I was truly helpless.

"You were very brave to escape the way you did," Alistair says. I open my mouth to argue and hear the others do the same, but he goes on. "I promise that as soon as it is possible, I will find for Curram the justice he deserves. I wish that moment were now."

There's silence for what feels like a long time, and I can hear my heartbeat.

"You have to do something," Marion chokes, finally speaking up. "We think Curram may be looking for us, and this was the only place I knew to come. We thought you would help. . . ." She trails off, and Alistair rocks back on his heels, watching us.

"You've put me in a difficult position," he says sternly, staring Marion down, "with a man who has it in his power to ruin everything we've built here." Marion's hands tremble slightly, but she doesn't cower. "If Zachariah Curram believes that I've betrayed him by hiding you all, he can say a word to Carr and the entire army will surround us in moments."

Silence again. "Are you asking us to leave?" Phoebe says sharply.

Alistair looks at us long and hard, contemplating. "No," he says finally. "But I will expect your cooperation if I ask for it. We can discuss this further at another time. In the meantime, I can assure you of my protection while you remain here at Eisendrath."

It's clear we're being dismissed, but Des doesn't budge. "You don't know anything about a girl Curram keeps, then, separate from his manor? Or of a place he might hold someone?"

Alistair shakes his head. "I do not," he says, rounding his desk and taking a seat.

"Your deals with him are funding the capture of girls like us," I say, shaking.

Alistair kneads his brow. "I understand," he sighs. "But

my job is to think of the greater good." He looks between us once more. "If you'll excuse me, I have business to see to."

I storm out the door and the others follow.

"That can't be it," I say, pacing back and forth. "He can't just let Curram go on as before. People are *dying*."

"I thought he'd want to help," Marion whispers, looking like she might cry. Then she looks angry as well. "He must have other ways of getting to Carr. He can't just ignore what we told him. So many times he's talked about justice and the oppressed, and—and—"

"If he won't help us, we'll have to do something on our own," I say, barely thinking about the words. Everyone stares at me.

"Like what? What could we do?" Val's eyes are wide.

"I don't know," I admit. "I'll have to think about it. And Des has to heal. But we can't rely on Alistair Swain when clearly we're not his priority."

We make our way down the hill without speaking. My mind wanders and I'm only vaguely aware of where we're going. *How can we bring Curram to justice?* I think. *I need to start by finding out what he does with the girls he's finished with. The ones who still need saving. And what about the people he bought us from? No matter what we do to Curram, they'll still be taking girls off the streets and selling them to people like him.*

More than anger, disappointment seeps in. *We shouldn't have assumed Alistair Swain would help. As soon as we saw his name on those receipts, we should have known that our problems wouldn't be the priority of a man leading a revolution.*

Back at the common fire, we find berries and gruel in a giant pot hanging above last night's embers. Valentina passes a bowl to each of us, but I don't have much of an appetite. I force mouthful after mouthful down my throat, but I'm sick with uncertainty. *What if Alistair changes his mind and decides to give us up to save his camp? What if Curram finds us here? What if he never pays for what he did, and buys more girls and ruins more lives?*

Phoebe slides closer to me on one of the logs that surround the fire. "Don't be discouraged," she says, frowning. In the firelight, her hair and skin glow like gold. "We'll make him pay. We'll avenge the girls who didn't make it." But the longer I think of Eugenia, of Cecily, of the nameless girls and their screams, the harder it is to feel the same hope that she does.

"Isla," she says firmly, "you're doing everything you can."

"I'll be back," I say, getting to my feet and heading toward the barracks.

All the way there, I finger the sleeves of Tam's coat, pretending it's his arms around me instead. I pass the smithy, and pause. It takes the farrier only a moment to solder my chain back together where Curram broke it. Standing so close to the fire pit, watching the blacksmith take hot metal rods out of the coals and hammer them into line pulls me back to the day in the warehouse, my hand held flat, the red brand searing my skin. I leave the moment the chain is ready, tucking it into my pocket until it cools.

When I finally reach the pavilions, someone directs me

to Tam and I find him sitting on a cot, buttoning the collar on his uniform shirt.

"Isla," he says, standing when sees me. "What are you doing here?"

"I wanted to talk," I say, realizing as I do that he's probably busy.

He glances around. "I'm expected for drills in just a few minutes. Can I walk you back somewhere?" I nod, trying to be grateful for even a few minutes.

As we walk, he looks above him into the dense branches of the trees. "Have you climbed any of these?" He gestures around us. "They can't be that hard. No harder than your gutters and railings, huh?"

I shake my head. "Easier than that, I'll bet."

His grin splits his face. "Oh yeah?" he says.

"I'm wearing a dress, Tam. I can't climb if you're standing underneath me."

He blushes furiously. "Sorry, right! I could go first, if you like?"

I nod. "Sounds perfect." It takes Tam a minute to find what he deems to be the best tree, with low, thick branches that bow outward before growing upward and a rough trunk that's good for gripping. He grabs hold of the first branch, which is shoulder height for him, and hoists himself up until he's perched like a monkey on the most level section. When he starts to climb to the next branch, I see him wince; his leg, no doubt.

The branch is level with my head, so I have more trouble

getting a grip and pulling myself up. It takes me a less-than-graceful moment to straddle the branch and catch my breath before I mount the next bough and settle beside Tam, trying to disguise my heavy breathing. "Not so hard," I say.

There isn't much space between us, so our legs and shoulders knock together, but I don't mind. "Who taught you to climb trees?" Tam asks. "Not that fellow you ran off with this morning, right?"

"What, is Tam Lidwell jealous?" I nudge him, but the movement unbalances me. Tam throws an arm out behind me so I don't fall, but my heart is racing. "You should meet Des, actually. I'll bet you'd like him." We're both quiet for a moment, and I realize his time is ticking by.

"We should go," Tam says, shifting slightly. "I really should get back. After you?"

I climb unceremoniously out of the tree, my legs shaking like reeds by the time I reach the ground. Tam is beside me in a moment.

"You know what you still haven't told me," he says, leaning in almost conspiratorially as I lead the way back toward the common fire, "and I keep asking, why'd you come here? How did you even know about the rebellion? I hadn't heard of it until I joined the army. Nobody ever talked about it at home."

"I'm not surprised," I say, my mind racing to find the right words for my story. "The cities are controlled by the rich men who benefit from Nicholas Carr's partiality."

"So now you're a politician?"

My face feels warm. "I've seen cruel people, rich and powerful men who are dishonest and wicked."

"All since I left? I thought mine was the surprising story." I glance up at Tam, who's still waiting for my explanation.

I change my approach, my words tentative. "Do you remember that girl at school, Eugenia Rigney, who everyone said looked just like me?"

"I don't think she looks like you," Tam says matter-of-factly. "You're much prettier than Eugenia Rigney."

I blush, trying not to be deterred. I don't mention that he's probably the only person who thinks so. "Well," I continue, "after you left, something, um, happened to Eugenia. She . . . somebody took her."

" 'Took'?" He stands straighter. "What do you mean, 'took'?"

"Kidnappers. They took her and several other girls from the city, and they sold them to rich, filthy men, and to brothels, I think." I'm shaking. "Nobody can tell me what happens to the girls after they're disposed of, except that I know some of them are killed. There were dozens of them taken . . . I think it happens all the time, on a schedule."

I look down when Tam's hand finds mine: the right one, free of scars.

"Is that why you're here?" The words I need to say are stubbornly refusing to be loosed. I try to cough them up, convincing myself that this is the moment to tell him. But then he goes on. "You want to find justice for Eugenia and others like her?"

And I find that I'm nodding, because, I tell myself, it's the truth. But really, it's because it's the easy answer, to agree to the far simpler scenario Tam is supplying for me.

"You finally found the right adventure," he says, with a hint of a sad smile. "I'm so proud of you, Isla." I don't know what to say, but his focus shifts to something over my shoulder. "Isn't that your friend?"

I look up, and Des is slowly making his way toward us. "You should probably be getting back," I say, still worried that Des will make a casual remark that will ruin everything.

"I should introduce myself at least," Tam insists as Des reaches us.

"I hope I'm not interrupting anything," Des says, looking pale. He glances between Tam and me, his eyes suspicious. "But I need to speak with you, Isla."

"This is Tam. Tam, this is Des. He and I were . . . he's . . . he's my friend." I can feel Tam sizing Des up as he moves a little closer to me.

"It's nice to meet you," Tam says, a little standoffishly. And then, "I'm glad Isla has made friends here already"— Des gives me a funny look—"since she's never been good at interacting with other human beings." I elbow Tam, and he laughs, but it's tense.

"Isla's mentioned you," Des says, narrowing his eyes. "I look forward to seeing what sort of man you are." Des leans in toward me. "Can we speak in private?" He watches Tam out of the corner of his eye.

"You should go on, Isla. You know I have to get back."
Tam smiles, but I can tell he doesn't mean it. He lifts his
hand like he's going to touch my shoulder, but drops it awkwardly instead. Finally, with a somewhat less-than-friendly
glance at Des, he slips past us, leaving me with a lurch in my
stomach.

As soon as he's gone, I whirl on Des. "You could have
been nicer! What was that? Did you hobble all the way over
here just to make things awkward?"

"I take issue with the term 'hobble,'" he says, unfazed by
my frustration.

"No, Des, no. Answer my question. Why weren't you nice
to him? You scared him away!"

"I hope he doesn't scare that easy," Des groans, rolling
his eyes. "I just want you to know that I'm here to make
sure you don't get hurt."

"It's Tam, Des. I've known him all my life, I told you.
He'd never hurt me." I take his arm and we start walking. I
can feel that he's grateful for the support, even though he
tries to hide it.

"I take it back, by the way," he says. I look at him sharply.
"I did hobble." He watches me sideways, the grin that mocked
the soldiers and first made me like him creeping slowly onto
his face.

"You're an ass," I say, but I can't help but return the grin.
"Did you . . . well, what did you think of Tam? Don't say
you hated him, please?"

Des pretends to search for an answer. "He's kind of a

pretty boy, isn't he?" I punch his shoulder and he doesn't even flinch.

"That was supposed to teach you a lesson," I moan, wringing my hand.

"Oh, sorry. Hit me again; I'll pretend it hurts. No, really"—he starts laughing—"really, I will. Go for it. Try again."

"I don't ever want to speak to you again."

"What if I promise to be nice to your true love?"

"Maybe if you're especially sweet." He's definitely improving, but he grips my arm as we walk and clenches his teeth every so often at the pain. "You should probably be resting," I say. He glances at me and rolls his eyes.

"I'm fine. I'll be ready to leave any day now."

My vision gets blurry suddenly. "Don't say that yet." He stops and looks at me. "Just let me pretend you're staying for a little while, all right?"

"I thought you were coming with me," he says, smiling slightly. He brushes the side of my face with the backs of his fingers, snagging a tear before it can fall. "You're my partner, remember? I don't have any other family until I find Lillian."

I wrap my arms around Des and bury my face in his shoulder. *What will happen when he finds her? Will we go our separate ways and never see each other again?*

He startles me by pulling away abruptly. "Nope," he says. "Let's not do emotions yet, hmm? I'm no good at those." He's smiling one of his many smiles, the one that makes him look like a little boy.

I offer my arm again. "Sure." Then I remember. "What did you want to talk to me about?"

Des's face darkens. "Someone's here from the city, so Marion went to find out what the news is. Swain sent word that we should keep out of sight. They're all waiting at the infirmary."

twenty-three

Val meets us at the infirmary door, looking stricken. "Stay inside," she says, ushering us in. I look around at the others, confused. The little room where Des's cot is set up is empty besides our group. Des takes a seat, wincing.

"What's the news?" I ask, looking at Marion. "Something about Curram?"

"Boyne was here," she says, her voice hollow.

"Here?" *We're not safe after all. I won't go back to Curram's cellar.*

Marion nods. "He came to speak to Alistair, with a dozen men. He must be looking for us. Either he thinks we're a threat to Curram's reputation, maybe, or—"

"Or he wants revenge," I finish for her. Silence settles over our group.

"Did he see any of us?" Valentina asks. "Does he know we're here?"

"Not as far as I know."

"What should we do?" Val's face is pale, her knuckles white where they're gripping the side of the cot she's sitting on.

Jewel clears her throat. "Well, we're not staying here any longer," she announces.

Caddy nods. "That man, Abraham, said there's a group leaving tonight," she explains, "and we told him we want to join them. They go to different cities, not just Verity."

"What will you do?" I ask.

"Can't go back to the orphanage." Caddy shrugs. "We thought it would be safe here, but if Boyne can walk in at any moment . . . We'll find work, don't worry, selling flowers or something."

Jewel snorts. "We can find something better than flowers," she says.

I picture them alone and vulnerable in a city again. "But you'll look after one another? You'll be careful?"

They glance at each other. "Always have," Jewel says, as if it's obvious. *It wasn't enough last time,* I think, but I don't say it.

"Maybe we'll see you sometime," Caddy says, taking my hand and squeezing it gently.

"I'd like that," I say, but I know I don't sound hopeful.

Before I know what's happening, she wraps me in a long, tight embrace. "I'll miss you, Isla," she murmurs. Laughing, Jewel joins the hug for just a moment.

"All right, that's enough for me," she says, letting go, then straightening her dress and looking uncomfortable as Caddy hugs Valentina and Marion in turn. Then she turns serious for a moment. "We won't forget what you did for us, Isla. Thank you." I try to smile, but everything is blurry.

I could go with them. I could go back home, to Pa and safety. And maybe I could convince Tam that he really is unfit for duty, that he should come with me. We could go back to the way things were. But deep down I know we can't, not really. I know things won't ever be the same again. Curram is still out there, with no justice in sight. And I still don't know where to find Lillian. "Would you do me a favor?" I ask, and the girls nod. I rummage around in the satchel from Curram's study, which is stored under Des's cot, and hand my letter to Caddy. "Would you mail this to my pa? I don't know when I'll be back. I can give you money to post it—"

"We never left the money for the food," she blurts out, looking at the ground.

"Caddy," hisses Jewel, but it's too late.

"We didn't steal much, you saw," she goes on, her face darkening slightly.

"Leavin' the money like you said would have been ridiculous," Jewel says, crossing her arms. "Anyone could 'ave found it." Valentina looks mortified at having eaten stolen food, and Phoebe and Des are smirking.

"Well, take a bit more to help you get home," I say, rifling around in the satchel again.

Jewel accepts the coins gratefully. "Anyone else?" We all

look around at each other, but no one speaks up. "Well. We've got to let them know we're coming." She stands, and Caddy follows her.

"Be careful out there!" Valentina calls after them, and the room is quiet again.

After a long silence, Phoebe arches her back, looking around at each of us. "What do you think Swain told Boyne?" It's the question none of us wants to think about.

"He promised we were safe here," Marion says, but her words don't hold the same conviction they used to.

"We're not really safe until Curram is dead," Phoebe counters. "And probably Boyne also. We can't sit here like fish in a barrel and just wait for Swain to decide we're worth more as bargaining chips."

"Maybe we can talk to him again," I say, trying to be hopeful. "And if he won't help us this time, we'll do something on our own." I square my shoulders. "At least, I will. None of you have to help me."

"I'm not sitting around any longer than I have to," Phoebe says, guffawing.

One of the nurses pokes her head in, surprising us. "There's someone here with a message for you," she says, looking around. "From Mister Swain. Should I send her in?"

At least it isn't Boyne, I think, nodding.

A girl appears. She's around my age and dressed to blend in with the forest like so many here. "Which one of you is Isla?" she asks, and I raise my hand. "Mister Swain requires your presence first thing tomorrow morning."

My mouth hangs open; the others stare at me. "J-just me?"

"That's what he said."

"Thank you." When she's gone, I look around in confusion. "Why only me?"

"You're the one Curram probably has a vendetta against," Val supplies, sounding nervous. "Maybe Boyne asked for you?"

"You can't go up there alone," Des argues, shaking his head. "What if he's still here? What if Alistair made some sort of trade, and he's giving you back?" *I've already thought of all that*, I think, fear pricking my thoughts.

"I'll go with you," Phoebe says. "It can't hurt."

We all nod, our discomfort thick in the air. Outside, the light is turning orange from the setting sun. "I'm going to find us something to eat," Val announces, slipping past me and into the main part of the infirmary. *I was hungry a second ago*, I think.

A chill creeps over me, and I hug Tam's coat more tightly around myself. *Summer must be nearing its end.*

"What did Tam mean about you making friends here?" Des asks suddenly. "Didn't he know I was one of the ones who came with you?"

"I haven't told him . . . everything."

"Haven't told him about me? Or . . . ?"

"No," I say slowly. "About any of it." Des opens his mouth, so I hurry to add, "Yet. I haven't told him everything yet. I will. I just didn't tell him about Curram exactly, or my hand, or . . . or . . ."

I can feel their eyes on me. Des looks stern. "What did you tell him, then? Why does he think you're here, Isla?"

"Tam knows about the kidnappings, and the people who sold and bought the girls, and that I'm trying to find out what happened to the others, to get justice."

"But not that you were one of them."

Hesitant, I shake my head.

Phoebe glares at me. "This is because of what Valentina said, isn't it? You're scared that he'll—"

"It's not just that!" I say, wringing my hands. "It isn't easy, telling someone what happened, when I knew him before and I—"

"What did I say?" Val is standing in the doorway, balancing bowls of stew in her arms.

Phoebe is shaking her head vehemently. "He's your best friend, Isla. I'll tell him if I have to. He needs to know what happened to you."

Val's eyes widen. "Tam doesn't know?"

"You're the one who said 'damaged goods,' Val!"

She looks down at this, and I feel like I should apologize, but I don't. I storm outside, resting against the cool stones of the infirmary building. *I don't know, I don't know.*

Tam would want to know what happened to me, I argue with myself. It would be ridiculous to keep it from him. My hand slips into my pocket, fingering the locket.

But what if he thinks something is wrong with me?

I can't make the voices go away.

A moment later, Val joins me.

"I—I know I said I'd never tell anyone what happened, but Tam is different. Of course he'll understand. He'll probably be more upset if you *don't* tell him. Look at you; he let you keep his coat. He cares about you, Isla."

"And Marion's family doesn't care about her?" I mean to throw the words at Val as a rebuttal, but they come out small and quiet. "Her father can't look at her, you heard her. And *she* got away clean. I couldn't bear it if"—I feel my throat closing up, but I don't want to cry—"if Tam thought something was wrong with me, if he saw me as broken."

Val looks at her feet. "We're *all* broken, Isla."

I swallow, blinking at the trees. "You know when you're having a good dream," I say, "and you feel yourself waking up, so you try to stay asleep?" Valentina nods. "I'm trying to hang on to the person that I was before all of this happened. Not that everything was easy, but at least I knew who I was, you know? I went to school every day, and I had Tam and Pa. I was happy.

"Now I feel like I'm losing that person, or I already have. My old life is like a dream, and the harder I try to grasp at it, the faster it slips away. Even if I somehow make Curram pay for what he did to us, how will I be myself again after that? Maybe I'll stay angry and hurt forever, and never heal, even if I get justice." *But if I pretend that none of it happened, if I leave things unfinished, will my pain be worthless in the end? Without justice, will everything I suffered be meaningless?*

Valentina's eyes are wet. *She can never go back to her old life,* I think, remembering Davey, who's gone forever. "Maybe,

eventually, there will be more good news than bad memories," she says. She takes my hands, forcing me to look her in
the eyes. "Do you really want to go back? Was the old Isla so
much better than the new one, who saved so many lives and
wants to save more? You're brave, Isla, and stronger than you
know. I don't know what you were like before they took you,
but going back means losing something, too. Maybe there
are girls like us who haven't figured out how to save themselves yet. Maybe the only way they'll ever be free is if you go
forward instead." She smiles, though it's dark enough now
that I can't see her well.

"I need some sleep," I say, suddenly exhausted. "Will you
tell the others where I've gone?"

She nods, and we go in opposite directions. When I find
the tent that Phoebe and I are sharing, I crawl inside and
wrap one of the quilts around me. The ground is hard, full of
ruts I can feel through the blankets, but I'm too tired to
care.

*Tam has never made me feel worthless, even with all of his
teasing about my reading and shyness. This won't be any different, will it?*

*And Alistair Swain. What does he want to see me for? Why
not all of us? Has Boyne already left Eisendrath, or is he lurk-
ing here still? Will he be waiting for me in the morning, to take
me back?*

✦ ✦ ✦

Morning sunlight is seeping through the tent fabric when I
wake.

Lying still for a moment, I sift through my dreams to remember where I am. Beside me, Phoebe is asleep on her stomach, her face buried in her arms. I pull off my blanket and crawl outside. In the early-morning light, Eisendrath is almost peaceful. The air is full of the smells of pine sap and cook fires and the salty sea, and the trees are tall and lush, if a little bowed by the ocean winds.

Valentina is already awake, stirring a pot of porridge that sits toward one side of the fire. She smiles tentatively at me, and I do my best to return it, despite the hollow feeling in the pit of my stomach when I think of the morning's uncertainties. The porridge is flavorless and burns my tongue when I try it, but I force it down, hoping some of my sharp edges will round out if I keep eating.

"Can you tell Phoebe I'll be back, that I haven't forgotten?" I ask Val, heading off in the direction of the barracks.

The walk is a familiar one by now, and it feels too short. "I need to tell you something, and you need to promise you won't be upset," I rehearse aloud. *But that's ridiculous, he'll be upset no matter what.* "You need to promise to hear me through," I correct myself. *Why is this so hard?*

My stress is all for nothing, though; Tam's unit is on a training run in the woods and won't be back until the afternoon. "Can you tell Tam Lidwell I'm looking for him?" I ask the man sitting at Harlen's desk with all of the schedules. He looks irritated, so I add, "It's very important; I'm on my way to speak to Alistair Swain about the matter first." Reluctantly, he nods.

As I make my way back to camp, relief pulls me one way, and tension another. *If I don't tell him soon, I never will.*

Phoebe is standing by the fire when I return, smoothing her dress and tucking her hair behind her ears. "Ready?" she says, sounding more eager than I feel. "If we don't come back . . . ," she says, trailing off dramatically and looking around at the other girls. By Valentina's face, it's clear she doesn't approve of the joke.

"Be careful," she says, and Phoebe and I start on our way. But Val's words from the night before ring in my head. *I can't let all of this be for nothing. I have to go forward.*

When we reach Alistair Swain's office, we're let in by a gruff woman who replies to my questions with little more than grunts. Alistair sits behind his desk, watching with narrowed eyes as Phoebe and I approach. Another chair has been brought in, one that looks as if it used to be regally upholstered, but the velvet has since worn thin, and clumpy cotton, yellow with age, is peeping through the seams. Alistair makes no move to provide another chair for Phoebe, nor does he comment on her attendance.

"Please, take a seat," he says.

"I'd prefer to stand."

He continues to study me, and I stare back. "You intrigue me, Isla," he says. "You're the mastermind of that little group, aren't you?"

"I'd hardly say m-m-mastermind," I stammer.

"You're driven. I wonder if the same can be said for all of your friends."

I don't answer.

For a long, awkward moment we wait for the other to speak. "When we met, Isla, you seemed very bent on bringing Zachariah Curram to justice."

"Did you call me here to tell me that Boyne is looking for us? Or to hand me over to him? Because I'm guessing it's not that you've had a change of heart in the past day and want to help us after all." I can barely keep the bitterness from my voice.

"Then you'd be wrong," Alistair says. "As a matter of fact, I think I've found a way that we can help one another." Phoebe and I glance at each other. "You're correct that Josiah Boyne paid me a visit yesterday, and with a message from his master. He is, in fact, searching for you still, and thought Eisendrath as likely a place as any for a group of runaways to end up. He asked me if I had recently sheltered any new recruits, and he described your motley crew." He presses his hand over his eyes, sighing. "His master doesn't trust me, I can feel it. I think he believes I'm harboring you out of ill will. Perhaps because I left his little party earlier than he had expected." I can feel my heart pounding in my chest.

"What did you tell Boyne in response?" I ask, my voice tight.

"Nothing yet." Alistair settles back in his chair with his arms folded behind his head, watching me. "I told Boyne I would look into it, ask my men. He left me with an interesting proposition, actually. By his master's reckoning, you and your friends stole some of his property, which I'll take to mean yourselves, but he says he'll be lenient. He claims to have something of great value to your friend who deals the cards, Mister Morrisay, I believe, and said that he'd be willing to make an exchange." My breath catches.

"Des's sister, I'm sure that's what he means. What does he want in return?"

Alistair watches me very carefully. "He described you, Isla, and said that he would trade your debt for hers."

I feel as if everything is spinning. "M-me," I say.

Alistair nods. "I'd like to know what you did to make Zachariah Curram so hell-bent on getting you back," he says, looking almost like he'll smile.

"I cut his face with his shaving razor when he tried to rape me, and then knocked him out with a bust of his own head." Alistair surprises me by laughing.

"If I'd been inclined to turn you in, that might have swayed me," he says, a scheming glint in his eyes. It's the most at ease I've seen him. I feel a swell of pride that he thinks well of me, and suddenly I understand why people follow him. Despite everything, his approval feels like a prize.

But will he help us? I let out a long breath. "So what do you plan to do? We can't leave Lillian to—"

"Our rebellion is nearly ready to soar," Alistair says, leaning forward and cutting me off excitedly. "Our troops have rallied in Kingston and Adderly, and I am told that we could now attack. At this stage, it looks as if we don't need Curram's supplies any longer."

"Just like that?" I frown. "A day ago you told me he was next to essential. That our problems weren't important enough." Next to me, Phoebe crosses her arms.

"I didn't have the reports from Kingston and Adderly when we spoke," he answers, reining in his excitement and sitting back slightly. "And Harlen wasn't convinced that our mismatched army of deserters was ready to take an entire city." Anger flashes across his face, but he schools it back, grinding his teeth. "And to be perfectly honest with you, I didn't appreciate Curram's *manservant* waltzing into my headquarters feeling that he could make demands within my jurisdiction." *There it is, that's what's really bothering him.* "We have no use in a new government for an arrogant man whose loyalty can be bought for a handful of gold. You see my dilemma."

Phoebe guffaws. "Now you want to get rid of Curram. I don't see how that's a dilemma."

"He has powerful connections, and those benefited us not only in the weapons market. If I disavow him with the rest of Carr's government at the end of all this, I'll sabotage myself. Curram's friends will come to his aid, or call him a martyr and refuse to support me when it's important. The last thing I need is a mutiny within this revolution. I cannot be responsible for Curram's death, not in the eyes of the public." He watches me again for a moment, trying to read my thoughts. "The choice is entirely yours, Isla. Would you like to take Curram up on his offer of a trade?"

Phoebe makes a startled noise, and my mouth drops open. "You don't mean—"

"We could make a show of it. He knows war is coming; he's holed up in his manor at the moment. But he wants you. He'll open his doors to get you back. I'd send two of my men to escort you, and the trade would occur at night when there's less chance of a servant witnessing what happens. Once your friend's sister is secured, my men will see to Curram. Though they can make it as painful as you say."

Curram's life, in my hands. "What if something goes wrong? What if he doesn't have Lillian, and it's a trap?"

"That's a possibility. He may be arrogant enough to believe himself an integral part of the rebellion, but he's not a fool. He must see all of the angles. If he mistrusts me already, I cannot send a dozen men to make a simple exchange. He'll never let them in the door. If he's expecting foul play, it could be dangerous."

I'll just have to come up with a contingency plan of my own, then.

Me, going back to Curram. I suppose that was bound to happen if I wanted justice. But the thought of setting foot in his house again makes my head swim. *What if I don't escape this time? What if he keeps me, in place of Lillian?* I feel clammy. *But those girls, those nameless girls: Who will avenge them if I don't?*

I swallow. "Could I choose one of the soldiers, so that—"

"The army is Harlen's jurisdiction. These would be my

own men, not soldiers. I'm sorry, but this job calls for a particular skill set."

"And what about Boyne?" Alistair's brow furrows at my
question.

"Once Curram is dead, my men will find him and secure
him. He'll have his master's information, but none of his
dangerous social status. Don't worry about him. Is there
anything else you'd like to know?"

I shift back and forth on my feet, feeling Phoebe's eyes on
me, and glance around at the moth-eaten drapes and cracking walls. *For all those girls who didn't make it out, whose fates
still hang in the air, unfinished.* "I'll have an answer for you by
the morning," I say.

twenty-four

We can't tell Des," I say to Phoebe as we leave the fortress behind and make our way back toward the camp. "If Curram is lying about Lillian, it'll crush him."

"So you're going to do it," Phoebe says, not looking at me.

"Do you think I shouldn't?"

"I didn't say that. I think it's the best chance we're going to get at this point. Unless Curram is stopped now, his power will only grow. At least this way we're not on our own."

✦ ✦ ✦

We find the others sitting around the fire where we had breakfast. "Boyne's gone," I say when I'm met with relief on every face at my arrival. "We don't have to worry about him. Alistair has changed his mind and has a plan to do away with Curram after all."

"He's Alistair now?" Des snaps, startling me. "Since when did the two of you get to be so chummy?"

"I understand that you don't trust him—"

"And you do? You saw it yourself, he works with Curram. However he managed to win you over, it's just manipulation, take my word for it. These powerful men are all the same, Isla. Swain, Curram—"

"Alistair is *not* Curram," I say.

"Just be careful with him, all right?"

"I can handle myself, Des." My head aches, and I shut my eyes for a moment.

"Did Alistair tell you how he's going to handle Curram?" Valentina ventures quietly.

I brace myself for the backlash. "He wants me to act as a decoy, as a show of faith. Alistair's men will bring me to Curram's manor, and once we're inside, they'll kill him." Val's eyes are wider than ever, and Des looks angry. "That's what Boyne came here about," I hasten to add. "Curram is still looking for us, for me."

"I can't believe I'm hearing this," Des says, shaking his head and refusing to look at me.

"Did you agree to it?" Marion asks.

"Of course she didn't," Des answers for me. "She wouldn't be so stupid."

"What choice do I have?" I say.

"As long as the bastard's dead, what does it matter how?" Phoebe adds. "I'm not sure I trust Swain myself, but at the moment, at least, we want the same thing."

"What if he's just using you?" Val asks, glancing between us all, her brow furrowed.

"I'm sure he is," I say.

Des throws his hands in the air. "And you're all right with that?"

"We're using each other! He didn't want to help us until it benefited him, and I can't risk going back to Curram without protection. We're both winning, Des!"

He rakes his hands angrily through his hair. "Tell me what Swain told you. Did you already agree to go? What exactly is his plan for using you as bait and not getting you killed somehow?"

"I—" I start, and Des stares at me, his eyes wide.

"You're not even thinking about it. You've already decided, haven't you?" He gets to his feet, stands right in front of me, and shakes his head disbelievingly. "You're free, Isla. You're *free*. You've risked your life enough. Let Swain find someone else to do his dirty work."

"I should have killed Curram the night we left!" I shout at him, feeling like I'll cry. "For all we know, he's already got another cartload of girls in his cellar, and that's *my* fault. *I* had the chance to put an end to his atrocities and I *didn't*, Des, I *didn't*. That's on me." He takes my face in his hands, stroking my cheeks with his thumbs.

"But it's not safe," he pleads, his eyes impossibly pained. "I can't tell you not to feel guilty. I haven't figured it out myself. But I can't let you go back there. I can't let you die."

"Hey," I say, not breaking eye contact. "None of us will have to feel guilty after we beat him, right?" I want to tell Des about Lillian; the words are ready to overflow, but I hold them back.

"Bad timing?" says a voice, and I turn to see Tam standing a few feet away, looking flushed.

Des drops his hands, and I try to stutter an answer, but Tam strides off without another word.

"Tam!" I shout, racing after him and trying to picture what he saw. "Tam!" I catch up, but he doesn't stop until I move in front of him and put out my hands. "Wait, Tam." He stares at me for a moment while I catch my breath, hurt or anger in his eyes, or both. "I need to tell you something," I say, trying to take his hands.

He pulls back, taking a step away from me. "I don't think I really want to hear, all right?"

"Tam, I—"

"How long have you even known him? Your"—his throat catches—"your 'friend'?"

"Only since just after you left, he's—"

"Huh. You seem awfully close already."

"He's just being protective."

"Right, yeah." Tam looks around, refusing to meet my eyes. "I didn't mean to pry into your personal life."

"You can. I mean, there's nothing I don't—"

"Look, you don't need to explain yourself, or whatever. I know I was gone."

"Tam, it's not what you think."

"I have to go, Isla," he says, looking above my head.

Everything. I have to tell him everything. He won't understand my new friends, my new scars until I do.

"Please," I try again, and he looks down at me, impatient.

I falter for a second. I don't know where to start, so I let my thoughts spill out and hope that Tam will sort them out on his own. "There's a lot I haven't told you yet, because I didn't want anything to change between us, and I was afraid you would see me differently or wish I hadn't told you, or that, I don't know, you wouldn't want me to change. But I need you to listen to me for a couple of minutes, all right?"

He doesn't answer, and nervousness floods my thoughts. I don't have the words that I need. I don't know how to say that I was kidnapped and sold, that I was somebody's property and that I felt like I was as good as dead for all that time Tam was gone.

So I take out the locket instead.

"This," I choke, holding it out to him. He clenches his jaw, suddenly angry, and I don't know why, so I press on, panicking. "It's about this locket, in a way—"

"I can't believe you still have it," he cuts me off, drily. "I lost mine right after I left."

I feel like I'm falling.

He looks around, thrusting his hands into his pockets, and gradually I become aware of the breeze snaking up my dress and sending a chill through me, and how neither of us is speaking any longer. *How . . . how could he? No, how could I? How could I think he meant so much by giving the locket to me? Does he still have the spyglass I gave him?* I don't think I want to know.

"It was just a trinket," he says, making it worse with

every word. "Cost me a couple of pennies, Isla. Don't make it mean something it doesn't."

I fought to keep this, I want to tell him, clenching the locket until my fingers burn. I want to yell the words in his face. I'm still holding the locket out to him as if he'll take it, as if something will change. *It meant everything to me.*

But he doesn't take it; he isn't even looking at me any longer. I take a step back, and then another, leaving him where he's standing. *What just happened? What am I supposed to think now, supposed to feel?* I stumble through the trees, hardly caring where I'm going. I wonder if Tam is watching me go, or if he has already rejoined his friends. I don't look back, because part of me wants to believe he's watching, that he regrets what he said, and that he'll come find me and apologize.

But if what he said is true, whispers a voice in my head, *what does regret matter?*

Uphill. That's all I know. Up to my library, to peace and quiet and a dark hiding place where no one will look for me. Even though the trek feels steeper and longer than ever, I refuse to stop, despite the smell of the ocean and the sounds of the gulls calling to me beyond the fortress. But when I reach the library and its window seat, all my energy drains away. I cry long, ugly tears onto the books that haven't been touched since Tam found me here, my sobs echoing around the empty room. *Why do I have to care so much?* I ask the voices in my head, but they're gone now that I need comfort. *Why did I have to be so sure that he felt the same way I did?*

Why does it have to hurt so much that he doesn't? What does it mean for tomorrow, and the day after?

I try to distract myself with the books, as the light begins to fade and my stomach growls for supper, but it's no good. I don't care about the fishermen who climb the cliffs to harvest abalone from the rock face. I don't care that fifty years ago, I could tell an entire room what I was feeling by batting my fan either more or less rapidly. I don't even care about the knight saving the girl from her murderous fiancé and their happily ever after. I'm half convinced she'd be happier in the long run if she just saved herself and kept the knight out of the picture entirely.

✦ ✦ ✦

I wake when the sun rises, straightening my dress and rubbing dried tears from the corners of my eyes. *I've survived worse than a broken heart,* I tell myself, even though it doesn't feel like the truth. I'm still holding the locket, but I don't want to look at it. I tuck it into my pocket, until I can decide what to do with it. I walk in circles around the little library, working the feeling back into my feet and weaving my hair into a neat braid down my back. With a book under my arm for later, I go downstairs to wait for Alistair.

Feel nothing, I tell myself. That will be better than this throbbing pain just behind my ribs.

When Alistair finally appears, he looks half asleep, with his hair pushed up slightly on one side and dark circles under his usually bright eyes. He's surprised to see me. "Early riser?" he asks drily.

"I said I'd give my answer in the morning."

He wakes up a little at this. "And?"

"I'd like to leave immediately."

He moves toward me, his hand gentle on my arm. "You don't *have* to go, Isla. I can find another way; you don't have to agree." I can't tell if this is a subtle trick, a manipulation to win me over, or if he genuinely cares about my safety. But no matter; with every word, I'm more and more sure of my decision.

"I'm certain."

He smiles warmly. "I'll walk with you. You can leave within the hour." As we go, he talks quickly. "If Curram is suspicious, he'll have my men searched and make them leave their weapons outside. The only way we can be certain of a moment with him unguarded is if he perceives there to be no threat. However . . ." Alistair's eyes glow, making him look younger than he already is; I doubt he's older than thirty-five, but the responsibility he bears makes it seem like more. "If Curram believes you to be a prisoner, he won't have you searched. You can conceal a weapon on your person and my men will do the rest."

When we reach the stables, they're ruins like the infirmary: crumbling stone structures with tarps spread across the tops. While Alistair speaks to the stable master about sending word to the men who'll be accompanying me, I wander from one stall to the next, trying not to shy away when the giant animals poke out their heads to see who I am. I remember reading about draft horses years before. *Hearty, steady, strong, faithful. Perfect for pulling a cart or a plow, among other things.*

The books didn't tell me what their tongues would feel like on my hand—rough, warm, and sticky—or that I could look into their dark, glossy eyes and find all the understanding in the world. "Why doesn't Tam care?" I ask the last horse as he exhales warm, wet air onto my hand. His ears swivel toward the sound of my voice, and I could swear there's sympathy in his great big eyes. I stroke the animal's cheek, and he blows softly on my face. "I thought the locket was his way of tying us together before he left."

He never said that, whispers a voice in my thoughts. *He never said there was anything special between you. That kiss was a good-bye, and nothing more.*

twenty-five

Alistair's return saves me from my dark train of thought.

"My men will be here momentarily," he says. Standing on the damp grass with sunlight making his hair even lighter, he looks more relaxed than in the dusty, intimidating cavern of an office. "Here, this is for my men"—he hands me a small pistol—"and this is for your own protection." It's a knife, small enough to hide in my boot, the blade only as long as my index finger.

"Thank you," I say, and he nods before going on.

"Tensions in Verity may be mounting, but my men will be able to get you in and out. I've given them documents containing my seal and that of a lawman who helps us with these sort of situations, should you have any trouble at the gates."

Everything is waiting already. "What if I hadn't agreed?"

His eyes twinkle. "I hoped you would." I imagine the

rousing speeches Alistair must have made here over the past months or years, perhaps while standing at the entrance to the fortress, or even walking among the people, gaining their trust. No wonder Marion's faith in him is so great. When he adds, "I have every confidence in you, Isla," I feel I could go into battle if he asked me to.

After a moment, two men appear, and Alistair quickly introduces them as Caffrey and Gilbert, prison escapees like a number of the men at camp. They're young and strong, but Alistair makes it clear that they're not at Eisendrath to play a part in the battle in the same way that the soldiers are. His less-than-subtle comment about saving them for tasks more suited to their history, like this one, makes my mind reel with possibilities of what their prison sentences might have been for.

"Each of you has my sincerest thanks," Alistair says as the stable master leads two horses to us that are pulling a cart not unlike the one in which the other girls and I arrived. The men toss in blankets and satchels and the one called Gilbert jumps up to the front, volunteering to drive for the first stint. Caffrey stretches out in the front of the wagon bed as if he'll go to sleep. "Godspeed," says Alistair, raising a hand in farewell.

Gilbert slaps the reins against the horses' backs and we start moving, but guilt tugs at me for not saying something to Val, Phoebe, or Marion. *I'll be back any day now,* I think, but how can I be sure of that?

"I forgot something at the common fire," I tell Gilbert,

and ask him to stop. He tells me we're in a hurry, and I promise to be quick. The girls are already awake, but Des is nowhere to be found. *Probably for the best,* I think, but my heart aches at the thought of leaving him to worry.

"Where'd *you* sleep last night?" Marion asks, her tone a little teasing.

Of course—the last they saw of me, I was running after Tam to explain. We were all wrong about how that would turn out. "I fell asleep reading, would you believe it?" I say, forcing a smile.

Valentina laughs lightly. "In that library of yours? Phoebe told us. I'm a little jealous you found a place to hide away like that."

"I was lucky." I shrug, trying to swallow away the tightness in my throat.

Phoebe watches me carefully, seeing through me, no doubt.

"You hungry?" Marion asks, gesturing to a pot over the fire's embers.

"Actually, I've got to go and see Des," I say. "We didn't leave things in the best way. I'll find you all later." I almost embrace Valentina, but she'd be suspicious, so I hold back. I try to memorize each of their faces before I turn and walk back toward the waiting cart. *Just in case,* I tell myself. *Anything could happen.*

"Ready?" Caffrey asks when I climb back into the wagon.

"Ready," I say.

But we've barely started moving when I hear a shout and

Phoebe appears behind us, running to catch up. "Nice try back there," she gasps, jumping onto the back of the wagon next to me and trying to catch her breath. Alistair's men shoot her questioning looks.

"I'll only be gone a few days."

"And you could use some backup." I open my mouth to protest, but she waves my words away. "You're not going to cut me out of the action *now*," she insists. "There's too much chance that things could go wrong. You need me, Isla Powe."

I roll my eyes, but it's comforting, having her beside me. Strange, considering that the first time I saw her we were also on our way to Zachariah Curram. Only then we seemed destined to be more enemies than friends.

"So," she announces loudly, "who's doing the castrating? I'll take a shot at it if any of you are uncomfortable."

"Have you forgotten about the killing part?" I say, nudging her.

"But that doesn't need to happen right away," she presses, grinning at me. "What did Tam think about you driving off for a week with two strange men?"

I can feel my expression fall. "I didn't tell him I was leaving."

Phoebe sits up straighter. "Why not? He'll probably go mad, looking for you."

"I doubt it."

"Isla." I meet her eyes, reluctantly. "Don't be an idiot."

I don't answer her. I watch the ground instead, sliding beneath us, and try to forget that Tam lost his key and didn't care. Finally I feel Phoebe's eyes leave me, but the hollow feeling doesn't leave my stomach.

Caffrey's eyes are closed, but I can't tell whether he's sleeping, and Gilbert is quiet at his post on the wagon's seat. I'd like to ask what the crimes were that put them in prison in the first place, but the long, winding dragon inked into Caffrey's skin makes me too nervous to speak. My eyes wander along the tattoo, hypnotized by the way the dragon weaves together with its own flames, from Caffrey's neck, down his arms, and coiling around his wrists. *For all I know, they were mass murderers and I'll be adding to the list of crimes on their records by helping them.*

We drive late into the night, only stopping to let the horses rest after the air turns cool. Phoebe falls asleep quickly, and I'm left to lie awake and wish for real walls to keep the wind out, and weak tea in chipped mugs to warm my hands as I sit across the table from Pa, and the certainty of seeing Tam the next morning as we walk to school.

The next day, Phoebe takes a turn driving, following directions that the men give her when necessary. A few times I jog beside the wagon to stretch my legs, until Caffrey asks if I want to drive.

"I've very little experience," I say in warning, but I join him on the bench. As he tells me what to do—which isn't much—he lays their map out on his lap and traces our approximate route with his broad fingers, showing me where he hopes we are and then what signals the horses respond best to for direction.

"I have a question," he announces eventually, giving me a sidelong glance. "How come Swain picked you for this? We coulda gone in and taken care of everything ourselves, but he said it was important to make this trade, and that you were the only one it would work with. What's all that about?" Phoebe turns slightly to listen.

"I . . . have a history with Zachariah Curram," I say slowly. "He's the reason I ended up in Eisendrath. I came with Marion Colter. Do you know her?"

"Couldn't say," he mumbles. "So you used to work for Curram, then?"

"Not exactly."

"She's one of the girls who escaped from his manor," interrupts Gilbert from behind us. I jump; I had thought he was sleeping. "You know, the ones he buys all hush-hush." *How many people know? Could Tam find out through gossip?*

Caffrey's face shows understanding, and a little color. "Of course! Right."

There's silence for a moment. "Did you come with one of the prison groups?" I ask. "From one of the breakouts?"

"I did." Caffrey doesn't give me anything beyond this, and when I steal a glance at him, I see that he's watching me with amusement. "And you're wanting to know what I did to be there in the first place?" I blush, nodding reluctantly. "What's the worst you'd believe of me?" he says, and I know he's teasing, but it doesn't help.

I wait to see if he'll give in, but he is silent. "Did you kill someone?"

He waggles his eyebrows but shakes his head. "Guess again."

"Steal something?"

"Oh, worse than that, sweetheart! Come on, guess again."

I'm not sure whether I'm nervous or amused. "I—"

"He got drunk and assaulted a lawman," says Gilbert drolly.

"You didn't have to spoil it!" laughs Caffrey, reaching around and trying to knock his friend, but nearly toppling into the wagon bed instead.

Apparently resigned to not sleeping, Gilbert sits up. "Are you curious what my crime was, then, Miss Isla?" I nod, trusting that he won't put me through a guessing game to find out. His is a more serious air, refined and straitlaced. He's the opposite of Caffrey, with all his muscle and tattoos. Gilbert has a carefully shaved chin, neat clothes; still, both have an edge to them that I assume comes from prison.

"I was too political for the likes of our nation's great leader. I spoke a little too loudly and a little too freely, and so they took me from my home and beat me and told me that I'd been caught stealing money from some company or other, and they sent me to prison. I had another five years to go when the rebellion freed me."

"Then why did Swain—"

"Assign us to an assassin's mission?" I nod. Gilbert smiles mirthlessly. "In prison, you can become a different person. I killed one of the guards with a shiv I made from a bedpost splinter. They didn't even notice until they searched my room the next day. Caffrey took three out by himself." I shudder, and they probably notice. "That was before the rebellion. That was when we were on our own."

Day passes slowly into night, and we drive late again. "Are you really all right?" asks Phoebe, her face close to mine as we curl up under our one blanket in the darkness. "Going back to Curram's, I mean."

Too late to pretend I'm asleep, I decide. "I'll be fine," I whisper. *But I'm scared.* "This is the best chance we'll get. The fact that he came to us—"

"That's what worries me. What if it's a trap?"

"It is. He thinks I've already been caught by Alistair." Then, more for myself than for Phoebe, I add, "It's different this time." *But what if he has a dozen men guarding Lillian and demands that they hand me over first? What if he never lets Gilbert and Caffrey inside? No, it will be fine. We'll save Lillian, we'll kill Curram, we'll get whatever we need from Boyne to find the other girls and learn who he bought us from in the first place.*

"I won't let him keep you," Phoebe whispers.

"Thank you," I murmur, and roll over, pretending to fall asleep. But my thoughts persist. *Maybe this was a mistake,* they say. And I can't help it, I start to believe them.

✦ ✦ ✦

I wake to a pale pink sky and help Gilbert feed the horses. The day passes slowly; I try to be engaged in the book I brought, but it's about land ownership laws and the sentences are as dry as dust. *Has Tam noticed I'm gone?* I keep wondering, trying to convince myself that he's not worth worrying over.

Finally, we begin to pass farmhouses, half-hidden among the trees. I haven't seen the town where Jewel and Caddy stole the food, which leads me to assume we've taken a different route. It isn't until evening that we leave the cover of the trees and finally see the city in front of us, stretching far to the left and the right, walled in and powerful. When we reach the gates, Gilbert produces the papers from Swain and the sentries let us pass.

Once inside, we drive quietly in the fading light, trying not to attract attention, and I manage to calm my anxious heart. But when the sky gets dark and Gilbert stops the cart at the gates to Curram's manor, I realize I'm shaking. *Why did I agree to come back?*

Lillian, I think. *I can do this, for Des.*

Caffrey climbs to the ground and calls through the gates. I hold my breath as pale, bodiless faces appear on the other side of the bars, talking quietly before the gates swing open. "You'd better hide, Phoebe," Caffrey mutters as he climbs back onto the driver's bench. "They want to check that we've brought Isla and they'll be suspicious if there are two girls."

She slips under the blankets as a sentry comes around to the back of the cart. I sit perfectly still, my hands crossed in my lap where Gilbert tied them loosely so I could slip out easily as soon as the need for pretense has passed. The man, whose face I can't see well, leers at me from different angles before looking satisfied. "Wait inside the gate," he says, motioning us into the courtyard.

While we wait, my thoughts turn around and around. *How different was I from all the others that Curram wants me back so badly? Was I the first girl to really give him hell? And to escape?* I feel as if I've fallen into a recurring dream, one with an ending that keeps changing. *Will I win this time? Will I escape again?* Caffrey makes a show of hauling me to the ground, but my legs are shaking, so I lean against the cart as casually as I can to hide it.

While the sentry goes to the manor to announce our arrival, Phoebe slips past me, touching my shoulder. "We don't belong to them anymore," she whispers. "You can do this."

"Wait until we're inside and find a way into the cellar," I tell her. "If there are more girls locked up, get them out."

She nods, patting one of the pockets of her dress. "I've still got the knife," she says. "In case . . ."

"Robbie." I nod. She disappears into the shadows of the courtyard.

"Ready?" Caffrey asks as the door to the manor opens.

No, I try to say, but I can't make any sound. *I don't want to be here, I don't want to be here, I don't what to be here.* The knife from Alistair is tucked safely in my boot, the pistol in one of my pockets, concealed by my bound hands. My escorts stand on either side of me and take hold of my arms, leading me toward the front of the house. A man stands in the doorway, a man in a round hat, a man I know. Boyne.

I can't do this.

It's too real. Too recent.

I try to breathe as we reach the steps, and I can see him smiling. "Welcome," he says, looking between the two men before letting his eyes fall on me. "Mister Curram is expecting you." There's a glint in his eyes before he turns to lead us into the house. "If you'll just follow me this way."

Gilbert glances at me when Boyne's back is turned, nodding as if I'm supposed to know what he means. *That everything is going according to plan? That he's sorry he's gripping my arm so tightly?* I don't know. My throat is tight with fear; every footstep is a struggle.

We pause in the foyer, where two new sentries step toward us, glancing at Alistair's men. "Oh, and you'll need to leave any weapons here," Boyne says, clearly enjoying everything about this. *No wonder Alistair was so irritated.* Caffrey argues that they came here in good faith, and Gilbert says it isn't fair, both playing their parts as offended emissaries well. Eventually they acquiesce and leave their personal weapons with the sentries, and we're led onward.

I know this corridor, I think as we get closer and closer, and then, *I'm going to be sick on the carpet.* Then we turn and we're in the library of all places. And he's there.

He looks even taller than I remember, but thinner, too, and older. His beard has grown in, showing flecks of gray that I hadn't noticed before, and there's a pale line across part of his face that I know is the scar I gave him. But he's smiling, condescendingly, and for a second that's what I hate most about him. His eyes tell me that I'm helpless and pathetic, and I believe them. I have to believe them.

I try to breathe, but I can only manage short gasps.

"I hardly dared believe I'd see you again," he purrs, as I hang like a fish between Gilbert and Caffrey. "You know I only received Alistair's response a matter of hours ago. Hardly enough time to prepare myself for this pleasure."

I hear a whimper that must be my own; Curram moves toward me, and I'm vaguely aware of Boyne leaving the way we came in. *Kill him,* I think, wondering when Alistair's men will make their move. *He'll touch me if you don't do it soon.*

He's right in front of me suddenly. "Not much to hold her," he says to Caffrey, his eyes roving over my hands.

"She didn't put up much of a fuss," Caffrey says, shrugging.

Zachariah Curram smiles knowingly. "She likes to surprise you," he says. He steps back, clasping his hands together. "As a matter of fact, I seem to remember regretting the last time I underestimated this one." He steps toward me again, pulling at one end of the rope and unraveling it easily. "Strange. If I didn't know better, I'd say that wasn't really meant to be much help." I can feel Gilbert and Caffrey shift uneasily, and my heart races faster. Before I can lunge at him to cover for them, Curram seizes a handful of my dress, his hand closing around the gun before he pulls it out of my pocket.

"Guards!" he shouts, and a dozen armed men stream in,

as if they had been waiting. "Get them out of here," their master says casually, gesturing at my friends. I look between them wildly as they struggle against his men.

"Look, I don't know what you think—" Gilbert says, but Curram cuts him off.

"Either you're very stupid yourselves and never searched her, or you take me for a fool," he says coolly. "I am not a fool." Gilbert's eyes dart to my face, and Curram smiles. "I thought as much. Please escort these men to the cellar until I'm ready to send them on their way."

No, no, no.

The soldiers haul my friends, shouting and struggling for all they're worth, toward the door. But their efforts are for nothing. I try to make a break for it, but Boyne's meaty hands grab hold of me. His arms wrap around my stomach, holding me fast while I kick and try to tear myself away. "Not this time," he hisses in my ear, sending a chill through me. I bite and thrash until I'm worn out, but it's useless; the door closes behind me and the sounds of Gilbert's and Caffrey's struggles fade.

Suddenly Curram is right before me again, running his hands along my dress, between my legs, never breaking eye contact and smiling as I start to cry despite myself. "At least you keep things interesting," he purrs. *Ignore my boots,* I think frantically. But his too-thorough hands reach them next and he finds the knife almost instantly.

In a blur, he tosses it across the room, where it clatters to the floor. "So you thought you'd get away again, hmm?"

he asks, straightening up and stroking my cheek with the back of his fingers. "You didn't just miss me?"

I spit in his face, and he wipes it away, chuckling.

Once again I try to lunge out of Boyne's grasp. He's not expecting it this time, and I break free. But before I can get far, new hands grab hold of me and Zachariah Curram draws me up in front of his face.

"No matter the reason, I'm so pleased you came back," he says through clenched teeth. His hands hold my arms tightly to my sides, while his eyes undress me. When he looks at me, I'm covered in shame again, heavy, ugly shame that I don't deserve. "We have unfinished business, my dear. I don't even know your name."

"And you never will," I say as calmly as I can. *"Pig."*

For just an instant, Curram lets go of my arms, stunning me with a smack across my cheek that leaves my ears ringing and my eyes filling with tears. My vision is blurry as he pulls me close to his face again, and he's laughing. "You're unarmed now," he sneers, his smile increasing. I hear Boyne chuckling, and my throat tightens as I try to swallow. "So I think this time we're really going to have some fun. I never did get my money's worth from you."

twenty-six

T*hink your way out instead. Breathe. Think.*
 I tell myself that I'll survive this as I have everything else.

That I will be fine.

That there will be a tomorrow for me.

*But I can't do this, can't be here, can't see his face so close to
mine. Can't let him touch me one more time.*

Curram looks at Boyne and jerks his head, and Boyne
slides forward, the rope from before in his hands. *No, no.* I
try to kick Curram, but he only holds me more tightly, turning my back to him and wrapping his arms around my body.
I can't reach his arm to bite him, can't even spit at him again
with my back against him. Not for the first time, I feel small
and helpless in his hands. And my strength is fading. I try
to scream, but he slams his hand under my chin, holding my
mouth closed and leaving me dizzy from the force. My struggle becomes pitiful.

But I have to live. He can't win again; I can't let him.

Boyne grabs my hands and ties one end of the rope around my right wrist, tight enough to break the skin; then, smiling at me, he starts to wind the remainder around my left. I spit in his face through gritted teeth and throw myself backward against Curram, distracting the two men just enough that neither notices when I twist my hand and wind the cord three times around my right wrist.

Boyne angrily wipes his face on his sleeve and ties the left even more tightly, but doesn't realize that I've afforded myself a foot or so of slack if I untwist my wrists. I try to breathe evenly through my nose, storing up my energy again. "Leave us," Curram tells Boyne with a smile, and I feel a flicker of hope. I could never have beaten them both.

I can do this, I think. *I have to, or I'll die.*

The door closes behind Josiah Boyne, and his master turns me roughly to face him. I try to call up Tam's face for strength, or Des's, but it's not enough.

It's Eugenia's that comes to mind, for some reason. Eugenia Margaret Rigney. And then it's her cries, echoing in my head. I see the saucer-size eyes of the girl in the warehouse, and remember Cecily's shouted plea, that we get word to her family. I see the girls who were dragged upstairs on the night of the party, the ones who never came back. And here, right in front of me, is the man responsible for all that. The man who imprisoned us, ordered floggings, made a game out of our fear, and hunted down our innocence. The coward who might as well have marked my flesh himself, who took my locket for a laugh and tried to take so much more.

I should be terrified by the greed and intensity in his eyes, but I'm not, somehow. A strange certainty surges through me now. My heart drums in my breast.

I'm strong enough.

I'm brave enough.

I won't be his. Not ever.

Curram takes a fistful of the front of my dress, tears it open so that my corset is exposed, and shoves me to the ground. He pushes my bound hands above my head and climbs on top of me with a horrible grin on his face. "Now," he breathes heavily, as I furiously try to unravel the slack of the cord about my wrists, "let's try and enjoy ourselves, hmm?"

I try to kick him, to deter him, to shove him back with my legs, but he's laughing, fiddling with the top of his trousers, then reaching for the bottom of my corset to tear it open. Then my hands have all the slack they need, and I loop the cord over his head.

His moment of surprise is all I need; I twist my arm over his head so I'm cutting off his breathing, and he sputters, tries to break free, to pull the rope away from his neck. His eyes are wide, shocked. He struggles for all he's worth, but he's already losing.

I hold on, for my life, wrapping my legs around him, twisting about so I'm nearly straddling him, while he gasps and claws at the cord, swats at me and swears and tries to shout but chokes instead.

"I'm going to kill you," I grunt into his ear, also breathless, pulling, pulling, pulling. His breathing catches, coming in short gasps, his hands clawing at me a little longer with the last of his strength, his fingernails leaving bloody lines along my hands and face where he can reach. I keep pulling, keep holding on. Then his frantic hands become weak and sluggish; I can feel the life slowing in him just as if it were my bare hands wrapped around his throat.

Curram tries to say something again, falters, and the breath rattles out of him as his eyelids droop. Even after his head falls and he ceases to move, I keep my grip on the cord. I can see the red line on his pale skin, like a noose mark, but I don't let go.

I stay on top of him, half expecting him to sit up and overpower me somehow. But he doesn't move. He doesn't breathe.

When I do finally let go, it's because I'm too exhausted to hold on any longer. Vision blurry, I work at the knots on my wrists; I can't let my guard down yet, no matter how much I want to. I scramble off Curram's body, every breath like a shuddering earthquake, and find my knife on the ground, pulling my knees up to my chest and brandishing it, just in case. When I try to stop my tears, my hands come back covered in my own blood, from the marks he left with his clawing. I wipe my hands off on my dress, which is so torn the front won't close. I feel tired, and spent, and small, and the familiar sensation of filthiness that comes from Curram's touch is already creeping over me again.

But I saved myself. The words ring through my head, bittersweet triumph.

Is he dead? Is Zachariah Curram dead?

I don't want to move to find out. I don't want to touch him again. What I want is for someone to wrap their arms around me and let me cry. I want to rest, really and truly. I want my pa, and my room. *But Boyne could return at any moment,* I tell myself. I tear strips of cloth from my dress and wind them around my hands to stop the bleeding, and then crawl back to Curram's body. Closing my eyes so I won't have to look at his face, I lay one ear against his chest.

Nothing.

This time his body is empty and silent, and I don't have to worry that he'll wake up.

I scoot backward as fast as my trembling legs can take me. *He will never touch me again,* I think. *He will never claim that I belong to him, never undress me with his eyes, never make me feel small or weak. I won.*

But I still need to find Lillian.

My legs are unsteady as I stagger to the door. The manor is still and quiet, and the corridor is dark after I close the door behind me. I don't realize I'm not alone until someone seizes me from behind and a soft, fleshy hand wraps around my mouth when I try to scream. Boyne, again. His other hand holds down my arms, and I try to wriggle free, but he's stronger than I expected, and I'm weaker now. "Not so fast, bitch," he snarls in my ear, squeezing me tighter. I can't scream, can't even kick because he's holding me so close.

With the crack of a gunshot, everything changes. Boyne lets go of me and falls to the ground, screaming and whimpering. I look wildly around, my ears ringing from the shot, but my eyes haven't adjusted to the darkness. I scramble backward as figures loom closer, but I reach the wall and can't move any farther. I slide down and pull my legs up to my chest.

Then someone is before me, crouching down to my level, cupping the side of my face in his hand. "Isla," he says, so gently. "It's all right, Isla. Everything is all right."

"Tam?" I sniff, trembling. *But he can't be here. He's three days' away, in Eisendrath.*

He slides an arm under my legs and behind my back and picks me up, like I don't weigh anything at all, and holds on to me tightly. "I'll protect you," he says softly, kissing my forehead. "I promise." *Am I dreaming?*

"Where are the others?"

I start at Valentina's voice. "Wh-what are you doing here . . . ?"

"Shh," says Tam. "We came to find you, of course."

"But—" *How are they here?* I stare up at him, letting my eyes adjust to the darkness and trying to convince myself that this is really happening. I don't understand.

"Did they leave you to take on Curram alone?" Val sounds indignant.

"No, he suspected a trap."

"What happened, Isla? Who did this to you?" Tam's eyes

move over me, taking in the bloody bandages on my hands and the torn front of my dress. He could put me down, but he doesn't. "Are you all right?"

"It was Curram," I say very slowly, still trembling. "He tried to—" Then I realize Tam has no idea who I'm talking about. "He's the man who took Eugenia." I take a deep breath. "And me, he took me, too. I was with her. They kept us here." I feel like I can breathe again without the words weighing on my chest. "I didn't know how to tell you."

"Where is he?" Tam's voice is tight with anger. "I'll kill him. I'll beat his brains out if I find him." He's shaking, but he hasn't let go of me. He hasn't recoiled like something's wrong with me.

"Tam?" He looks down at me, his face inches from mine. "How did you even know to come?" He eases a little.

"Des realized you'd gone," he says. "He told me to come."

"Of course he did," I moan, but I'm not sorry.

Val crosses her arms. "We've been trying to catch up since you left."

My eyes flick to Tam's face; his mouth is set in a grim line, his eyes hard, not looking at me. "I couldn't let you walk into danger on your own, even when I thought it was just about Eugenia," Tam says, softening when he talks to me. He sets me gently on my feet, wiping my bloody cheek with his thumb. "What did he do to you?" I falter a little, leaning against Tam and feeling weak again. *He came.*

"Curram is dead," I say, my voice quiet. "At least, I think he is."

"Where?"

"I'll show you."

I move toward the door, but Tam hesitates, looking at Boyne, who is moaning and whimpering, clutching his leg near the knee. "We'd better do something about him first." Tam picks up Boyne's pistol from the ground and pockets it. "Someone must have heard by now. Let's bring him with us."

When we're inside, he drops Boyne's arms, leaving him on the library floor. Between moans and groans, Boyne spits insults at us, but he seems incapable of pulling himself together and bearing the injury. I watch Tam take in the room and scold myself for thinking he didn't care. *But why act so cruelly? Maybe I didn't understand what was going on. Maybe he's not as easy to read as I thought.*

He's wearing his army uniform, rust-brown pants and shirt, heavy black boots; I imagine he'll be in trouble for leaving, if they realize he's gone. "Will you be—" I start to ask, but then I realize that he's looking at Curram, the cord still tangled about his neck.

Tam looks furious, his jaw tight, his face flushed. "You did that?" he asks. I nod, and he looks me up and down, seeing my bloody hands and face, my ripped dress, all over again in the light. I feel like I should cover up, or tell him I'm fine, or that he doesn't need to be upset because nothing really happened.

He leans down and kisses me, suddenly, pulling me toward him with a hand against my back.

I make a surprised sound, and he pulls back, leaving me
stunned. My mouth tingles and my stomach lurches. I wish
he'd kiss me again. "I've been wanting to do that for a while,"
he says. He watches me for a moment before adding, very
seriously, "I won't let anyone hurt you again, Isla." And then,
with a slight smile, "Even if it seems you can defend yourself
pretty well without me."

"I'd rather I didn't have to," I think I say. It's hard to tell
with my head spinning.

There's a commotion outside the door and Tam whirls,
stepping in front of me. Caffrey and Gilbert burst in, each
brandishing a knife and a pistol. They take in the scene
quickly, lowering their weapons, their jaws dropping in surprise. Phoebe appears behind them, with Marion beside her.

"Are you all right?" Gilbert asks, looking me over.

Caffrey looks angry. "Evidently Curram had it out for
you," he says.

"I survived," I answer, without the energy to say more.

Gilbert's expression is grim. "I had no idea he'd guess at
Alistair's plans, Isla; I'm so sorry."

"Who had the honor?" Phoebe asks, gesturing to Curram and looking between Tam, Valentina, and me. I laugh,
but it comes out as a strangled sort of sob. Tam's arms come
around me and I bury my face in his shirt. When I eventually pull back, he meets my eyes, serious.

"Will you be all right?" he asks. I nod, but it feels like a lie.

Then I see her. Past Marion and Phoebe, still in the shadows outside the door. From her sharp, attractive features like

his and dark hair like mine, I know instantly that she's Des's sister. She stands like she's afraid she'll break, her arms held straight and close to her sides, her steps hesitant like she could fall through the floor at any moment. Des is behind her, his own hands hovering awkwardly as though he wants to guide her movements, but never touching her, as if he, too, is afraid she'll break.

"You mean Zachariah?" she says, stepping closer, and only as she moves into the light do I see the haunted look in her eyes. They take in everything, from my bloody hands to Tam's arms around me to the still-whimpering Boyne trying in vain to claw his way away from us across the floor to Curram's motionless body. The others part to let her past, Des hanging back with worried eyes as he watches her every move. "He's dead?"

"I think so," I say.

"Justice has been served, then." She puts bitter emphasis on the first word, her voice breaking as it grows louder.

"Lillian," Des starts, but she ignores him.

"Yes," I say, taking an uneasy step toward her. The room has gone perfectly still.

"Good," she says, her voice leveling. She's faking the calm. I know because I know her brother. Very slowly, she takes another step forward, and then another. And before anyone knows what's happening, she grabs the pistol from Gilbert's hand and fires into Curram's chest, the crack of the gunshot ringing in my ears.

I want to press my eyes shut against all the blood, but then she's holding the gun to her chin and Des is shouting. "He's dead, Lil, he's dead, it's all right," he's pleading, reaching toward her frantically. She backs away from him, shaking her head as her eyes fill with tears.

"That's not enough," she says, very quietly.

"Lillian," I say gently, inching toward her. She turns, the gun flailing in my direction. I swallow, keeping my eyes on Lillian's, as Tam tries to reason with her, Val and Des plead for her to listen, and Boyne moans in the background. I push all the confusion out of my head. "Lillian, please."

"You have no idea what it's like," she says, her voice hoarse and hurting. "You think—"

"I do, Lillian, I do know. He took me, too." I don't want to patronize her, but if I stop talking it'll be worse.

Her eyes widen. "You don't know anything," she chokes, aghast. "You were one of the lucky ones."

"But he's dead," I go on, taking the smallest of steps closer. "He's dead, you can start over, you're free. You can try to forget."

Her face is thin and gaunt, her eyes rimmed in red. "He spent three years making sure I'd never forget." She's stock-still for a moment; then her arm drops, the gun hanging limply by her side. "Not the first time, or the second, or the tenth, or the hundredth after that." Her eyes, so full of sadness, look vacant, like she's lost somewhere else for a moment. "He took things from me, made me get rid of—" She's shaking her head fast, the tears streaming down her cheeks. "A baby would have been inconvenient for him, and I didn't want to have his child, I didn't, but he made me, he brought a man—" Her words pick up speed until they slur together.

She takes a trembling breath and looks at Curram's body again. "I wanted it to be enough," she says, "but it's not." Then she pulls the pistol up to her chin again, and Des throws himself at her as the sound of another gunshot cracks the air.

twenty~seven

They hit the floor and the gun goes spinning away. I rush to Des's side, dropping to my knees, but Lillian is curled up, shaking with sobs. There's no blood; Des knocked the pistol aside in time.

"Hey," he's saying over and over, as he pulls his sister into his arms and holds her tightly even as she fights him. Gilbert steps carefully past them and pockets the gun, even though it's probably harmless for the moment. *That would have been me,* I think, staring at Lillian. *If not in the cell, before Curram disposed of me, then after we made the trade. I would have been his next Lillian, a plaything, always at his disposal.*

"He must have sent all the staff home tonight," Gilbert says quietly to me when I stand. "Only the guards were here. With your friends' help, we managed to incapacitate the ones who took us, and now they're in the cell underground."

Phoebe steps closer to me. "You were right," she whispers. "There were other girls. They're in the vestibule now;

we couldn't send them out because they'd only be stopped by the men at the gate."

"How did you get in?" I ask, turning to Tam.

He looks sheepish. "Climbed the wall. Couldn't think of a clever enough lie to get past the gates."

I take his hands. "We can pay off the guards with Curram's money if we have to," I say.

"You've always had enough brains for both of us," he says, swallowing hard and glancing at Des and Lillian once more. "Come on. We should let them alone for a moment."

I look once more at Curram's body and realize with a jolt that I've only half succeeded: I've lost my best chance at getting answers. Tears well up in my eyes. "Maybe it's still not enough," I say, looking at Phoebe. "We don't know where he sent the others, or who he bought us from in the first place. I doubt he kept records of that sort of thing. Curram's dead, but that doesn't mean they'll stop taking girls every day off the street and selling them to someone else."

"Isla," Tam interrupts quietly, pointing at Boyne, curled up on the ground. "Would he know?"

Caffrey and Gilbert offer their help instantly. "This one's pathetic. He'll tell us whatever you need to know," says the latter, holding Boyne to the ground when he starts to kick and squirm. He sounds like a whining dog. Standing over him, Caffrey looks double his already formidable size.

"What did you want to know, sweetheart?"

"Who was Curram's supplier? Who did he buy the girls from?"

"You heard the lady." Caffrey grins, raising one foot over the bullet hole in Boyne's leg. Boyne hesitates, and Caffrey stomps hard on the wound, making him scream.

"He was there, he knows," I say, still staring at Boyne.

"Of course he does. And he's about to tell us."

"If you j-just—*aauugh!*" More pressure.

"The name of the place, the leader, give us something, anything," Caffrey says good-naturedly. He swivels his foot, grinding it into the bloody mess that covers Boyne's pant leg. "Just a word, and I'll let you be."

"Drisdale!" he sputters, crying out again at the pain. Caffrey removes his foot but stands ready to readminister it.

"Is that a place?"

Boyne nods frantically, but Caffrey looks disbelieving. He stamps his foot into the wound again, and Boyne tries to pull away, moaning and writhing. "In the red district! There's an inn! I swear it's the truth! I swear it!" He looks like a baby, sobbing on the floor. "Mercy presides over it. She's the one he buys the girls from, and sells 'em back to. The Merry Little Maid, the inn's called. Mercy has other sites, but that's where you can find her. I can help you, whatever you need. I know everything he did, everyone he dealt with. If Swain wants me to talk—"

"I know the place," Phoebe says quietly to me. "I can take you there."

I turn to her with questions, but no chance to ask them. "We need to go," Gilbert says, silencing Boyne with a glare.

Boyne curls in on himself, sniffling and pitiful, his eyes darting among all of us.

"We'll need to bring the body. And that one"—Gilbert points at Boyne—"for Alistair's decision." He turns to Caffrey. "I'll find a sheet; can you go and take care of the sentries at the gate?" Caffrey slips past us while Gilbert wraps Curram's body in the sheet before seeing to Boyne's leg. Lillian's sobs have subsided, but Des still cradles her against his chest, murmuring things I can't hear.

Tam looks down at me. "Come on," he says. Marion plants a kick in Boyne's side and flashes him a smile before following us out the door, and from there, Phoebe leads us to the vestibule.

It's poorly lit by just one lantern on a table, probably taken from the cellar. In the dimness, I can see figures: small, bent figures, huddled together in the middle of the room. "You can leave," I tell them, my voice echoing off the high ceilings. "Take anything of value that you see, use it to get home. The guards won't be a problem. Go on." They stare back at me with wide eyes, not moving, and I try not to be irritated.

But then I remember the awful, paralyzing fear that came with my captivity. Guessing that they carry similar scars, I hold out my left hand so they can see the brand. "I came from this place," I tell them, keeping my voice gentle. "I was taken off the street, and they put this on my hand before I was brought here. He's dead now. That's why I came back, so that you don't have to belong to him any longer."

One of the girls looks down at her own hand; she's so thin and so small, her cinnamon-colored skin smudged and dirty. She looks up again, meeting my eyes. "This is not who you are," I say as sternly as I dare. A girl with red-gold hair and freckled cheeks gets to her feet. She steps timidly forward, keeping her eyes locked on mine. She can't be older than fifteen.

"Thank you," she says hoarsely. "I didn't think . . . I thought there wasn't any . . ." She doesn't finish, and I nod. She moves to one of the tables along the side of the room and begins opening drawers. Encouraged by her action, the other girls move about the room, and I watch them with satisfaction swelling in my chest.

Tam says something about helping Caffrey and slips past, touching my shoulder as he goes.

"I tried to say good-bye to my parents," Marion says, watching the girls go, "but I couldn't get the words out. I'm sure they'd have tried to stop me. They must have noticed I'm gone by now."

"I'm sorry," I say.

"They'll be fine eventually." She shrugs, not looking like she believes it.

"How did you find Lillian?"

"They'd put her in the cellar, where we were kept," Valentina says. "We got in that way and saw Phoebe and those men fighting the guards. Tam joined the fight and it was over pretty quickly. I don't know where Curram kept her before, but she looked like a scared rabbit and hardly moved when we let her out. It was like she'd never been outside. I've never seen Des so shook up."

"I don't know how I forgot how awful it was," Marion says, her eyes wide. "The smell and the stickiness . . ."

"Was Robbie still there?"

Phoebe grins. "I swear he pissed himself when he saw me," she says. "Must've thought I was a ghost, coming from the shadows. He went down easy. He's in the cell again; I wonder if he's getting used to being beaten by a girl, and the same one twice at that."

Caffrey reenters the house and passes us. Valentina offers to help the girls on their way, then leads them nervously outside. When the last one disappears through the door, I look at Phoebe. "You said you know the place we're going?"

Her expression turns serious. "The brothel Curram was selling them to, it's not the only one, all right? If you really want to do some damage, it won't be easy."

"I never said I thought it would be."

It feels like a long minute before she goes on. "I grew up in the red district, with brothels next door and doctors' assistants selling laudanum under the bridges. It's just life, there. You're lucky if you take care of yourself, if you're not owned by a man with a bed for rent, or worse. If you close one whorehouse, they'll just open another. It's like a sickness, buried deep. Changing things will take everything you've got."

"I can't go back to my old life," I say, "not after all of this. I thought when Curram was dead everything would be over, but he wasn't the only one."

A smile works its way onto Phoebe's mouth. "That's how I've been feeling," she says. "But we'll need help. We can't take down the industry with just a handful of people." She furrows her brow, murmuring names and ideas to herself.

She would have left me behind to die if it had meant her own freedom, that first day I met her in Curram's cellar. Even in the train car, her only thought was for a way out. I see now how small of me it is to think that I am the only one who has changed, who has become strong because of what happened.

Tam appears in the doorway. "Ready?" he asks.

There's a commotion, and Gilbert and Caffrey appear, carrying a linen-wrapped body between them. Boyne, his bound hands tied to Caffrey's belt, stumbles after them, yelping in pain and limping. Behind them, Des eases Lillian along, his arm around her shoulders, his footsteps keeping slow pace with hers.

"We'll be loading up what's in his treasury," Caffrey says, smiling broadly. "Swain wouldn't want us to waste it, I'm sure."

"Of course not," I say.

"Is this good-bye, then?" Gilbert asks, putting down his end of the awkward bundle.

I nod. "There's still a lot to do," I say.

He tips his head to the side. "I hope we meet again."

"Good luck, Isla," Caffrey says. "Take the cart. We'll tell Swain you slipped away."

When we step outside and the cool, fresh air hits us, I feel free all over again. Lillian hesitates just inside the threshold for a moment before stepping out into the open air, her arms wrapped tightly around herself, her head tipped back, her eyes on the sky. The stars are bright, and the moon brighter. It's like a new world.

It's only when we reach the cart, parked near the wall, that I see the two guards from the gate lying on the ground, their hands tied behind their backs. I give Tam a questioning look and he shrugs. "Caffrey made a good point. Why waste the gold?" he says. "And there was rope coiled up there at the wall. What were we supposed to do?"

I bend down to see their faces. "Your master is dead. Lawmen will be here to search the place in the morning, no doubt. When they arrive, feel free to tell them about your friends that we locked in the cellar."

Marion hauls the gate open, and Phoebe climbs onto the driver's bench.

"I know a place we can stay tonight," Phoebe says. "Curram's dead and that's a good thing. But he wasn't the mastermind behind the operation that took us in the first place; he was just one of many buyers. If we want to really damage the industry he benefited from, we're going to need reinforcements. We can discuss a plan tomorrow, but if any of you would rather not be a part of saving lives"—she looks pointedly around at everyone—"we won't make you stay."

No one objects, and she looks satisfied. "All right, then," she says as Marion climbs up beside her, "Drisdale it is." Tam offers Lillian a hand into the cart, but she shies away from him, clambering in on her own. Even when Des takes a seat next to her, with Valentina on his other side, she keeps her distance. *Will she ever be all right?* I wonder, watching her in the near darkness. *In her mind, has she even fully left? Will she ever be free of those years of abuse and darkness?* And there must be so many like her.

I can see the others behind my eyelids: Eugenia, Cecily, the one with the darkest skin, Winifred, and the one with all the freckles. One of the girls said she missed her brother, and one was afraid of the dark at night, when Dunbar took the lantern with him. And before those was the skinny, frantic girl at the warehouse with her wide eyes and bony wrists.

There were so many, and even though I know I couldn't have helped them, it still hurts to remember.

I sit on the loading trap, my legs swinging over the edge, my heart heavy. Tam jumps up beside me, and we start to move. The streets are mostly unlit as we begin to weave our way through them, but Phoebe seems to know the way well. For several minutes, Tam and I sit in silence, and I don't know what to say.

Should I still be angry with him? I'm almost too tired to be upset. But he hasn't apologized, or said anything about our last conversation. His coming here proves that he cares, but it doesn't make everything magically better.

"There was a water pump in the garage," he says a little awkwardly. He holds out a handkerchief, and when I take it I realize it's soaking wet. "You . . . your face," he explains, gesturing. I mop away the blood; the lines drawn by Curram's fingernails feel raw, but at least they've stopped bleeding. I can feel the tenderness of a bruise starting to form on the side of my face where he struck me. When I'm clean, I look over and see that Tam is watching me.

"You wanna walk for a second?" he asks, gesturing behind us.

"Don't go too far," I call to Phoebe, jumping to the ground. Tam does the same, and we let the cart stretch ahead of us before following. When he doesn't say anything, I take a deep breath.

"It was when I went to say good-bye to you," I start, swallowing the lump in my throat. He looks over at me, still silent. "You saw the crowds; I could barely spot you. I didn't even know what was happening until I was being dragged away from the station." Instead of disappearing, the tightness in my throat only seems to be getting worse. "I thought you saw it happen. For all those weeks, I told myself you'd come to save me." He opens his mouth to say something, but I hurry on, afraid if I don't finish now, I never will. "They branded us all, and then Curram came. He bought us, Tam. I didn't—I can't tell you how it feels to know someone owns you, someone who can just dispose of you at any moment.

"You saw those girls in the cellar, so you've probably guessed the rest. He kept us down there until it was our turn to be taken upstairs. It was hell, seeing one girl after the next go upstairs, wondering if they'd come back. Eugenia did." My chest is tight. "She was so upset, he killed her." The words hurt, coming out. Saying them aloud drags me through every emotion, every nightmare all over again. But Tam doesn't flinch, or change the subject.

I tell him about the girls I want to believe could still be alive, and when I get to the part where we found Eisendrath, he shakes his head, frowning. "Isla, why didn't you tell me?"

"I was scared of what you'd think of me. I didn't even know what to think of myself."

He stops walking and leans down to kiss the top of my head. When he pulls back, he puts his hands on my shoulders, making me look at him. "What I think is that you're brave and fierce and brilliant." I feel like I'm sinking, somehow. "I need you to know something," he goes on, sounding nervous. *Tam is never nervous.* He reaches into his breast pocket and draws something out, holding it toward me.

I cup my hands and he drops a jumble of metal into them: the chain with the key to my locket, and the miniature spyglass I gave him. I turn the objects over in my hands, waiting for his explanation.

"I've had them with me since the day I left. I never let them out of my sight because they made me feel connected to you. I knew I would see you again if I was strong enough to survive everything around me." The words to tell him I felt the same are pushing against my lips, but I force myself to wait, to let him finish. After a long moment, he clears his throat. "But after the army . . . I wasn't sure of anything anymore. I thought you liked Des," he says, sounding like a little boy, ashamed of something he's done. "I thought that while I was gone, you'd fallen for him, and I didn't want you to think that I expected anything from you, or that you should feel obligated to me, so I let you believe I didn't care."

"You were really convincing."

"I could tell," he says miserably. "And I'm . . . I'm so sorry. I wanted to let you off the hook. I didn't want to make you hate me. I can see how stupid that was, and I'm so sorry that I hurt you."

I can't speak around the tightness in my throat; I try to smile, but it threatens to turn into a sob. Tam pulls me close, like he did that last day on my roof. "I've never been any good at saying the important things," he says into my hair. "I registered for the army weeks before I left, but I didn't have the guts to tell you until it was time to ship out."

"Well, you're *not* as brave as I always thought," I murmur against his shoulder, breathing in deeply.

"Hey!" He laughs, and I can feel it in his chest. "Only when it's about you, all right? I'd have told you years ago, only the words always felt like rubber when I tried to get them out."

"Told me what?" I demand, pulling back slightly.

"Y-y-you know," he stutters, and I'm sure he's blushing.

"No, I want you to say it."

"You're not as clever as I always thought, either, all right? Do I need to kiss you again?"

"I wouldn't mind," I say with a grin.

He plants a quick kiss on my nose.

"Cheater," I say, feeling everything settle into place inside of me.

But the longer we walk, the quieter Tam becomes. When I look up at him, he turns away. "I'm not sure where you got this idea that you need me, Isla," he says. "Seems like you've got everything pretty well sorted on your own."

"I wouldn't go that far." I laugh, but he's serious. "Fine, then. Can I keep you even if I don't need you?" His fingers lace through mine, and I smile, stepping a little closer to him. A year ago, my stomach would have erupted in butterflies if our shoulders had touched when we sat next to each other.

It wasn't long ago at all that I shied away at the thought of standing up for myself, of seeing new places and challenging the way things work. And Tam always thought that no matter where he went, it would be a beautiful and perfectly grand adventure. We'd both gotten such different things than we imagined we would. "Just think," I say, spreading my free arm like Tam used to and putting on my best impression of him, "of all the amazing things we'll do, the lives we'll save, the sights we'll see."

Now it's his turn to tease, affecting astonishment. "Isla Powe, asking for an adventure? I don't believe it."

"If you think all of this sounds like too much, I'll understand."

He watches me for what feels like an eternity. I used to

worry when he looked at me for so long: *Was I as pretty as I could be? Did he notice all of my imperfections? Was I talking too much?* This time, none of that crosses my mind, and not caring makes me love him more than ever. Slowly, he shakes his head. "I don't know why you'd choose me," he says finally, taking me by surprise.

"What do you mean?"

"Even when we were kids, I wondered why you always stood next to me when any of the other boys would have loved to take you to the dances or share their lunch with you." I almost laugh, but he means it. He doesn't see me like everyone else always has, as ordinary and small. "I'm scarred, Isla, and different. I told you the things that I did, when I was with the army—"

"Tam," I say, stopping and pulling my hand away from his and holding it open to him. "I'm marked, too. I wanted to be the same when I found you, but it didn't work out that way."

He's quiet again, tracing my X in silence. *I'll never be rid of it,* I think. But then he brings my palm to his mouth and kisses it gently, in the center of the brand, sending a shiver through me. I trail my fingers along his cheek, the skin still tight and pink from the burns. "We each have scars," he says, smiling slightly.

I touch the locket absently where it sits in its rightful place around my neck again; he's already hung his key just under the collar of his uniform. "I guess I feel like I grew up," I say finally. "As if . . . I don't know. We've changed so much."

"It doesn't have to be bad," Tam whispers. The space between us and Curram's manor grows wider and wider. *Curram is dead,* I think. It isn't his manor anymore. It's just a house. "We were bound to grow up eventually. No more hiding behind me, all right?"

"It's a deal," I say, and Tam grins like a little boy, his eyes crinkled and brimming with promises.

Tam's arm comes around me and he pulls me closer, resting his chin on the top of my head as we walk. It's getting colder; summer must be nearly at its close, and it's strange to think that this will be the first autumn of my life that I won't be starting down the cobbled streets to school each morning, pretending to have something in my shoe so that Tam will catch up and we can walk side by side, or letting him think he has surprised me with a handful of dry leaves raining down on my head.

Somewhere at home, in the old paper hatbox that was Mum's, I've got the best leaves from each year: the ones Tam stuck in my hair and the ones we tried to make a pile out of on the sidewalks, from all of the poor, skinny city trees growing in manicured boxes. If my absence wasn't noticed before by my schoolmates, maybe it will be now.

But that life feels strangely distant now, and all of the safety and predictability in the world couldn't lure me back. Here, now, with Tam's arm around me and a new purpose pumping my heart behind my ribs, I have what matters.

Tam stops walking again, and the cart drifts on ahead of us. "I love you, you know," he says, laying his hand against the side of my face and stroking my sore cheek ever so gently with his thumb. I can feel my pulse in the slash marks, racing faster all the time. Then he leans in and kisses me, his lips soft and eager, and my fingers tangle in his hair as my eyes drop slowly closed and my heart soars high.

acknowledgments

I lay all the blame for my love of stories on my mother, who read The Chronicles of Narnia and *The Arabian Nights* and innumerable others aloud to my siblings and me growing up, making magic a part of everyday life. Between the countless hours spent in the library putting holds on Gail Carson Levine novels and Andrew Lang collections, and my own whimsical imagination, I believe I was always destined to pursue storytelling in some form. I certainly didn't think I'd see my name in print on a novel before I was twenty-five, though. For that great, impossible-seeming gift, I thank the marvelous people at Swoon Reads.

Firstly, Holly West, my editor. I don't know how you know what needs to go and what needs to stay, or which characters aren't necessary, or how to hone my voice. I think it's an actual gift. Thank you for the ingenious insights and the phone calls to talk me off of panicked editing ledges. For making *Finding You* what it is, for seeing the heart of my story and working your magic so others can see it, too, I am forever in your debt.

Lauren Scobell, I think I've had a crush on you since we met. Thank you for rooting for *Finding You* and helming the ship that has brought it to where we are today. You are brilliant and insightful *and* you love *The Night Circus*.

To Jean Feiwel for believing in my book when it was almost double this size and had so, so many troubles. I'm indebted to you for taking it on anyway.

To Emily Settle for your patience and helpfulness and responses that are much more prompt than my own. To my copyeditors, who made *Finding You* make sense, and to Rich Deas for the beautiful cover art that made it all feel real. To the Swoon Reads staff for making my publishing dreams come true.

Also to my readers, who have pushed this book to where it is today—its baby years, chapter-by-chapter on figment.com, and then in the Swoon Reads community, where your kind and constructive words were responsible for this physical book becoming a reality.

To my stalwart comrades, Savannah, Reagan, Kristin, Janelle, Patrick, Cara, Hannah, and the rest of our Figgies Underground. Thank you for the love and word sprints and virtual pear cheese. To Kim Karalius, the whole reason I'm here today, for texting and calling when I'm lost, for loving my characters more than I do sometimes, and for sharing Swoon Reads with me in the first place. To Samantha, to whom I've almost dedicated this entire book a millions times over. *Finding You* would very literally not exist without you. I am deeply grateful for you, mighty woman of valor; I cannot tell you in words. Isla owes much to you as well.

And to the people who kept me sane during the last crazy

years of trying to figure out who I am and what stories I was supposed to tell—Meghan, for believing in me *way* too much, calling me when I'm panicking, and loving me when I'm a mess; Brittney, also for your belief, for keeping all of my secrets, for being the big sister that I never had; Rachel, for writing with me via nerdy blogs and long emails; Sarah, for the moral support that reaches all the way to tattoo parlors; Aidan, for earnest encouragements and Keira Knightley imitations; Abigail, for sending writing memes and taking way too many headshots; and the rest of my unofficial support team who I couldn't do without: Raleigh, Alli, Michelle, Tiandra, Kristi, Autumn, Sharon Duffy, who believed in my writing and really took it seriously years before I did, and the Warner family, for reading my books before they were ready for the rest of the world. To my family at Aletheia Church (especially Donny & Janna, Adam & Hope, Kevin & Kelsey, and Becca), for enveloping me.

To my grandma and grandpa, who have encouraged me and my dreams at every turn and in every possible way, and all the family who have been telling strangers that I was a writer long before it was close to being legitimate (looking at you, Auntie Sharon).

And of course to my family—Mum, who taught me to love stories and wouldn't let me graduate until I stopped procrastinating and finished a novel (unconventional homeschooling win) and has read every one since; Daddy, who never doubted that I could do anything I put my mind to and has always encouraged me and teased me and pushed me; Jake, who made me start writing in the first place so I could be like him and has been my biggest supporter ever since (sorry I stole the name Valentina); Emmy, my best friend in the world, who loves me unconditionally and reminds me I have value and stories to tell; Ben, who reads my books aloud on road trips in outrageous accents and doesn't let me take myself too seriously but is always proud of me; and Katie, my beta reader, my first and foremost fangirl, who makes me feel like a real author every time she yells at me for something that happens to my characters.

To close, I have to thank Beatrix Potter, for making me want to tell stories; as a first-grader struggling to learn to read, I thought Tom Kitten was going to be eaten and felt my stomach tighten into knots and thought, "How can she make me feel something real with just words?"

And more than anyone, my creator and savior, Jesus Christ, who puts stories in all of us—behind us, so we can share, around us, so we can empathize, and in front of us, so we can hope. I'm so glad he decided that I get to tell a few of my own.